Yabbies

Fragments: possession,
passion and purpose

Tom Graves

Published by
Tetradian Books
Unit 215, Communications House
9 St Johns Street, Colchester, Essex CO2 7NN
England

http://www.tetradianbooks.com

First published June 2011
ISBN 978-1-906681-32-6 (paperback)
ISBN 978-1-906681-33-3 (e-book)

Contents

Acknowledgements

Amongst others, the following people kindly provided comments, suggestion and feedback on ideas, themes and descriptions in the various drafts of this book: Isabela Abreu (BR), Alex Burns (AU), Shawn Callahan (AU), Catherine Caulwell (IE), Joseph & Inga Chittenden (GB), Paul Devereux (GB), Pat Ferdinandi (US), Alexandre Gabriel (PT), Linda Moore Gentile (US), John Gøtze (DK), Bob Gray (AU), Marty Gregory (US), Martin Hungerford (AU), Palden Jenkins (GB), Simon Ashton Jones (GB), Kitty Juniper (AU), Beck Kelly (AU), Joe Kisch (AU), Cynthia Kurtz (US), Kevin & Karen Masman (AU), Andrea McCarthy (AU), Alanna Moore (IE), Kerrie Patmore (AU), Cindy Pavlinac (US), Liz Poraj-Wilczynska (GB), Helena Read (AU), Guy Richards (AU), Jose Ramos (AU), Roberto Severo (BR), Kevin Smith (GB), Michael Smith (MX), Peter Tseglakof (AU), Colin Vincent (AU), Ian Waldron (AU).

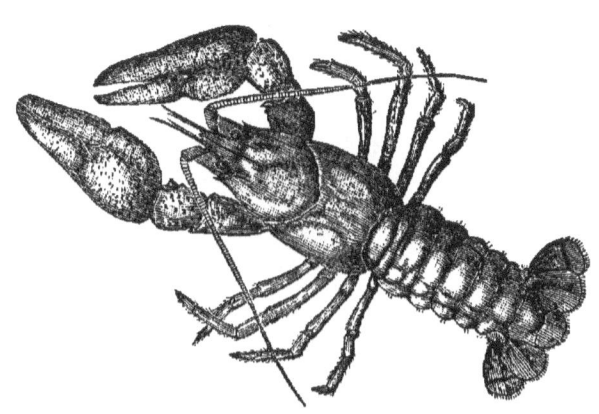

Don's thesis

"Towards a System of Sustainable Law"
James Donald Mercer
Doctoral Submission 14012/84
Derwent University
Melbourne, Australia

Abstract
Current Australian law is based on the Westminster system, which is of relatively recent origin by comparison with the legal systems pertaining prior to European immigration. A problematic characteristic of Westminster statute-law is its volatility, requiring constant maintenance by the legislature to keep pace with changes in society. By contrast many tribal or 'traditional' systems of law have remained stable for long periods, in some case for millennia. A variety of traditional legal systems from around the world, and from different periods in history, are assessed in order to identify principles and characteristics that would assist stability and sustainability. A hypothetical system of law is presented that integrates these principles into a framework for use under current societal conditions.

Steve arrives

Too tired to think straight. But glad it's almost over.

The engines' howl slows to a whine, then a whisper, and finally stops. Silence at last – outside at least.

Inside, it's the usual chaos at the end of a long flight across the ocean. "Please remain seated until the captain has switched off the seat-belt sign", says the chief steward's voice over the speakers, but her grating Michigan tones are ignored as perhaps half the passengers climb out of their seats, heave open the lockers, dropping other people's bags to the ground in their frenzy to grab their property and get out of the claustrophobia and the canned air. Crammed in the centre of the row, Steve unclips his belt, rises, signs as if to move out, join the crowd. But his seat-partner waves him down.

"Don't worry the self, mate", comes the laconic drawl. "We ain't goin' nowhere till they get the bloody doors open. And we ain' gettin' out the port till they get the bags out." A wry smile. "If the Yanks wanna be stupid, they can go ahead, but it ain't gonna make any bloody difference. Just slows everyone down."

Steve grins. "Yeah, you're right. They been stuck on too many US flights, I guess."

He sits back, and watches. His companion's right: it's only the foreigners who are crammed into the aisleway, bags in hand, the stench of irritation and frustration wafting off them in waves. The ones who seem to be locals hardly seem to have noticed they've arrived: still sitting, or quietly stretching, chatting over seat-backs.

Not bothered: no need to make things other than they are, I guess.

Minutes pass, then the line starts moving. Two decks, two aisleways each, eight hundred passengers: it always takes time. The usual pleasantries, the mechanically friendly goodbye from the cabin crew; a waft of warm air at the edge of the jetway gives a first hint that this is a different continent, a different world. Pack held over one shoulder, Steve is swept along, still crowded, cramped, squeezed together on the way out through the narrow tube, and through the double doors into the main passage, merging with people from other flights in a surging human flow.

It takes several moments to notice: something's missing. Steve turns to his companion from the flight; a whisper.

"Where are all the guards? The uniforms? The guns?"

A sardonic laugh. "Where you come from? – you been in the States too long. This is *Australia*, mate!" He shakes his head in dry amusement. "You blokes are crazy – we don't do that kinda crap here."

"What – no dogs, even?"

As if in answer, Steve feels a nudge in the back of his leg. He looks down, into the mournful eyes of a green-jacketed beagle.

"Don't mind us", says the handler. "Just looking for quarantine. Dog thinks you got fruit on you. From the flight, yeah?"

Steve nods, pulls out an apple.

"Dump it in the bin over there, will you? Thanks."

Steve does, and returns to his companion, as the crowd arrives at the baggage hall.

Don alone

Don stands in the doorway and waves as the last well-wisher leaves.

A long sigh. He takes a last look at the sky – overcast, unusually, but so appropriate for this day – and turns inside, closing the door.

Alone at last.

Alone with his grief.

Flowers everywhere, some of them drooping already in the dull heat of the day. He'd asked for none, but people had brought them anyway, for Mary. It's right, in a way: she'd loved colour, in every form. Past tense already, he thinks: 'loved', not 'loves'. And yet I love. I know I will always love. Present, past, future: they're all the same to us.

And still the tears will not come. Still too early and too public for that, even now.

He glances at a piece of paper one of the visitors has left: an ugly print-out from one of the new-fangled 'web-sites', it seems, from the Tapestry Guild. Other people's memories of Mary; but none of his own.

His hands drift over the table, seemingly of their own volition, touching, stroking, caressing fabrics and other small gifts. A different kind of memory: more real in its way.

In his study, a clutter of papers and student assignments: they tug, demanding attention. But they can wait: this is a different day, a different world. Another newspaper cutting, on the desk: stark, cold, factual, it mentions the car and little else. A statistic. Nothing human; no sense of the *person*, the woman, partner, lover, friend, behind the name. Or the family left behind. Even if most of it is just a family of one, now.

Not quite a family of one. A small wry grin crosses his face as a clatter at the back door announces the kitten's return, now that the strangers are gone. A plaintive call for the woman who's no longer here, no longer able to provide the food-bowl and the warm lap in which to curl up for the evening. A plaintive call that brings it all back: the dark night, the knock on the door, two sombre figures, the uniforms, caps respectfully under arm, the low voice explaining. And yet he'd known, somehow, even before the squad car had arrived: a feeling in the air, something very wrong; a broken thread. The tapestry of the Three Sisters, Clotho, Lachesis, Atropos: one spins, one weaves, one cuts...

He scoops up the kitten, holds it gently under his arm, stroking, as his eyes fill at last. The kitten clambers up his arm and perches on his shoulder, rumbling contentedly in his ear, as he walks the narrow passageway to Mary's studio, empty now, and silent. He sees her in her chair, turning, laughing in the bright sunlight, as she so often did; but there's no-one there. Yet even in this grey light the room is a blaze of colour; swatches of thread and fabric samples lie everywhere in glorious profusion, glorious confusion.

But no-one now to bring a subtle, joyful order to this chaos. A stab of anger, frustration: he wants to sweep it all aside, bury it, destroy it, burn away the pain and loss. Abandon himself in abandonment at having been abandoned in this way, is how it feels. Another sad smile flickers across his face. The anger is real; yet so is Mary's presence here. And he knows which he'd prefer to keep.

"This isn't right, is it, dearest? We can't leave this unfinished. But I don't have your touch: you'll have to show me what to do."

His hand settles on one pile of fabric scraps. Picking up a needle and bobbin from beside them, he leaves the room, with a brighter glance at the woman who nods approval at his choice. Mary's chair; Mary's room; her space, not his; that much remains the same. Possessive in her own way; yet she'd always understood. Another bright, sad smile.

Returning, fabric in hand, he clears a space on the kitchen table and spreads out the patches. He sits, reaches out, finds two pieces that seem to make sense together. The kitten climbs down and settles into his lap, purring, whilst the tears form and fall. Making anew to re-pair; new stitches to hold together a new patchwork quilt, in the old frayed fabric of the world.

Steve's diary

2 November, for what it's worth

I want her. I'll start with that. I bloody want her. I've always wanted her. I'd say I *need* her, but she'd probably say that ain't the same thing. But what bloody difference does it make? – I still want her, but don't have her.

And I can't. Can't have her. Simple as that.

And it bloody hurts.

She says write it all down, get it out of my system – that's what all this is about it, ain't it, though I doubt it'll help. So here goes, dear effing diary. Start from the top. Or somewhere.

Okay. I'm Steve. I can manage that bit. Steve Hallam, for what it's worth. Twenty-eight years old, and still living with me bloody parents, here in bloody Bolton. Guess they'd say I'm the failure of the family: me sister's followed me mum into teaching, and me brother's gone one better than dad and got his full engineer's ticket from uni, and me, all I've got is a fitter-and-welder cert from the tech and a dead-end job at Hobart's like the half the other scrags in this dead-end town. Least I'm better than production-line, cos that really would drive me mad.

Dead-end town. Dead-end job. Dead-end life. Certainly feels that bloody way.

And – no, can't even write her name in here, even that hurts too bloody much right now – Anyway, she and I grew up together. Always liked her. Then a lot more than just liked her. And she always liked me too, I know that. She still does – I know that now too. That's what bloody hurts. We never did get it together – having mum in the same school was bad enough, but she was our class teacher every bloody year through that school, so that screwed any chance I might have had with any of the birds there. Let alone with her. And the only other birds I've known are into it just for what they can get for themselves and nothing more, take a guy to the bloody cleaners and never give nothing back, and I seen too many of my mates get ripped to shreds that way. So I got into drinking with the lads as the only bloody thing I could do, and walking the hills when I wasn't drinking, and she got into studying and drawing and singing and all that stuff, and then she was gone.

Till last month, when I saw her back in town. With a kid on one arm, and a guy on the other. A Traveller, by the look of him, and she looked it too. Travellers, making a few quid here and there, singing at pubs and that, and then always moving on afore someone gets pissed off with them and trashes all their gear. She sees me, recognises me, comes running over, gives me a great big kiss – and yeah, that brings it all back. Even writing that brings it all back.

The baby's still a squeaker, but she introduces her guy, name of Rouge or something like that, decent enough lad which makes it a bit better, I suppose, but of course I hate him just because he's where I've always wanted to be. With her. Jealous ain't easy. And we talk a bit, the usual crap about the time of day and such, and then she waves, and he waves, and even the squeaker waves, and they're gone.

And we meet up again a week later at my usual, the Monmouth, where they've got a gig. I've been playing a bit of keyboards there too – feels like it's the only bloody thing I can do now other than drinking – bluesy stuff, a bit of casso and such, nothing much but at least it keeps me sane and off the booze a bit when I'm there. So we get a chance to talk a bit while her guy's up on stage with the rest of their crew. Doesn't make it any better – just reminds me what I ain't got – but I agree to meet up with her again at some kind of gathering they've got at one of the old places down south.

Which we did, a couple of nights back. Can't remember the name of the place, a tiddly little village with just the one pub, in the middle of a bloody great circular ditch and some huge old stones like up the back end of the Peaks. We talk some more, but that's it, really. I want her, and she wants me, but I dunno that's good to know that at last, because it ain't going to change. They ain't got much, those Travellers, but they not far off own each other, those two, and the kid owns her, there's no doubt about that at all. I don't figure in that equation.

And she's a Traveller, for god's sake, she's got the life she wants. Best I could offer her is a two-up-two-down box in the scrag end of Bolton with the cops' sirens howling all the bloody time and the kids having to scram out the way afore they get flattened by the heavies and the drug-heads. She'd be gone in a week, or be a strait-jacket job in two.

So I want what I can't have. Story of my bloody life, really.

I'm going to have to get out of here. Have to get out of here. I can't face seeing her in the street again. And even if I do push off out of Bolton, chance is that I'll bump into her on the streets of Edinburgh, or Solihull, or bloody Milton Keynes or wherever.

Feel like I'm bloody possessed by this.

But what the hell can I do? Where the bloody hell *can* I go?

Scattered fragments

In the background, in the unseen distance away to the right, beyond the end of the corridor, the screams settle down from terror to simple fright and fear of the unknown. Jeni sits on the floor, silent, slumped, leaning against the wall of the corridor. Exhausted. Exhilarated, perhaps. Released. Overloaded, certainly.

She's perhaps thirteen. Perhaps tall for her age, short hair, scarily thin, but with an energy that exudes far beyond her small frame. Scattered all round her are plates and fragments of plates, some still spinning and settling to the floor. Shattered plates and shattered glass all round the swing doors from the school's kitchen area. Whoever threw those plates – or whatever threw them, perhaps – there was no small amount of force behind it. Yet the half-open door, still swinging on its hinge from the impact, shows there's no-one in the kitchen. Hasn't been for some time. The place is empty.

A crash as the doors are flung open at the far end of the corridor. To the simpering chorus of wails continuing from behind her, a heavier-built girl, perhaps a year older, runs in, skids to a stop in front of the slight girl on the floor, kneels down. An arm around the shoulder; words whispered in an ear. Jeni allows herself to be helped upright. Stops for a moment; looks in wonder at the chaos around her.

"Don' worry about that, darls, we'll fix it…"

"I did it, Kimmie – I *did* it!" Exhilaration; wonder.

"Yeah. You did. An' those slags won't bother you about nothin' no more. Not for now, anyway." She holds Jeni's hand, gives her a gentle tug. "C'mon, girl – gotta get you outta here afore any of the teachers come."

Jeni allows herself to be lead down the corridor, away from the sound of angry questioning that begins to be heard beyond the far doors.

Don Mercer and Tony Morrison

From Walther Hannau, *Tony Morrison: Nurturing the Revolution*

It was at Derwent that Tony finally found the mentor he needed. James Mercer – affectionately known by all his students as 'the Don' – had recently joined the faculty as a full-fledged lecturer, after completing his doctorate the year before, and had been tasked with developing the new Philosophy and Theory of Law unit. He and Tony hit off their friendship immediately, as Don recalls:

> "It was actually my first time on an interview panel, and I think Tony would have been about the fourth or fifth prospective student we assessed on that day. I remember him as a striking young man even then, tall, with an engaging smile and an unusually sharp intellect, even amongst the calibre of students we expected at Derwent. What impressed me most, I think, was that at age eighteen, with no formal legal training, he'd already arrived independently at the same conclusions as I had about the failed relationship between law and sustainability in possession-based economies."

This was, of course, the theme for Don's doctoral thesis on sustainable law, the first seeds of the revolution. Even in those early days, long before sustainability issues came to the fore of public attention, it was not unusual for students to recognise some of the problems, particularly around the impact of corporate law; but Tony, says Don, was one of the few who could take it beyond the level of gut feel and into fully detailed and reasoned legal argument. The legal argument, in turn, was always grounded in an astute grasp of human psychology and social relationships.

By the start of his second semester at Derwent, Tony was the most active member of the Theory group, and already contributing key ideas towards the subsequent SusLaw model. For example, the Derwent archives include this formal query between Tony and Don on a Theory of Law assignment, with perhaps the first clear reference we have to the question of rights versus responsibilities that was to underpin so much of the earlier stages of Tony's career:

Don

I know everyone else is working on content for a Bill of Rights, but I don't think it's the right approach.

The problem I see happening is that with a Bill of Rights people tend to think that they're the only ones with rights, or at best their own rights have priority over everyone else's. Even more, there's an assumption because the Bill defines and guarantees those rights, individuals can assume that the onus for their protection is always the responsibility of others rather than themselves. Because responsibility is so often equated with blame, anyone who does accept responsibility for anything tends to be blamed and punished even for entirely unrelated incidents, as evidenced in the litigation-centric culture in the US. So not only is there no active incentive for individual responsibility in a Bill of Rights, there are strong disincentives against taking responsibility.

But as I see it, without responsibilities, nothing works. Without responsibilities, there are no rights.

Geoff and Lynn suggest that we solve this with some kind of charter of social responsibilities as an addendum to the Bill of Rights, but to me it still places too much emphasis on the supposed rights. A 'right' is a declaration of a desired outcome, but without any indication of how we could achieve that outcome. So we can't derive responsibilities from rights. But we can derive rights from responsibilities, by structuring relationships between responsibilities to achieve the desired outcome.

For example, in traffic law there is no actual right of way. Instead, there are defined sets of responsibilities to give way, which interlock to create an effective 'right of way' for each potential point of conflict. Potential for unfair 'rights' is reduced by ensuring that any asymmetries are resolved over time. In the same example, we give way at a red traffic light because we would have priority on our green, or we give way to an emergency vehicle on our green because we might be the one needing the emergency vehicle next time, and so on.

It also seems to be simpler to define legislation in terms of responsibilities rather than rights. Each potential asymmetry requires only a description of the desired outcome, a link to the overall outcome, and a defence that demonstrates how the asymmetry is resolved over time or in some other way.

The difficulty is that this suggests there is no valid defence for supposed 'rights' that are inherently asymmetric, such as Karin Fairchild's proposal for a Bill of Women's Rights. In fact, in terms of this approach, her proposal in its current form would be interpreted as an attempt to enshrine automatic priority in law for women and legally-enforced abuse against men, because it assigns all responsibility for women's protection to men alone, along with all of the blame. This cannot be seen as defensible in legal ethics, though I know she will disagree with me on this. But I am certain that the problems there are political rather than legal.

So to me this approach seems more sustainable than a Bill of Rights, and would lead to fewer arguments over priorities.

May I develop this direction as my paper for the assignment?

Thanks – Tony M.

As can be seen, the query also presages the incident that was to launch his career as a politician. The clash with Karin Fairchild and the Women's Rights caucus at the National Student Conference that autumn won him few friends and many enemies, though given the dominant ideology-driven political-correctness in that milieu it was unlikely that his insistent challenges on the ethics of the caucus' proposals had any chance of success. His diary shows that he was badly shaken by the vehemence of the personal attacks against him, and clearly felt he was greatly and perhaps intentionally misunderstood. But he gained the respect of many in the legal profession and elsewhere for his calm demeanour and flawless presentation of reasoning, in the face of perhaps the most savage diatribes of his entire career.

At this time, Fairchild herself seemed set for a meteoric rise. But as with so many of her peers, feminism's self-contradictions and inherent self-dishonesty later proved to be her undoing, and her career ended in disgrace when she was convicted and jailed for promoting perjury as a deliberate policy in her Women's Legal Resource Centre network. This confirmed to the letter Tony's explanation and warning of the logical end-point of the 'women's rights' ideology, though the foreknowledge of this outcome would have brought him little satisfaction. Instead, after this first rude awakening to the dishonesty and irrationality that pervaded so much of the politics of the time, he became determined to recover, to research, and to learn.

Steve's diary

I got to get out of here, out of Bolton, out of this dead-end life. And real soon now, too, before I go off my bootle. But still don't know how.

Tried the bloody job-agencies, no dice there. There's jobs around, but most of them are up here in the midlands or the north, which means I'd still see her. And they all want an arm and a leg for their money, pretty much your whole bloody life it seems. Not as bad as a bloody Yank closed-debt contract, of course, nothing could be <u>that</u> bad, thank god we've still managed to keep those bastards out, but still too bloody close to it for my liking. So I'm still stuck at Hobart's for now.

Gave meself a bit of a laugh and had a look in a travel agent's. Got a bit of money aside, could give meself a bloody holiday if nothing else, and it'd be better than getting myself lost in the booze as a way to forget her, I'd guess. Went through a whole bunch of brochures and stuff about a whole bunch of different places, but nothing seemed like it would work, just spending money for the sake of spending money, really. Went through pretty much the whole bloody store looking for ideas, they even suggested Australia, for god's sake. And yeah, odd, it did kind of stand out, I guess, but only because everyone knows they're bloody mad there, cuckoo-clock ain't in it, the whole bloody country's supposed to be clean round the twist. So no, I ain't crazy enough to go <u>there.</u> I'll think of something.

But better be soon.

Home Matters

Radio 3QJ: *"Home Matters"*, Tuesday 8th March

Transcript of interview with Dr Donald Mercer: Part 2

Jane Ruhr [presenter]: Welcome back to Home Matters. If you've just joined us, our guest today is Dr Don Mercer, senior lecturer in law at Derwent University, who's just added another item to his already formidable list of publications. This week his latest book, "Traditional Quilting", was published by Alpha Press, at $14.95. If you haven't seen it yet, go out and buy it: Don's work is really beautiful, and the book is very well presented.

Earlier in the show, Don, we talked about your techniques and the various traditions from different countries that you've brought together in your work. But there's something I suppose every woman listening to this show will want to know: what's a man like you doing writing a book on needlework?

Don Mercer: Now that's a bit of a sexist question, isn't it? [laughter] Seriously, though, I'd have to say that it's a sad story with something of a happier ending. Textiles were Mary's work, of course, but I suppose I've always loved the feel and texture of fabrics too – it's one reason we came together in the first place, I think – and we collected tapestries and quilts and the like from all over the world. Our cleaner hated them: said they were good for nothing but collecting dust! [laughter] Mary loved the *doing* of needlework, too: she was always making something to hang on the wall, or to decorate some piece of furniture.

But when she died five years ago, after a car accident, as you know, I found myself on my own, in a house full of memories and half-finished fabrics. I needed something to do, to take my mind off things, as it were, and it seemed wrong to leave everything unfinished – I knew Mary wouldn't want that. So with the help of one of our friends, Anne Murray, I set out to remember what I'd learnt about sewing, all those years ago, from my grandmother back in Somerset. I spend my

professional life thinking, you see – it's very therapeutic to do
something with my hands! One thing led to another, as they
do, and I had my first exhibition at the Needlework Guild, in
memory of Mary, in August two years ago.

JR: That caused quite a stir, didn't it? And not just because you
were exhibiting.

DM: That's true! [laughter] At that time the Guild was still called
the Needlewomen's Guild, and – quite reasonably, I thought –
I suggested that we really ought to change the name to bring it
up to date. Most of the members are women, of course, but
there are quite a few men, too – Geoff Anstey, who's Proctor
at the university, is another well-known one. Unfortunately,
several of the more prominent women members didn't see it
that way, and weren't very happy about it – or us. Looking
back now, all those arguments seem so unnecessary, but it
didn't seem so at the time. Changes like these are important –
sometimes very much so.

JR: Yes – I do agree. And I gather that in much the same way
you're also quite famous – even notorious – amongst your
colleagues for something called the 'Sustainable Law Project'.
Could you tell us a bit about it?

DM: Oh, that! [laughter] It's actually an offshoot of our course on
philosophy of law at the university. It started life as a student
project – my doctoral thesis, in fact – but we've used it ever
since as a test case for our students to practice on, and it's
become quite a respectable body of law in its own right. The
idea behind it is quite simple. Current Australian law is based
on the Westminster system, but we Europeans have only been
on this continent for a couple of centuries or so, and our laws
have to keep changing all the time, trying to keep pace with
changes in society.

JR: Can you give us an example of this?

DM: Oh, certainly. One which many of our listeners would know
about is the changes in life-patterns which gave rise to equal-
opportunity legislation. Around the end of the nineteenth
century one of the main themes of our society was 'Populate
or Perish': Australia simply didn't have enough people to
keep going. With all the advances in medicine since then, it's
hard these days to realise just how serious that was. For
example, if you were living then, Jane, you would probably
have had seven or eight children by the time you'd reached

your present age – and buried more than half of them already. And there'd be a real chance that you'd already be dead, too.

JR: That's horrific!

DM: Exactly – to us, now. But in fact it was almost accepted then: that was the way things were. To give you a personal example, Mary's great-grandmother went to work one morning, leaving her six happy, healthy children with her mother, as was usual enough in those days. By the time she came home that night, only one child was still alive: the rest of them were dead, from diphtheria, which had swept down the street and killed most of the children there in a single day. That kind of tragedy wasn't unusual then: more people died in the great influenza epidemic of 1919 than had been killed in the whole of the Great War that preceded it. To make matters worse, one woman in ten died in childbirth. These were real problems: too real, in many ways.

So for the children to survive – for the nation to survive – something had to be done. From society's perspective, that meant that new law was needed. The women's movement of the time argued that children could only be cared for properly by their mothers – this was also a time, you'll remember, when the old extended families were breaking down, with immigration, and the general move to the cities. So legislation was passed, which effectively reserved most jobs for married men – not so that women would be forced to be dependent on men, as some of my feminist colleagues still seem to believe, but so that mothers were supported in staying at home. In those days marriage generally meant children, usually quite quickly: so as a woman, the day you got married was the day you left your job – because your real job, from then on, was to help your children thrive. All well and good – for those times, and for most people, anyway.

But then things changed. With improved medicine, thankfully, children simply didn't die in the way that they had: so there were fewer of them needing women's full-time care. Then the men were sent away to another lengthy war, leaving jobs that could only be done by the women – and they did them well. When the men came back from that war, there was the expectation for a while that things would simply go back to the way that they had been – but things had changed. And by the 1960s, the old legislation, allocating jobs by gender, was simply absurd – so it was repealed, and replaced by equal opportunity legislation. Which still needs quite a bit more tinkering before it really is equal, but that's another story!

But I think you can see what I'm getting at: in response to what people say they want, the law tries to define how things should be, but it's always aiming at a moving target – which, apart from anything else, means that it's almost always out of date. And so it goes on.

JR: I do see what you mean. But what do you mean by 'sustainable law'? And what difference would it make, for people like our listeners?

DM: The original idea for the sustainable law project came from permaculture, which most of our listeners will know about, I think. Permaculture aims to interweave the needs of people with the needs of the environment, so that all needs are met in a sustainable way – hence permaculture, you see, permanent agriculture. Permaculture was pioneered here in Australia, back in the early 1980s, and has since become something of a practical revolution, a real success story. But it can't really be sustainable, at the level of the whole society, unless there's a system of law that fully supports it – which is where the idea of sustainable law comes in.

JR: I don't see what the difference is. Doesn't the existing system – the Westminster system, you called it – do this?

DM: No, it doesn't: that's the problem. One of the principles of permaculture is "protracted and thoughtful observation rather than protracted and thoughtless action" – and I think we'd all have to admit that 'protracted and thoughtless action' does describe our present system rather too well! [laughter] At present, the law changes almost at random, following the whims of fashion in politics and the world economy. In some ways this instability is hardly surprising: politicians in particular can rarely afford to think any further ahead than the next election. But that's the way things are: and being realistic, I think it would take a catastrophe of worldwide proportions before that would change.

JR: It certainly seems like it! [laughter]

DM: Yes! But it seems to us to be worthwhile to at least allow ourselves to indulge in some 'protracted and thoughtful observation', as it were, and see if we can find any way in which the results of that observation could be applied to things as they are. In particular, we're aiming to learn from other people who've been along the same path, as it were, trying to create a system of law – or principles of law, at least – that would stand for centuries. And the systems that really have stood the test of time are those of the old traditional or tribal societies – for example, in this country, aboriginal law, though there are plenty of others that are of interest, from around the world, and throughout history, such as the ancient Irish system.

We can't apply these old legal systems directly in the modern world: we have to think carefully about how they could be adapted to suit our needs in a sustainable way. For example, almost all those societies were highly gendered, in that – for simple reasons of survival, such as the child-health issues I mentioned earlier – men did one set of jobs, women did another, and no-one crossed the boundaries. But in our society most of that is no longer necessary, and the freedom of choice is something that, as a society, we obviously want to keep. So there's a lot of thought needed: 'protracted and thoughtful observation', just as with permaculture. That's what the project is about.

JR: That seems reasonable enough – so why do some of your colleagues get so upset about it?

DM: They don't like it because they don't like what it's showing us about our society as a whole. And I must admit it worries me at times, too.

JR: Why's that?

DM: What we've come to realise is that our current system of law – in fact the entire economy that goes with it – simply isn't sustainable. We can't go on indefinitely doing what we're doing now, because it doesn't work. I mean, it does, after a fashion, obviously, but it's ridiculously inefficient in its use of resources of all kinds – people, time and materials especially. The whole system is so fragile that, quite honestly, there is a real risk that it could collapse at any time, in a really big way. We already know that it tends to break down anyway, quite often – such as in the Depression years of the 1890s and 1920s, or the computer-driven stock-market crash of 1989 – but what we're seeing is that those problems are inherent in the system, so to speak, and that the whole thing is held together by little more than wishful thinking. We're not exactly popular in some quarters for saying this, as you can imagine! [laughter] But our research does demonstrate beyond reasonable doubt that the problems are real, and it seems at least prudent to research alternatives that genuinely are sustainable.

JR: What would those alternatives look like, then? And, again, how would they affect ordinary people – the mother of two children, for example?

DM: As we see it, there need to be at least two absolutely fundamental changes to our current system of law, to make our society and our economy sustainable. But in many ways they really wouldn't change all that much for – as you put it – ordinary people. There'd need to be a big change in attitude, though, which is often the hardest thing of all to create – which is why all of this is still no more than a research project, though a very interesting one.

JR: I'm sorry, I don't understand: what are these changes you're proposing? What change in attitude?

DM: A change in attitude to property: what belongs to you, what belongs to me, what belongs to someone else, what belongs to everyone. It's a bit difficult to explain, but our present system of law describes property in terms of exclusive possession: if I own something, I can do what I like with it, without having to ask anyone else, or care about what effect it has on anyone else. In other words, without any responsibility to anyone else. Mostly, that is: we have all sorts of law – an enormous amount of law – about nuisance, and pollution, and so on. But all of that law – all of it – actually arises because of a fundamental problem with the notion of ownership. It's a problem that doesn't exist in tribal law: they have a completely different notion of property. For example, there's much more emphasis on sharing: it's obviously much more efficient in use of resources than our present system, where sharing is thought of as rather odd and unwise, whereas in many native American tribes, for example, to hoard something, and not share it, was thought of as a mental illness. So there's usually a sort of communal ownership in tribal law, but it's not like what was attempted in the communist states: that one simply doesn't work, because the attitude is that it belongs to everyone, hence belongs to no-one, and everything falls apart because no-one cares. What we see instead in tribal law is a concept of stewardship, of responsibility: we own something because we use it and maintain it, and for no other reason. I think it's beautifully expressed in the old aboriginal statement that "we belong to the land: the land belongs to no-one" – in other words it belongs to itself. Misunderstanding the true meaning of that phrase led to the mistaken claim that Australia was 'terra nullius' – land belonging to no-one, hence up for grabs – which created all sorts of problems we're still living with today.

So the change in attitude that we're suggesting needs to be supported in law is quite simple: I own something because I use it and am responsible for it. But it actually belongs to everyone: and if I'm not using it, it's my job – my responsibility – to ensure that it goes to someone else who can make better use of it than I would. That's the most effective use of our resources as a nation: and a system of law that supports that is sustainable law.

JR: Are you serious about this? It sounds horribly close to the kind of 'collectivisation' that happened in Stalin's Russia, you know...

DM: No, no, it really is quite different. We're talking about a system of law that actively supports your ownership – your stewardship, rather – of something as long as you're using it. That's your personal choice and personal responsibility, and it would be little different from what we have at present, in practice, though the law describing it would be much simpler. Only in the case where you're not using something, or not using it well, could someone formally request the use of that resource from you – and a sustainable law would support them in doing so. Again, it's expressed particularly well in some systems of aboriginal law: the idea of 'singing the site', where within the framework of a formal ceremony you're allowed to demonstrate that you know the songs of a place better than the person who currently has use of the site, and hence you claim to be better suited to maintain it.

So you see there would be very little change for most of us, for most things: the only big 'losers', if you like, would be people who currently possess far more than they use. And even then they wouldn't really lose anything, because if they're not using it, it effectively doesn't exist as far as they're concerned. All they're doing is preventing others from using it – which, as I've said, isn't efficient in the overall use of our resources.

JR: Whew! I can see why people get upset at this! [laughter] But that's just one of your two 'fundamental changes': what's the other one?

DM: Quite simple, but probably quite impossible: an end to money.

JR: Seriously?

DM: Yes. I know it sounds mad at first...

JR: You're not wrong there! [laughter]

DM: ...but if you think about it for a while – and believe me, we've thought long and hard about this – you'll see that it's nothing like as crazy as it sounds.

JR: This isn't some kind of moral crusade, is it? – you know, "money is the root of all evil", and all that?

DM: No, no, we're talking about something quite different. Our only objection to money, from the standpoint of sustainable law, is simply that it doesn't work. Or work well, rather. Think about it for a moment. A vast amount of current law is concerned with money, and protecting money, for money's sake – and nothing else. Having an economy based primarily on money is also a startling waste of resources: for example, something like a third of all jobs are involved primarily or exclusively in the transfer of money – banks, taxes, welfare, insurance, cashiers, guards and so on. That waste simply doesn't happen in tribal law. It doesn't even happen in your own home, if you think about it: for example, your son's six, isn't he? – does he pay you to do the cooking, or the washing-up?

JR: I wish! [laughter]

DM: So it is with most other things in the home – and in the rest of society, in fact. Think of all the volunteer groups, and all the work they do, unpaid – yet it's all essential to our society. The word 'economy' literally means 'the management of the household' – and the money side, as you'll know, is only a tiny part of managing a household. The easy bit, in many ways. It's only in recent times that 'economy' has become so synonymous with money. As I say, it doesn't occur in most tribal law: there's something a bit like money often used in exchanges between groups, but not within them – it simply isn't necessary. Money is really a standardised form of barter: but if, as we're suggesting, we come to understand that we don't actually own anything – we use it, but we don't possess it – then there's no legal basis or need for barter, and hence no need for money.

JR: I think I see what you mean there...

22

DM: Another problem with money, as a basis for the economy and the law, is that it's a very poor way of managing resources over a lifetime. If you think of the stereotype life-cycle – you know, from infant to child to adolescent to young married, then with children, and then with teenagers, and on into middle age, retirement, and so on – you'll notice that there's an almost perfect mismatch between monetary income and monetary needs. If you're lucky, you'll have money available whenever you don't really need it; but whenever you really need it most, it just isn't there.

JR: Ain't that the truth...

DM: We're supposed to bridge the gaps by 'saving' – which again doesn't work at all well. Sometimes people get lucky; more often they don't. And the savings tend to evaporate anyway in charges and fees for layer upon layer of middlemen who add little if any value at all. So for the nation as a whole, it really would be much more efficient to do away with it completely.

JR: Certainly be nice to do away with taxes!

DM: Yes, indeed! [laughter] That's something everyone wants, I'd guess! [laughter] Unfortunately it's not quite as simple as that, though it would take quite a time to explain why.

Coming back to money, though, a big complication is that – certainly as far as the law is concerned – we currently depend very heavily on money not just as a carrot, but as a stick to beat people with if they don't conform to society's demands. By that I mean things like fines, and so on. Tribal systems of law either don't bother with any equivalent – they rely on customs and attitudes instead – or else use what we would now think of as barbaric forms of coercion, such a spear-challenge, or cutting off the offender's ear, or hand. Or head. Not surprisingly, we don't want that in any modern system of law; but the problem of conformance and coercion is real, and it's one that still needs to be resolved.

JR: Again, are you serious about all this?

DM: Oh, yes. But only in the sense that we think it's a worthwhile research project. It certainly gets our students thinking, anyway...

JR: I'll believe that! [laughter]

DM: ...and they do come up with some very good ideas of their own. But you honestly needn't worry: we have no expectation that our 'sustainable law' would ever be used. It's strictly an academic exercise – though it's amusing to see the emotional outbursts it arouses! As I said earlier, there's so much investment in the current system that it really would take some kind of worldwide catastrophe before anyone – any government, at least – would dare to put it into practice. And I don't think that's very likely.

JR: But – honestly, now – do you really believe it would work?

DM: Yes, I do. It would be hard, for a while, but after that I honestly believe that no-one would want to go back to what we have now. The present system is so ridiculously inefficient, in every way: our research has shown that for certain. And it would be much more effective – and, I honestly believe, much more satisfying, for everyone – to belong to a literal 'commonwealth', in which resources are owned simply in terms of use, and are used as needed. To go back to what we first talked about, it would be like a patchwork quilt, a tapestry, if you like, with each person's life as a living thread within the fabric, weaving and interweaving with that of everyone else. And yes, as far as law is concerned, it really is as simple as I've said: for example, we really could replace every single monetary transaction with the simple phrase "What do you need?"

JR: Whew! Well, I think what we need most right now is another short break! I'm talking with Dr Don Mercer, about quilting and sustainable law, and we'll be right back after these messages from our sponsor...

This transcript copyright © Radio 3QJ, Melbourne. All rights reserved.

Mercer's law

From *The Age*, Letters page, 19th Sept

Mercer's law

I must say, I do like Prof Mercer's description of a world without money ("Sustainable Law", The Age, Wednesday). But if I follow his ideas, does that make me a mercernary? And if I don't, would he call me mercerless towards the needs of others?

Tod Ryland, Mt Dandenong

Women and guns

From *The Courier-Mail*, Wednesday

"A woman's best friend"

By our US correspondent, Maggie Combin

Only in the USA, perhaps. I'm looking at a full-page advert in the only nationwide newspaper, which begins with the caption "A woman's best friend is the pistol in her purse".

Since the end of the Cold War, reduced orders from the military have left gun-makers here struggling to meet their profit targets. To make up for the lost sales, they've turned to a previously untapped domestic market: women.

And it looks like this new clientele is taking the hook. Handguns are flying off the shelves as never before, whilst the magazine *Women and Guns* is now the hottest seller in most of the Southern states.

The industry has a multi-pronged campaign for new converts to their cause – and new sales to satisfy their shareholders.

There's the feminist position, of course. Gun-control, we hear, is nothing more than a patriarchal plot to keep women in chains. So even if you have no idea how to use a gun, just owning one will demonstrate your self-empowerment. Proof indeed of your right to count yourself amongst the leaders of the sisterhood.

And then there's the fashion angle. No smart woman could consider herself properly dressed without her Smith & Wesson 'Ladysmith', complete with its diamante trim and interchangeable hand-grips to match any style and outfit.

It's illegal to carry a concealed weapon in more than two-thirds of the US states. But that hasn't deterred fashion-houses from joining the gun-makers' charge. No ugly holster for women, please. No, the new vogue is for plush inserts for handbags, or a padded clip to go inside that subtle fur stole.

No surprise, though, that the main thrust of the sales-campaign is fear. Paid 'advertorials' crop up in every newspaper, warning every woman that she and her family at high risk of assault by strangers. Think-tanks and politicians alike have received hefty contributions from shadowy lobbyist groups for promoting the same fear-laden line.

But the facts don't support the sales-pitch. Far from it. New figures released by the Federal Bureau of Investigation show that just 45 women in the entire country used a handgun in 'justifiable homicide' last year. But for each woman whose life was saved by that "pistol in her purse", more than two hundred women died, most often killed by her own gun.

Despite the gun-lobby's myths, most of the more than 25000 gun deaths here last year were from suicide, not homicide. And like homicides, most suicides are committed with whatever weapon comes to hand. Until recently, women most often attempted to take their own life by poisons such as amphetamine overdose. But this tactic has fallen by the wayside with the increased availability of handguns.

Last year, 45 percent of women who killed themselves did so with firearms. And unlike Britain, where young males kill themselves almost three times as often as do females, here young women are killing themselves at almost the same rate as the men.

Some have called the steep rise in female suicides an 'epidemic'. But if it is, it's a man-made epidemic, and the blame lies squarely with the gun-makers and their sales-tactics.

The NRA's grand slogan "guns don't kill people" has always sounded hollow, cynical, self-serving. Yet as the stones rattle on the coffin of my friend's 16-year-old daughter, who killed herself last week with the pistol she found in her mother's handbag, that hollow sound will no doubt echo in her family's ears for many years to come.

Steve's diary

I must be going mental or something.

Had a dream last night, like I was sitting on one of those big grey laid-down stones at that village-place, like we did last time I saw her, and it kind of shook itself, kind of woke itself up a bit. Like the real one did when we was there, and I still don't know what the bloody heck happened there. And next thing, in the dream this is, I'm on me tod, sitting on the stone still, but the grass ain't there any more, it's not green, everything's gone kind of orangey-red, including the stone itself, and it's bloody hot instead of bloody cold, and all that. And I'm shrinking and I'm shrinking, or the stone's growing or something, till all I can see is the surface of this bloody enormous stone I'm on, and other rocks or mountains or whatever in the distance. And there's a pathway down, so I take it, till I'm down at ground, in amongst a whole load of trees, and though they look a bit odd they're all normal height, so it's the stone that's changed, not me. And it's quiet, real quiet, kind of calming quiet, but way out in the distance there's a kind of clacking sound, like someone banging two sticks together, in a kind of funny rhythm, a kind of funny edge to it, sort of ta-ka-ta-ta-ke-ta, like it's leading somewhere. And I move over a bit and the sound's coming from a different direction, with a different rhythm, and so on. Does this about a dozen different times, a dozen different ways, without hardly moving at all. Then I hear voices coming, talking in some funny kind of clickery language that don't make sense, so I try to hide, and then I wake up.

Yeah. Bloody mental. But it was so bloody real it wasn't funny.

What's even more bloody daft is it sounds like that bloody great rock thing they've got in the middle of Australia. Can't get bloody Australia out of my mind at the moment, but at least it means I'm not stuck thinking about her so much.

But I ain't that crazy. Not yet, anyway. I am not going there, and that's flat.

Developing the skills

Have we seen this girl before?

She's perhaps fourteen, and at first we see her only from the back, sitting in a chair in this cluttered place – an electronics lab, by the look of it. But there's a sense of familiarity about that slim body, the scruffy jeans and loose sweater-top, the birdlike stance: we *know* this girl.

Perhaps we shouldn't.

There's an air of uncertainty here, of tension, of strangeness beyond comprehensibility. A faint hum pervades the quiet focus in the room, but that in itself seems no cause for unease. There are two other people here – a middle-aged woman beside the girl, also birdlike, tall, thin, all emphasised by the circular wire-rimmed glasses; and a younger man, off to one side, intently watching the dials on a simple fascia perched amongst a tangled nest of wire. A twisted rope of ribbon-cable leads away from the rack to the helmet the girl wears: once an ordinary industrial hard-hat, it seems, but now adorned with extraneous electronics, including a standard sensor-mike and a bare see-through projection-holograph display-panel seemingly pulled out of a discarded laptop and tacked into place with hot-melt resin. Another cable threads its way to a well-worn joystick crudely clamped to the chair-arm below the girl's left hand. A typical lab-prototype lash-up, in other words: a little odd, perhaps, but nothing that much out of the usual there. Still no explanation as to why this all feels, well, just plain *weird*…

And then, as our hidden eye moves round, to the side, toward the front, we see it. A small wooden ball, no more than four or five centimetres across, each quadrant painted in different bright colours, red, blue, white, black, yellow, green. And floating in mid-air, with no visible support, gently quivering, directly in front of the girl, and perhaps half a metre from her face. Something that clearly should not be possible; and yet, here, now, in this place, clearly is.

Madness.

Certainty falls away, as the ball stays firmly in place. Is *held* in place.

In a calm, certain voice, the woman murmurs quiet instructions to the girl.

"Good... that's good... now rotate left... good... and right..."

At each command, the girl's knuckles whiten, as she adjusts the joystick in her hand. A moment later, the ball twists slightly, as if on some puppet-master's hidden wire. Except there's no wire there: *we know* this now.

"Now up... rotate up and away from you... very good... now stop the rotation... now ten centimetres to the left... twenty... thirty... and back to the centre again... *very* good..."

Seemingly following the words alone, the painted ball performs its matching pirouette in the empty air...

An urgent beeping comes from another instrument-rack off to one side. The young technician quickly reaches out to silence it, but too late. Distracted, the girl spins round – and the ball instantly drops to the ground.

"Blast! Sorry, Jeni, my fault, you were doing really well there."

"Can you get it going again, Marko?" asks the older woman.

"Yeah, give me a minute, just need to reboot the VR server."

The girl lifts up the visor on the helmet, pushes a wayward strand of dark hair out of the way.

"I can do it without the bender, Cory – look, I'll show you...?"

Without moving from the seat, she reaches down toward the floor. A moment's pause, then the ball leaps up, seemingly of its own volition – but bounces off her outstretched fingers, hitting the window-pane with a crack. Cory moves to retrieve the wayward object before it rolls underneath another cluttered desk.

"We know how much mass you can move, dear. And you're getting better every day. But you also need practice with *precision*, and that's where the bender will help right now." She smiles. "If Marko can get it going again, that is."

"Just a mo'... nearly there... yep, we got greens on all channels. When you're ready, Jeni?"

The girl pulls down the visor again. Cory gently throws the ball toward her; it stops in mid-air. And does not drop.

As this strange, impossible practice-session continues, we make our silent, invisible way back out of the room. The image fades, as if in a dream.

Was it just imaginary? Or real?

And if it was indeed real – and it certainly seems that way – just who *are* these people? How is it possible they can bend our everyday reality so easily in this casual-seeming way?

And where do they come from? Or when, perhaps?

Steve's diary

I really *am* going mental about this Australia thing.

Even went out and <u>bought</u> a copy of that *New Australia Travel Guide*, didn't just get it out of the library for free like anyone else would.

And I don't even bloody <u>want</u> to go there, that's what's so bloody mental about it.

Don't know what's up with me at the moment, I really don't.

Saber-rattling

Class: RESTRICTED::USEO
From: COL Andrew T. Brewer, TACRESPAC, San Diego
To: GEN Thomas J. Keene, DEFPUBREL, Pentagon
Date: July 18
Re: *MMRA and Australian uranium*

Tom

Thanks for warning me about Kohlker at MMRA. I know it ain't gonna be fun, but can you find some way to get him off our ass about this?

I do know he thinks he's short on raw for weapons-grade. And yes, I -do- know our job is tactical resources. And I sure don't disagree that uranium is a tactical resource. But we've told him and his goddamn competitors over and over that there's more than enough in the old stockpiles. So they can darn well re-process it. So what if it'll cost more? – they can't expect to make a goddamn fat profit -every- time, can they? I ain't buying it: this is his problem, not ours, and we intend to keep it that way.

Please remind him the Aussies aren't mining the stuff any more. And with the crazy way they run things over there these days, we can't see any way we can force them to. Can't buy 'em off, that's for sure.

And he can forget any ideas about our doing another Davao: I am -not- going to sit in front of Congress again and explain that we've sent in our troops – or anyone else's – to do his dirty work at taxpayer's expense. So Kohlker can go saber-rattle all he likes, but we are -not- going to start a war with the Aussies over this.

Our military links over there are thin compared to the old days, but they are still our allies, in PacRim and elsewhere. And they do enough UN blue-beret work to cause us -big- problems in that quarter if we end up playing Kohlker's patsy.

In any case, the view here at TacRes is the Aussies are a definite no-no for resource raids. There's something real weird going on there we do -not- want to mess with. They may -seem- like a bunch of woo-woos half the time, but there's a real nasty feeling that if we try going in heavy with them like Kohlker wants, we'll come out of it with egg all over our faces.

Remember two years ago, that Indon faction trying a sneak attack on Darwin, when they claimed northern Australia as their 'New Irian Jaya'? Sank their own entire goddamn fleet with friendly fire: five minutes and not a single warship left afloat. Survivors said nothing happened at all, no challenge from the Aussies, no nothing, until they crossed into Australian waters – then all hell broke loose, missile systems switching themselves on, refusing manual override, picking their targets and all launching in the same moment, while the on-ship defenses didn't even wake up till it was all over.

And we sold them those missile systems, too – exact same anti-ship setups as we use in our own Pacific fleet. That's what's got us rattled here, because no-one knows what the hell happened. The Aussies know, for sure, but they sure aren't telling. All they had to do was turn up as if it was some kinda accident, pick up the pieces in that smug so-concerned way of theirs, and walk away smelling like roses. Real scary shit.

We've had a taste of it, too, because they shit all over us when we were up against them at the last PacRim joint exercises. They had some kind of crazy comms gear that picked out every move we tried before we'd even started it, while all we could get out of the satellites was pictures of the Dodgers game in San Francisco. The sky was a mess – lost control of most of the spy-bugs the moment they hit the air, half our planes out of action with gremlins in the avionics, targeting systems couldn't tell north from south, all that kinda shit. Half the time we couldn't even get the goddamn GPS to make sense – yeah, something -that- simple – you can guess how much that screwed things up. And they knew it, too: you bet they laughed at us.

Since then we've tried every which way to find how the hell they did it, or how their stuff works. We acquired one of their boxes, of course, but we still can't make any sense of it: Ted Schickel over in ELINFO Sacramento can fill you in more on this. He swears their physics is total horseshit, either that or the SO boys got ourselves a dud; but we've even seen fully-shielded electronics go crazy when it's in the same room as this thing, sometimes when it isn't even switched on. Creepy as hell, I tell you.

So we need you to keep this quiet from the politicos. The Aussies seem so far ahead of us in this that I wouldn't mind betting the bastards could send even a tactical nuke to sleep, and send it straight back home. Believe me, I do not want to have to explain that one to Congress!

And yeah, I know damn well Kohlker won't like it. So I'll bet you ten to one what his next move will be: lean on Miller in Special Ops. He's spent too goddamn long wallowing in the boardroom, and read too many goddamn comic books: he probably doesn't realise we can't just "nip in under cover of darkness" and pick up ten thousand tons of uranium ore on the back of an SO stealth cutter. Warn Charlie we have an idiot on the rampage, will you?

Andy

Language

From *The New Australia Travel Guide*

Language

More than 160 languages are spoken in Australia, and in some states up to thirty may be used in public documents. The main language, though, is **standard English**. Australia being Australia, of course, there are a few local quirks and variations that can cause visitors some confusion or concern.

Spelling can be erratic, even on public documents. Officially, it is supposed to be an amalgam of British and American spellings, though usually closer to the British form. Expect '-ise' endings rather than '-ize', for example, and '-our' rather than '-or'. But you'll find 'labour' also spelt as 'labor' – the latter being a last remnant of the long-defunct Labor Party.

Structure can sometimes seem more like French than English, because of a common preference to avoid possessives such as 'my' or 'your' – hence 'the child of them', for example, rather than 'their child'. Many older people, particularly those who went to school before the Troubles, will still use the older possessive forms, but the usage is deprecated. With younger people, possessives are often used almost as an obscenity or an insult, so this can be one place where you do need to watch your language!

On the other hand, mild *swearing* is almost a standard feature of Australian English, so don't be surprised to hear 'bloody' this-that-and-the-other in almost any sentence, and from almost anyone. Even the word 'bugger' was officially sanctioned as acceptable language more than half a century ago, well before the Troubles, when a car-manufacturer used it in an advertising slogan. The general recommendation, though, is "don't compete with the locals" – listen to the local usage, tone it down a couple of notches, and you should be fine.

The other feature of Australian language which confuses almost every foreigner is a common tendency to pepper the dialogue with a breadth of *idioms* and similes that vary from the colourful to the flat-out incomprehensible. The range of graphic alternatives for 'vomit', for example, is truly legendary – perhaps from too much practice! Idioms for distance include the sequence:

- *out bush* – regional, some distance from a city
- *back o'Bourke* – rural, 'remote', by European standards
- *beyond the black stump* – remote even by Australian standards

See the *Dictionary* for other common examples; otherwise ask for a translation. We suspect, though, that many idioms are made up on the spot just to confuse tourists – you have been warned!

Prelude to disaster

From *The Independent*, London

Wholesale corruption – literally

The Australian election was thrown into turmoil yesterday with shock revelations that both major parties have been funding their political campaigns by large-scale drug-trafficking.

Senior police from several states have been identified as key players in a corruption scandal that has rocked the nation to the core.

A number of officers have also been implicated in the murder of Alexandr Topolski, the telecomms technician who accidentally recorded the incriminating teleconference between police and politicians on Wednesday.

Topolski was killed in a drive-by shooting shortly after delivering a copy of the recording to Canberra police. Highways Authority specialists identified the assailants' vehicle from motorway-camera footage as an unmarked police-car attached to the Parliamentary Protection Unit.

The Canberra copy of the tape is missing, presumed destroyed. But with the agreement of the Supreme Court, the original has now been lodged with representatives of *Four Corners*, ABC TV's current-affairs programme. The ABC have promised to publish a formally validated transcript within the next few hours. In the meantime, unauthorised versions have already started to appear on activist websites.

The government's justice minister, Attorney-General Andrew Pattinson, and opposition Shadow Attorney-General Alberto Morenzi have both been remanded without bail. Other arrests are expected as the urgent investigation continues.

Senior police already named in the affair include Commissioner Morag Campbell and the head of Queensland Police, Bob Murrell. Campbell was arrested at Laverton International Airport near Melbourne by military security officers yesterday evening whilst attempting to board a flight to Singapore. It is understood she was carrying a false passport and more than AUD$550,000 (€365,000) in foreign currency.

Early evidence from former officers indicates a "systematic culture of corruption and intimidation" at every level of police forces in all Australian states.

Two unnamed witnesses from Topolski's work-team have been offered protective custody by the Australian Army.

Topolskigate

Part of transcript from *Channel 6 News*, Friday

Max Amon (presenter): Now to Australia, where Claire Hammill has the latest on what's been nicknamed the Topolskigate affair.

Claire Hammill: Thanks, Max. Some details of the scale of the corruption are only now starting to come out, but we already know it was huge. It's alleged the Topolski tape describes a previously seized shipment of heroin with a street value of more than ten million euros that was to be sold on by police via a shadowy network of protected traffickers. First reports from police officers now in Army custody indicate this kind of transaction was happening almost on a daily basis.

I spoke with former Inspector Gavin Rowan, who was suspended without pay two years ago for alleged misconduct, after reporting possible evidence of corruption to then Deputy Commissioner Morag Campbell.

Gavin Rowan: You saw it everywhere, it was obvious there was some of kind of big secret going on. Anyone who was honest was either transferred, kicked out or framed for false disciplinary offences. It was the same with anyone who asked awkward questions, so you soon knew to keep your mouth shut. And whistleblowers, well, I'm one of the lucky ones, I'm still alive. Most of the senior people who got too close met up with fatal 'accidents', or were simply rubbed out.

Claire Hammill: Investigations have been reopened into the murders last year of Chief Commissioner Brian McKillop and Deputy Commissioner Maria Kowalska. Contract killer Lorenzo Martini pleaded guilty to both shootings, but his claims that the 'hits' had been paid for by police were rejected outright by the court. He's been asked to re-testify to a special inquiry which will be set up within the next few days.

Feelings are running high amongst the general public here, Max. These are just a few of the comments I recorded earlier this afternoon:

Public 1: New South Wales cops? Two hundred years and still the same bloody Rum Corps. Pack of thieves, the lot of them.

Public 2: Have you seen the Vic Police badge? It's an inverted pentacle. Symbol of the Devil, that is. They've been that way since the beginning.

Public 3: Disarm and disband, then start again from scratch. It's the only way to clean up this mess.

Public 4: There's a lot of good cops out there, doing good work, so don't tar them all with the same brush. But too many good'uns are silenced and shoved out by the crooks.

Claire Hammill: Gavin Rowan was one of those pushed out, and like many former members of the force, he's understandably bitter.

Gavin Rowan: The police like to portray that image of the solid blue line, but in fact it's always been way too much a job built on factions, on favours for mates, back-scratching and back-stabbing and such. I was the senior exec on the Catapult gangbuster team, I worked in homicide for a long time, and I've dealt with a lot of crooks, bad crooks, but fact is most of them had more morals than these people in our own ranks.

Claire Hammill: What impact all this will have on next week's election here is still anyone's guess. Back to you, Max.

Max Amon: Thanks, Claire. Well, there you have it: Australia the convicts' country, where the organised crime is run by the police.

Intuitive-technologies

Good evening, Nick, it's Don. Don Mercer, from Derwent.

Yes, quite.

And she's doing well, is she?

Good, good. Well, do send her my best wishes, won't you?

Look, I called about this 'intuitive technologies' thing.

That's right, your proposal for a new section to the SusLaw conference.

Quite, quite! Yes, since we added technology last year, and economics the year before that, we really ought to change the name, it really isn't just law any more, is it? Perhaps we should just call it 'Sustainability', I don't know. Though people do know it as 'SusLaw', of course. But coming back to your...

Yes. Well, you know, I really must apologise, I will admit I did think at first it was just an April Fools joke.

Oh good, so I'm not the only one who thought that? Thank you, anyway.

And yes, you're right, that was indeed my next response. Are we that predictable?

Yes, the whole idea is a bit challenging, isn't it? I mean, it's very close to, ah, *magic*, isn't it?

Really? Good heavens, I'd never thought of it that way round: "any sufficiently advanced magic is indistinguishable from technology". Of course, the original is Arthur C Clarke, if my memory serves me correctly? How intriguing.

But anyway, as you suggested, I asked Meryl to look up the references for me, and I really must admit I was wrong. I had no idea these things were so well established.

Yes, quite. Yes.

Batcheldor, I think. His work on psychokinesis was startling, especially with all the follow-on studies by Isaacs in the eighties. And Cory Osmer's done similar work here, has she?

Quite. Yes.

Oh, Sheldrake? Yes, I was most impressed with the thoroughness of his work. "Seven Experiments That Could Change The World"

– a good title, I'd certainly have to say it's changed mine. But seriously now, can they really be developed into technologies?

Really? Fully instrumented? With that level of reliability? Good heavens! That's that chap Marko whatsisname, is it, Marko Ivetic, whom I met with you last time you were here? A pleasant young man, quite.

Oh, he works with Cory, does he? Ah, that's the connection. And yes, by the way, I also managed to grab the time this weekend to read through Peat and Bohm's work on indigenous science.

Yes, fascinating, absolutely fascinating. Though I must admit that at the end I felt thoroughly chastened.

Why? It's because after all these years I'd thought I understood traditional law, but I'd had no idea there were all these other *dimensions* to it, you see. That law is not a thing apart, it's as much, I suppose, *interwoven* with the land and the science as it is with the people and everything else. You know, I'd never before understood the Elders' constant concern with secrecy and so on, but I suppose this puts it all on a par with our regulations on hazardous goods or occupational health and safety. Remarkable. I really had never thought of that aspect before.

Yes, quite. And I think we need to send this on to Stephen, too. It could help him in his negotiations with the Pitjantjatjara Elders, and we certainly need their involvement in the conference.

Quite. Quite.

So yes, I agree, please do ask Cory to prepare a paper and seminar, as per your proposal. Heaven only knows what it'll do to the conference's reputation, but I agree it's important. No doubt we'll have a few raised eyebrows, but that's nothing unusual for us, is it?

Wonderful. Quite. Well, do keep in touch on that. And thank you.

Best wishes to your Kate again.

Goodnight.

Steve's diary

Read the whole bloody *Travel Guide* cover to cover over the weekend. I know I'm going loopy about this, but sounds like that's nothing compared to those guys over there: they're not just loopy, they take the cake and the bloody biscuit too! Jesus! I knew they'd had to go a different way to everyone else cos of screw-ups in the Troubles, but that's nigh on thirty years ago, and they've gone crazier and crazier ever since then. Not just the no-money thing, I knew about that, but everything's different there. Loopy.

Not that it matters to me, cos I checked up and there's no way I can afford to go there. Going as a straight tourist is way too bloody expensive cos you have to do real hotels, not hostel-type stuff, and I'm too old now for a working-tourist visa. The only other way is what they called a workshare visa, a kind of trial-immigration, they said, and there's no bloody way I'm doing that.

Well, at least that's got it all out of my head, anyway. Dunno why the heck I got so screwed up about it.

Visas

From *The New Australia Travel Guide*

Visas

Visiting Australia is a lot easier than it used to be even a few years ago, but getting the right visa can still be a hassle. The problem is that because the social system is so different from anywhere else, by law all visitors have to have an Australian sponsor who will take responsibility for them. So to get a visa you need a sponsor – and not just any sponsor, but the right kind of sponsor.

A *Tourist visa* is easy to get. (The Tourist visa is technically a 'Visitor visa' – you'll find both names used.) It's applied for you automatically if you go through any of the standard travel agencies, such as STA or Thomas Cook, or a major airline such as Qantas. The agent acts as your sponsor, on behalf of the Tourist Alliance, and the visa's valid for six months from date of arrival. The catch is that you may not be able to change the travel arrangements the agent makes for you; and you're also not allowed to go outside Visitor Zones without an escort – see *Visitor Zones*. (Unlike other countries, you *are* allowed to work on a Tourist visa, but only in Visitor Zones – see *Working*.) If all you want is to see the city sights and go on the occasional package tour, or perhaps go to Uluru and Kakadu or see what's left of the once-Great Barrier Reef, a Tourist visa will be okay for you. But if you want to 'go bush' and wander on your own, or discover what it's like to live in a world without money, that type of visa won't do the job – and you'll need a more personal kind of sponsor.

Next on the list are the *Business visa* and *Academic visa*. For these the respective alliance (company) or academic institution acts as your sponsor. These visas are for people staying for some time and usually working with just the one organisation. (Ordinary short-term business visitors generally use the standard Tourist visa – the Business visa is only required if you need registered living-space or workspace outside the Visitor Zone.) You'll be expected to take part in the organisation's Workshare commitment – see *Workshare* – though often (if illegally) someone else will do this for you if you're a business visitor.

A *Personal visa* allows you to live outside of a Visitor Zone as a visitor, but only because your sponsor gives personal guarantees to act as your permanent escort. Your sponsor must be someone personally known to you, and has to apply for the visa on your behalf. Personal visas are used for visits to family or friends, or for 'green card' partners. If the length of stay is less than three months, there are no explicit Workshare commitments, though you'll usually be expected to do your bit. Any Personal visa for a visit of longer than a month in any one place needs quite a detailed formal assessment, to define the duration and conditions of stay: keep it less than that if you can, for your sponsor's sake! A Tourist visa can sometimes be turned into a short-term Personal visa while you're in the country: this is usually done for you through Workshare.

The only other standard visa is a *Workshare visa*, for which your sponsor is Workshare itself. This allows you to travel around Australia in whatever way you like, living as if you're a regular Australian citizen. The catch, of course, is that need to work like one too! Overall, you'll be expected to work an average of at least one day in three, including weekends, which gives most people plenty of time for sightseeing and generally lazing around. The visa's normally for up to twelve months, but can be extended indefinitely with Workshare's agreement.

There are two types of Workshare visa. If you're aged 18-25, you can apply for the basic type, which is equivalent to the 'working tourist' visa available in several other countries. There's a simple interview, and you're pre-registered for general work, such as fruit-picking, hospitality and general labouring, though you can do skilled work if you want to do it and it's available.

If you're 26 or older, you can only apply for the full Workshare visa, which effectively gives you temporary migrant status. To get the visa, you have to pass an interview, and be able to prove that you have skills which are needed in Australia. It's easier if you have someone to sponsor you, as for a Business or Academic visa. But you can do it on your own – though the interview has been described as 'gruelling'! There's also a similar process by which a Business, Academic or Personal visa can be changed into a Workshare visa in-country if necessary. If you're visiting to try out the idea of moving permanently to Australia, the full Workshare visa is the only way you can do it.

A quiet crusader

From *The Courier-Mail*, Saturday

A quiet crusader for social justice

By our US correspondent, Maggie Combin

It's the most comprehensive social study ever undertaken. Its credentials are impeccable, its logic is flawless, its results are undeniable. It could well be the answer to inner-city stress, the best way to eradicate the seeds of crime. And it's simple, cheap and effective.

So why are the US authorities so studiously ignoring it?

Perhaps it's because it doesn't involve guns and violence. It doesn't involve jail. It doesn't involve punishment of any kind. In fact it doesn't involve much of anything they'd know as 'crime prevention'.

Because the one thing that's been proven to reduce crime – and reduce it dramatically – is entirely at the other end of the scale.

Playschools.

Since the mid-1970s, members of the HighScope project have worked tirelessly with inner-city kids and their families in some of the most run-down, crime-infested districts of urban Detroit, Michigan. Over the years, more than 30,000 two- and three-year-olds have passed through their doors.

The results are startling. As children, as teenagers, and then as adults, HighScope kids have markedly different lives from their compatriots in other cities. On average, they are two-thirds less likely to commit a crime; their incomes are 40 percent higher; they are 70 percent more likely to marry, and much more likely to stay married.

It's good for the individual, obviously, and good for society too. But it also makes sound economic sense. The figures show that for every dollar spent on HighScope, the effective return to the community is at least seven times that much.

And all of this from just six months in playschool.

So how does this happen? When I visited HighScope's leader David Weikart and his colleagues earlier this week, what I saw going on in the small schoolroom behind us seemed much the same as in any other pre-school. There were more parents than usual, including fathers, engaged in the activities, but on the surface that was about it.

Weikart explained the difference. "The content of what we teach doesn't matter much. It's more about the context. What we show is that every action has consequences, and that everyone, even a two-year-old, has choices about those actions that can shape their lives."

Weikart's guiding mantra for the children is 'Plan, Do, Review'. "What works is helping people to understand that they alone have the choices that matter", says this quiet crusader for social justice. "Punishment doesn't work. It never has."

Britain's Home Office agrees. "HighScope is brilliant, we need to be doing more of it", said a spokesman there last week. "Prison does work, after a fashion, but it is way too late and ruinously expensive. If you increase the prison population by 25 percent, you can reduce crime by up to one percent. Prison should only be regarded as an option of last resort."

But it is advice that is falling on deaf ears in Weikart's homeland. The state of Michigan recently withdrew further funding for HighScope, and is instead launching an ambitious prison-building programme, aiming to complete two new prisons next year alone. It seems probable that the only people who will gain from this policy are the shareholders of the ever-growing band of private companies who will run the new prisons.

Last month the US passed a grim milestone: two and a half million people, or one percent of the entire population, are now serving sentences behind prison bars. And most of these prisoners are young and black, as in so much of HighScope's Detroit.

It is anyone's guess as to how long it will take the US to understand that Weikart is right, and that there is a better, cheaper way. As one who has seen too much already of the carnage in American society, that day cannot come soon enough.

Going independent

From the *Sydney Morning Herald*

Collapse of party-system accelerates

Veteran Liberal back-bencher Gary Brussard-Holmes has become the latest in a growing band of incumbents who are leaving their existing political party and turning independent.

The outspoken member for Parramatta, popularly known as 'GBH', was characteristically blunt in a statement aimed at party headquarters.

"We worked long and hard to rid this constituency of the filth of drugs, only to find that our greatest enemy all along has been our own so-called colleagues, who have lined their pockets from that misery, both in government and out. They have betrayed everything that our once great party stood for; as I see it, there is nothing left to save. So I'm gone: and long may they rot in hell!"

Former party workers have defected en masse to Brussard-Holmes' new campaign office on Pitt Street.

In related news, the Australian Electoral Commission has confirmed that next week's election will still go ahead. "With the resignation of the Prime Minister and the Governor-General's withdrawal of Royal Assent, we would have had to hold an election in any case", said a spokeswoman for the AEC, Sue Lin.

The AEC has set a Wednesday deadline for candidates who want to change affiliation or go independent. The cut-off is to allow time for ballot-papers for polling-booths to be re-printed.

Postal-ballot forms will remain unchanged. "The names and order of candidates will remain the same, so there will be no actual difference to the ballot itself", said Ms Lin. "But the re-print will allow voters on the day to gain a clearer picture of where their candidates stand in relation to the recent events."

The AEC has also confirmed that, because of the tight deadline, it will not allow parties to replace candidates implicated or alleged to have been implicated in the scandal. Substitution has been permitted in some previous elections, but only in cases where a candidate has died or become incapacitated through illness.

Steve's diary

Can hardly believe it's only a month since I started writing in this thing. Still, seems to be working, so keep going.

Got the papers off Wednesday, and interview tomorrow at the consulate. They move fast thank god, not like the bloody pen-pushers here.

Mum's going to go spare when I tell her – if they let me in, that is. Not looking forward to the rollicking I'll get at the Monmouth, either. Cross that bridge when we get there, I suppose.

Still don't have a bloody clue why I'm doing this, but it still seems right.

Goodnight Dear Diary, or whatever else I'm supposed to say.

Daft.

Emergency Management Act

From student notes, Faculty of Law, Derwent University

Excerpts and summaries from *Emergency Management Act 1986*: Act No.30/1986, with its various amendments up to 15 June 2000:

Objectives of the Act The purpose of the Act (section 1) is to provide for emergency management of and within the State; this is expanded (in section 4A) under the keywords 'prevention', 'response' and 'recovery'.

Definition of 'emergency* Section 4(1) defines 'emergency' as anything which threatens or causes actual harm to persons or property. It lists typical expected emergency-events – such as earthquake, fire, explosion, road-accident, epidemic, war, riot, or any 'disruption to an essential service' – but expressly does not limit it to any of these. It also asserts (section 4(1)) that in the context of the Act an 'essential service' can be *anything* declared as such by the State Governor (section 2).

Co-ordinator In Chief and Deputy Section 5(1) states that 'the Minister' [unspecified] is automatically the overall co-ordinator; however, the actual control must (section 5(2)) be passed to a deputy, who must be the Chief Commissioner of Police. The Co-ordinator In Chief is permitted to appoint an alternate deputy (section 7), though the conditions under which this may be other than the Chief Commissioner of Police are not stated. The Commissioner may in turn (section 21H) delegate 'any or all' of the Commissioner's powers to *anyone*.

Emergency Management Council Sections 8(1) and 8(2) require an advisory council to be set up, to advise the Co-ordinator In Chief, who may (section 8(2)(a)) appoint someone else to act as chair.

Head of government declares 'state of disaster' The head of government for the State is defined (section 23) as the only person who can declare or revoke a 'state of disaster' – an 'emergency which ... constitutes or is likely to constitute a significant and widespread danger to life or property' – and may do so at any time (section 23(2)). The declaration must be broadcast 'from a broadcasting station in the State', and be published in the Government Gazette (section 23(4)); such publication is legal evidence of the scope and terms of the declaration (section 23(5)).

Duration of state of disaster The Act (section 23(6)) states that the declaration of a state of disaster may remain in force for not more than a month, but may be redeclared indefinitely.

Priority over other law The Commissioner may, under a declared state of disaster, effectively overrule *any* existing law or 'subordinate instrument' (sections 24(2)(b) and 24(4)).

Sequestration or use of property The Commissioner may, under a declared state of disaster, 'take possession and make use of any person's property as the Co-ordinator in Chief considers necessary or desirable for responding to the disaster' (section 24(2)(c)). The Act defines no limitation as to the extent of such sequestration. Compensation for such sequestration and/or use is allowed for in the Act (section 24(5)), but only offers 'such compensation as is determined by the Co-ordinator in Chief'.

The Act acknowledges only *one* reason why anyone should have any need to remain within, or not be evacuated from, or return to, a declared disaster area: 'pecuniary interest in the land or building or in any goods or valuables on the land or in the building' (sections 24(7), 36B(2) and 36B(3)). [*By law, money is the only thing that matters*: nothing else – family, pets, livestock, treasured memories, things of emotional or spiritual value – is considered to have any value at all.]

For the context of *martial law*, refer to the equivalent federal Act. The key addition is that any use of the armed forces for disaster relief and/or maintenance of law and order shall be under the direction of the civil authority. At the local level, this would in practice be as authorised by individual police officers at their own discretion.

After the election

From Walther Hannau, *Tony Morrison: Nurturing the Revolution*

As the dust began to settle, after the furore of the election itself, it became clear that this would be a parliament unprecedented in Australian history. The Liberals and Labor alike had been reduced to pathetic shadows of their former might, with barely fifteen members between them; the largest parties were the Greens and the Democrats, with the Christian-fundamentalist Families First a distant third. But with more than half of new members declaring themselves independent, and often aggressively so, there was no way that any party could form a conventional exclusive government.

Now in his fourth term at the House, Tony at first kept himself in the background, looking on at the ensuing chaos both with amusement and with a sense of hope. "The classic conditions for emergence", he wrote in his diary; "the only place where real worthwhile change can start". But even he had under-estimated his own reputation as "the independent's independent". As the old party hacks and the new would-be revolutionaries jockeyed for position, "AM for PM" badges began to be seen in increasing profusion on tweed coats, city power-dress outfits and camo jackets alike. At the end of the first day, Tony stepped forward, if somewhat reluctantly, and, as he put it, "placed his hat in the ring".

It was Tony, too, who broke the deadlock, by using the Open Space approach that had proved so successful in policy-making and planning back in Melbourne. From this came one group's proposal for an 'anti-election', eliminating potential candidates for leadership on the basis of least trust. In effect, the resulting dozen members represented the entire House's choice for Cabinet; and they in turn asked Tony to take on the key coordinating role. Barely a fortnight after that diary entry in which he had pondered whether it was time for him to give up politics for good, Tony found himself walking through the great oak doors of Government House, where the Governor-General, on behalf of the ageing queen of a foreign country, would confirm his new position as the first-ever independent Prime Minister of Australia.

Then to the urgent business of government. First on the agenda, of course, was the ongoing nightmare of the Topolski affair. For this, Tony took the advice of his new justice-minister Jane Clement, and appointed the respected High Court judge Esther Bannock to head the investigation. This proved an inspired choice, as Bannock's combination of calm demeanour and curt determination quickly restored public trust in the judiciary at least, if not yet the police. This and other actions also helped to create overseas trust in the new government: the flood of foreign investment funds that had been haemorrhaging for the past two weeks slowed to a trickle, and then began to reverse.

In the meantime, even Tony's skills were stretched to the limit with the delicate diplomacy needed to manage such a disparate team. The new Cabinet included such lifelong adversaries as Gary Brussard-Holmes and Stavro Sipinksi, and career-feminist Patricia Corolli, who had once declared that "to work under a man is like the missionary position – it's tantamount to rape". But Tony was able to gain and maintain each person's trust, and each in turn had the trust of the whole House – a fact which was to prove crucial as the Troubles, still invisible yet already looming on the horizon, suddenly exploded on the scene a mere two weeks later.

Like the rest of the world, Australia would never be the same again.

Steve's diary

Dec 5

Yup, mum did her crust all right, dad was a bit better about it but not much, so I'm staying with Dave for the next couple of days. And Foreman Joe's bloody pissed off at me for leaving, though the Hobart's crew are doing me a send-off party at the Monmouth tonight. Someone threatened to bring a strait-jacket, and I'm not sure they're wrong.

They've changed me flight – the direct route is out at the moment cos the yips have got too trigger-happy again and nuked another airliner. So I'm going via the States – well, I always wanted to see the Big Apple, didn't I?

An upside-down Christmas in crazy Australia – well, I'll be there in time for that. Still sounds weird, don't it?

Closed-debt contracts

From *The Independent*, London, Thursday

US Supreme Court: 'yes' on contract-debt inheritance

In a landmark ruling, the US Supreme Court voted 5-4 yesterday to overturn its previous stance against the Moral America administration's controversial 'Contract-Debt Inheritance Act'.

Justice Lewis Goldfarb, appointed to the court last month by President Bradwell Cooper after the still-unexplained death of Justice Marsha Simmonds, cast the deciding vote in favour of the government and closed-debt contract holders.

The legislation permits contract holders to transfer a contractee's debt and contract to their spouse, children or any other 'related person' in the event of the contractee's death or permanent disability. Contract-holders are authorised to use "any means necessary" to enforce the contract transfer.

"This decision is a travesty of justice", said Aaron Toombs, a spokesman for the Colored Persons Defence League (CPDL). "The wording of the legislation is so broad that companies can choose whoever they want as the 'inheritor'. From this day onward, black people will live in permanent fear of the slaver's midnight hammer on the door."

The CPDL and the American Civil Liberties Union (ACLU) had taken class-action in March of this year against Blackwood, the largest contract-holder corporation in the US, to prevent the forcible arrest and ghetto-incarceration of forty-two relatives of deceased contractees.

Closed-debt contracts were introduced into the US ten years ago as a means to manage punishments for minor offences. All other US prisoners were transferred into closed-debt contracts the following year.

The convict's 'debt to society' is calculated in monetary terms and taken up by a contract-holder corporation, binding the convict into a legally-enforced labour contract with the corporation until the debt is deemed to be repaid.

Under current legislation, the contract-holder alone determines payments and labour-conditions for contractees and charges for services rendered to each contractee by the corporation.

The minority of the court defended the previous decision on constitutional grounds. In her lodgement of dissent, Chief Justice Anne Pollard quoted Abraham Lincoln, saying that "in any conflict between property rights and human rights, the latter must always prevail".

But the majority group ruled for the defendants on the basis that the legislation was essential to protect the future of American business. "What's good for Blackwood is good for the country", said Goldfarb.

Police completed the arrests of all forty-two inheritor-contractees on behalf of Blackwood late last night.

The greater villain

From an 18th-century polemical broadsheet

We hang the man and flog the woman
that steal the goose from off the common
but let the greater villain loose
that steals the common from the goose.

Contract-breach

From *The Independent*, London

'Shoot to kill' order for contract-breach

Washington, DC – Reuters

Despite strong objections from Canada and Mexico alike, the Moral America government today authorised 'shoot to kill' orders against any identified contract-breach offenders attempting to leave US territory.

"Contract breach is theft", said James Milner, a lawyer for Blackwood, one of the companies promoting the new legislation. "Any termination of assets is regrettable, but as owners of more than one million contracts, we must send a clear message to all contractees that theft in any form will not be tolerated."

In London, a spokeswoman for Amnesty International expressed outrage at the new development. "Closed-debt contracts are slavery, pure and simple. This is a black day for human rights: American corporations have now added state-sanctioned murder to their roster of crimes against humanity."

So-called 'closed-debt labour contracts' are unique to the United States. A person under such a contract is required by law to go anywhere and do any work under any conditions specified by the contract owner.

The contracts are automatically renewed in case of debt, and in practice it is almost impossible to get out of debt under the terms of the contract. For this reason, Amnesty has long claimed that they are tantamount to slave-labour, and should be banned by international law.

The contractee's voting rights and other citizen's rights are also transferred to the contract owner for the duration of the contract.

Corporations buy and sell the contracts en masse via the asset-exchange, as 'human resources'.

The contract-holder has the right to transfer the contract to children and other 'related persons' if the contractee dies. Most so-called 'contract-breach offenders' are attempting to escape such 'inherited' contracts.

Amnesty is classified as a terrorist organisation by the US government.

Related news:

- 'Underground railroad' arrests in US
- 'Underground railroad' – three Quaker groups charged with treason and asset-theft

Steve's diary

Dunno what the heck the date is, and I don't care as long as I'm getting further away from there

On the flight out from LA now, thank god. Fourteen hours to go.
Just two words to describe the States: Oh God.
Or Holy Shit! perhaps.
I have never been so shit-scared in my life. More later when I get a chance to cool down a bit.

Steve's diary

Either 19th or 20th if we've crossed the date-line yet

Couple of meals inside me now, but I'm still shit-scared we're going to turn round and go back. How any of the Yanks stay sane in that mess I just do not know. Probably they don't.

Okay, mum, for you, some quick impressions, as you put it:

- Guns, absolutely bloomin' everywhere (I'll put it more nicely for you, mum). Our cops just carry pistols, but their cops, or private guards mostly, they're carrying <u>machine-guns</u> with the safeties off (I looked). And they aren't just for decoration, they use them, like one poor sod they let loose at when he jumped a red light close by the Bronx Gate. I think it was just an ordinary backfire from a clapped-out truck-engine that started them off, I heard the bang and it was nothing much, but there was nothing much left of him by the time they'd stopped. (I know, mum, you'd say I shouldn't have been near the ghetto anyway, but I didn't have any choice, that was the way the airport bus went across town.) And what was scary was no-one batted an eyelid about it, they just went round the mess like it was everyday. Perhaps it was.

- Churches and preachers, also absolute bloomin' everywhere. And all they're after is your money, nothing else, like you pay for god like you pay (and pay and pay) for everything else. The more you pay them the better person you are, I suppose. The more money you have in this life buys you a better place in the next, you don't have to <u>be</u> a better person at all. And it shows, the few rich fancy-pants we did see came past us like they were Lord Muck and we were just some kind of scum in the road.

- Some really fancy places, a lot of money gone into there, but always out of someone else's pocket, I'd bet. Everything <u>felt</u> rich, but it also felt fake, like it was cardboard or something, give it a good kick and the whole thing'd fall over.

- Everyone's loud and noisy and smart-ass, but it's like everyone's also afraid of something. You could <u>smell</u> the fear – not just the Bronx ghetto, I mean, we could smell that even through the coach aircon, but felt the same with people everywhere else too. Kind of brittle, is how I'd put it, like really thin glass. Odd. Can't think of any other way to describe it.

- Back home there's white and black and brown and yellow faces, but here the only black faces I saw were in a line with their hands on their heads, getting into trucks just outside one of the small gates in the Bronx Wall, and a couple of street cleaners on Fifth Avenue, all with armed guards real close by. Even the two Paki guys in our party had a couple of close calls, nearly getting arrested just for being there till the group guide came to their rescue. I wouldn't want to be black there, that's for sure, though I don't know what happens to them.

- Guards and dogs barking orders at the airport, the bus terminal, at every checkpoint and street-gate, even at entrance to the hotel complex. Dunno what they thought they were protecting, because we felt so unsafe anyway because of them all that we didn't even try going outside the hotel at night, even to go drinking.

- Flashing signs and high-tech grabbers everywhere, always trying to sell something, so many of them you couldn't think straight. Jet-lag didn't help, but I had a splitting headache at the end of the first day just from trying cope with them all.

- And seemed like the only thing that was worth anything at all was money, people didn't matter at all. No-one wanted to talk about what we thought or anything, not for real, all anyone really wanted off us was our money. As long as they thought there was more to be had, it was all smarm and plastic smiles, as soon as they thought we were done, they treated us like garbage, couldn't get us out of the door fast enough.

I reckon it was the guns was the worst, but it'd be a pretty close call with everything else. Moral, all right, as long as you toe the party line, but god help you if you don't, cos they own god too.

I just hope like crazy that the yips and the freaks have stopped shooting at everyone when I head back, cos I'm scared stiff they'll send us back through there again.

Mitesh

A crowded medium-sized lecture theatre, with the auditorium angled upward in an arc, some twenty rows of thirty or more leather-padded seats. The place is full of students, both men and women, most in their early twenties, and almost all in un-student-like 'power-dress', sharp suits, padded shoulders and all the expensively gaudy trappings of the corporate clone. Everyone looks neat, washed, clean, attentive; the suburban dream. The sense of unrelenting opulence, though, is marred by the row of armed guards at the back of the auditorium, dressed in heavy leather uniform and riot gear.

On the stage stands a podium, flanked either side by a panel-desk, behind each of which sit hard-faced men and women of varying ages, all of them likewise dressed in the corporate-clone mode. The podium is fronted by a large wooden medallion, showing two clenched hands, though the sense of friendly greeting and equality is offset somewhat by its strangely fascistic style. And behind the podium is a large banner, showing a cross superimposed on a flag of stars and stripes, with the tag-line "One Country Under God" above and the label "America The Great" below. Below this, in turn, is a much larger, gilt-encrusted version of the same medallion, a symbol that we also see worn as badges by many of the students. The symbol, in fact, of the corporate-dominated party which rules with an iron fist over this divided land: Moral America.

Every face, we note, is white; every face and feature Caucasian in origin. Except one.

At the podium stands a figure whose free-flowing, bright clothes stand out in startling contrast against the all-pervading corporate grey. The name-panel on the podium identifies this person as 'Mitesh' – no title, and no forename, or perhaps no surname, it is impossible to tell. And the racial background, the age, even the gender of this person all seem equally blurred, fluid, uncertain. All that is clear is that whoever this may be, they are... different... and that sense of difference seems itself to be one source of the palpable tension that can be felt throughout this space.

Mitesh, it seems, has just finished speaking. There is a smattering of polite applause, but no more than that. Whatever the content of the lecture, it was not exactly popular. Mitesh bows, then turns to the panel. One of them, a man in his mid-forties, perhaps, with a name-badge bearing the label 'Dr Ross Parheim', gets to his feet. His voice betrays a tone of mild rebuke towards the students.

"Once again on behalf of all us here, I'd like to thank Dr Mitesh, who's come all the way from the Commonwealth of Australia to speak with us. Now, surely some of you have questions for our distinguished guest?"

Several in the audience raise their hands. Ross points to one, who wears a lurid purple tie beneath against the taut blue-white pin-stripe shirt of his flawless waist-coated three-piece suit.

"Yes – Mr Crosby?"

The young man stands, exuding an air of sneering self-confidence and inherent superiority.

"Mr, uh, I mean, ah, Dr, ah, Mitesh…"

Mitesh interrupts, in a calm alto voice that seems to emphasise the strange gender-uncertainty.

"Mitesh, please, just Mitesh. Where I come from, we do not use these honorifics."

Crosby nods. The sneer is overlaid by distaste at the need to ask of matters almost too obscene for words.

"Uh. Okay. Uh, Mitesh, then, is it, I mean, we've heard you even forbid the idea of rights in Australia?"

"Not forbid, as such. But I don't understand your question?"

"Uh, is it true you guys have no rights?"

"Ah. I think understand now. Not what you think of as rights, no, that's true. But this is because there are no rights, ever, anywhere. There never have been. Only the responsibilities from which those apparent rights arise."

"What about the Bill of Rights?"

"No. Instead, our law is built around a Citizens Charter, a charter of mutual responsibilities, which provides the same result as that you seek with what you call a 'bill of rights'. So no, it is true, we have no Bill of Rights."

"You guys cannot be serious! No Bill of Rights?"

"No, we are serious in this. To us, a Bill of Rights would be a charter for selfishness. Misleading. Dangerous. Evil, in the most literal sense of the word."

Confused mutters and murmurs arise from amongst the audience, as Crosby drops back to his seat, visibly shocked. Other hands are waved; Ross again points to a young woman with white gloves and red patent-leather shoes.

"Miss Silberstein, your question?"

She leaps to her feet in evident agitation.

"You must have property rights, surely? You can't possibly run an economy without them!"

"We do, and I assure you we have done so, and well, for some decades now. We find it works better that way, is more efficient for everyone, more effective. We do use a notion of property, a very strong sense of property, in fact, but perhaps not as you might grasp it: it is drawn from a declaration of responsibility, of stewardship, not some arbitrary 'title' or 'right' of possession. Once again, I urge you to understand this: rights are an illusion; only responsibilities are real."

Silberstein shakes her head, then returns doggedly to the attack.

"What about intellectual property, then? You've got to have that, you can't pretend you can possibly get away without it, I mean, this university, every business depends on intellectual property!"

"This notion of 'intellectual property' makes no sense to us. Decades ago physicists like David Bohm proved that all thought is collective, and as the great Isaac Newton once put it, we each stand on the shoulders of giants, the work of countless unknown others in the past and present. So how can any individual, still less any corporation, claim to be the sole possessor of an idea, or to have the 'right' to withhold it from others?"

Mitesh pauses for emphasis.

"I assure you, there is no plausible basis, no ethical defence, for what you call intellectual property. Or any other form of property that depends on exclusion. Once we look more deeply, every argument for such a 'right' turns out to be an attempt to justify dishonesty and greed. And sooner or later, any society which is foolish enough to base itself upon such poor foundations will surely fail."

More muttering in the audience, noticeably harder in tone, as Mitesh continues.

"So by both its name and by its nature, the Commonwealth does not accept or acknowledge any exclusive right of property, in any form."

A welter of emotions – confusion doubt, righteous indignation, a horrified disbelief, even a kind of nauseated fervour – pass in waves over Silberstein's face. The appalled strain in her voice is all too evident as she hurls one last question at Mitesh.

"No property rights at all?"

"Not as you see it. What you call property, we call it theft."

Sounds of indrawn breath and anger now from all around the auditorium. Silberstein surrenders to her fury.

"Our rights are our gift from God!"

Alone at the podium, Mitesh's expression forms a sad, wry smile.

"An interesting idea. But which god, pray?"

The soft voice suddenly turns sharper, firmer.

"Not a god of compassion, it seems. A god of rights, perhaps? Of our own self-centredness?"

The murmuring within the audience grows angrier; a scornful, sarcastic "who the fuck d'ya think you are?" breaks through the background buzz as Mitesh waves at the banner above.

"Tell me: is this truly under god – or merely under gold?"

The audience fast loses any pretence of self-control. Mitesh leans forward, pinioning Silberstein to her seat once more with the sheer intensity of the gaze.

"That god of rights, madam, is a delusion that may yet kill us all."

The auditorium explodes – everyone jumps to their feet, there are shouts of "atheist filth!", "kill the faggot!", and more, louder, louder, worse. The veneer of suburban nicety vanishes, exposing visceral hate and fear. Ross stands up and waves for calm.

"Ladies! Gentlemen! Please!"

– – –

A vibrant, busy upmarket mall, with moving, glittering displays everywhere – the very epitome of progressive affluence and technological prowess. We might note, however, that almost everyone in the swirling crowd of happy window-shoppers is Caucasian, white-skinned. As Mitesh, the one colourful exception to this apparent racial rule, comes past, a security guard stirs, ready to challenge the right to be there – then settles back again once it becomes clear that Ross Parheim is present to vouchsafe for this outlandish creature. Ross, it is clear, is still worried about the events on campus, barely an hour earlier.

"Well, you sure shook 'em up back there. But the University'd be grateful if you didn't do that again. We can't afford to risk the lawsuits. Or the fines."

"They would punish you so for speaking truth? Does money taint *everything*?"

"Uh... Guess you guys'd see it that way... but you don't have our problems, though..."

Ross stops as if to think it through, but is distracted by a flashing display showing an animation of some gadget.

"Gee, would ya look at that? Want one o' those!"

The price comes up on the display.

"Ah, shit, way more'n I can afford. Never have enough money. Or enough time. Work work work, it's what I do to pay for my play. But there ain't much time for play. Ah shit."

Mitesh looks at him, head tilted to one side, and sighs. Ross eventually notices the slightly exasperated 'don't you get it?' expression, and looks back at Mitesh in some confusion.

"Huh? Wassup, man?"

But the connection between the two lasts a mere moment before Ross is distracted once more.

"Hey, that's nice!"

He draws attention to a moving mannequin in a display, again indeterminate gender, with a striking coloured jacket. Mitesh nods in polite agreement.

"Tiki would see beauty in that."

"Tiki? Your partner?"

"The partner, yes. Not 'my' partner. We do not possess each other. No possession."

"You guys are sure weird about this no-possession stuff. Possession ain't nine-tenths o' the law – man, possession is every-thing. No possessions, you're screwed."

He looks past Mitesh in sudden surprise.

"Hey, what's that nigger doing here?"

A middle-aged black man walks out of a side-passage, dressed in tired once-good-quality clothes. He unfolds a sign, a quote from the bible: 'Care for the poor, for they will always be with you'. He stands still, calm, quiet, dignified, silently holding the sign. Within seconds, three armed guards in riot gear rush up. Two grab hold of him, pull his arms behind his back, cover his mouth and wrench his head back; the third pulls out a pistol and calmly shoots between the eyes. One pulls a plastic bag from a pocket in his uniform, unfolds it on the ground; the others drop the corpse onto the plastic, throw the sign on top, methodically zip up the body-bag. Everything's quick, neat, tidy, professional, no blood spilt on the sidewalk, not a word spoken between them; an everyday routine. Whilst the other two guards put the finishing touches to their package, attaching an ID tag and other items of paperwork – one of them an invoice to the mall's owners, it seems – their fellow squad-member holds up his hands to push away the small crowd beginning to gather at the scene.

"Okay, folks, nothing to see here, thank you, move along please."

He pulls out his radio, to talk to some unseen dispatcher.

"Control, this is Southside Four. Send a trash hauler to Seventh and Lion, we got us another charcoal for Dustyville."

Mitesh looks on in horror, while Ross firmly pulls away.

"Shit, I'm sorry you had to see that. But it's the only way to keep that trash where they belong."

Mitesh is aghast.

"Trash? The *only* way?"

Ross' irritation finally gets the better of him.

"Look, just ignore it, okay? Ya gotta harden yourself. It's dog eat dog out here."

Mitesh shakes his head from side to side in a mixture of disgust and disbelief.

"And yet you never ask why? You never ask why this should be so?"

Ross stops, staring at Mitesh in surprise and shock.

Steve's diary

Dec 21, I'd guess

Midwinter, back in England, and here it's Midsummer Day. Weird.

Funny that. This whole thing started out at Halloween, down in whats-that-place-called, and now it's the midsummer solstice half a bloody world away. Anyone would think I was going pagan like the Travellers or something daft like that. And I still don't know how the heck I got here, at all, let alone how I got here so fast. Feels like it had its own momentum or something. Or its own choice? No, that'd be even dafter.

Anyway, I'm here, for what it's worth. And though I'm still only in a Tourist Zone, it still feels pretty weird.

A lot of it's just the simple things, little things, mostly things that aren't there rather than are, really. Like no passport check at the airport – they said the airline had done it already before we got on, so what would be the point of doing it all over again? And there was food laid on in the baggage hall while we waited for check-out – but no-one to pay. Same with no-one to pay for the bus-trip. A few static signs and posters around the place, of course, but no grabbers trying to sell some kind of crap or other. No security gate on the airport, or on the turn-off to the city-centre. And not a gun in sight, not even on the cops – in fact I don't think I've even <u>seen</u> a cop yet. Yeah, it's <u>that</u> kind of weird.

And a heck of a difference from yesterday, of course – still can't get over that. Like it's safe to <u>breathe</u> again, or something.

Everyone says the Aussies are cuckoo-crazy, but I haven't seen anything much like that so far. About the only bloke who seemed a bit mental was the Customs guy at the check-out, big burly bloke like Uncle Jeff, so I certainly wasn't going to mess with him anyway. Nothing odd at first, just checked through my import form and so on, just usual sort of paperwork for any government stuff. Even showed me my record, bloody scary computer system, they got pretty much my whole bloody life-history on the screen in three seconds flat after I put my hand down on this kind of scanner thing. Anyway, he's looking at the screen, trying to sort out this here place for me, and I'm drumming my fingers on the desktop like you do, and he kind of turns his head sideways and looks at me a bit funny and says, Keyboards, is it? And that wasn't on me record, I could see that, so I dunno how the heck he knew, and it felt kind of weird him asking that, like he could see straight into me or something. But I says Yes, and he asks what kind of music I play, so I tell him, and he says something like "Black Cat on Fitzroy Street's good for casso, go up there sometime, they'll probably give you a gig if you ask". And that's it – just points out the door for the bus, wishes me good luck and all, and waves me out the place as if I was coming off a train, not a bloody airport. And how would he know about a good place for a gig – I mean, he's about the same bloody age as dad, how the heck would he know about casso, what's good and what's not? And yet he <u>knew.</u> And like he knew because _I_ knew. But I'd be going mental meself if I said that to anyone, sure of that.

Anyway, he set me up with this place, with no hassles at all, and they've done me well enough so far. Though I'll probably turn in now for a couple of hours kip, even though it's the middle of the day, cos I'm half off me noddle on jetlag. After that, all I'll need is to find someone else in the hostel to go drinking with, and I'll be well set up for the night.

Steve's in Oz – woo-hoo! Who'd a thought a that even a month or two ago, hey?

Transition – Last orders

Sure, mate. Two beers, comin' right up. It's twenty-three dollars twenty so far, okay?

C'mon, go the Pies! Get them bloody Bombers! Gerroutofit! Yeah!

Sorry mate, it's only on the radio. TV's stuffed, probably bloody cable down again, useless buggers. Yeah, I know it's crap, musta last switched this on five year ago, at least it's workin', okay?

Ah, no! Not a bloody Public Service Announcement? Right when our boys are about to score? Get off, get it off!

What they bloody talkin' about? International emergency? What bloody international emergency?

Shit? *Shit.* Can't be *that* bad? Are they bloody serious?

Shit, they are, too. That's a real bugger, no mistake.

Shit, is that it? That what it was? No wonder the bloody TV don't work. Jeez what a mess. Holy shit. Up shit creek alright...

Hey, you guys, better get over here, quick! – take a listen to this?

"Only alternative to martial law"? – what are they on about?

Oh. Oh shit. Well shit me sideways – jeezus wept what a mess...

"Federal Emergency Management Act"? – what the heck's that when that's at home?

Take *everything*? From *everyone*? How can they do that?

Shit, they can, too. Bloody 'ell. Okay, okay, can see the point, but bloody 'ell...

No money? How'm I s'posed to run this place? People still want the stuff but they ain't gonna pay for it?

Responsibility? "What you need"? Whatever dickhead dreamed this one up ain't never tried runnin' no bar.

Bugger this for a laugh. *Last orders*, jennelmen, please?

Transition – Stock trader

Fuck – the fucking network *can't* be down! Too much fucking money riding on this fucking put deal – I'll be down half a mill out of my own fucking pocket if we don't get it through today!

Don't you fucking computer clowns know that time is money? Get your fucking act together! If you screw us around, we'll have your fucking guts for garters, and no fucking mistake!

Shit – what *now*? Fucking pollies bleating about the economy? We *are* the fucking economy! Screw us around and you won't *have* no fucking economy – and then where will you fuckwits be, hey?

What? – they're blaming *us* for this fucking mess? How can they?

And *what*? What the *fuck* was that? No *money*? Nationalising the whole fucking *lot*? You call that a fucking commonwealth? Outta their fucking minds? It ain't a fucking common wealth, it's *my* fucking wealth, y'hear? *Mine!* It's *my* fucking house, *my* fucking yacht, *my* fucking Ferrari! *My* fucking money! I fucking worked for 'em! An' no fuckwit welfare waster is gonna fucking touch any of it! Ever! Get *that* in your thick fucking skulls, fuckwits?

Oh jesus. Sweet fucking jesus – the banks? *All* of them? *And* the forex? Futures? Even the fucking market? The whole fucking lot gone – *worldwide*? Shit, they aren't fucking about... looks like my fucking Stateside holdings are wiped, if all their systems are as fucked as that. Waste of a fucking bribe to the Finance Minister if the Indons are fucked too. *And* the Brits? – jeez, what's going to happen to Mitch and Kate, they'll be fucking stranded out there if they're all tied up in the City. Be good to see the Docklands fucked for change, though – the bastards done it often enough to us.

All right, I'll give him that – that fuckwit Morrison's got his head screwed on if it really is this bad. Thought he was just a fucking pinko when he came in, but this is fucking serious. Shit. Shit shit shit. What the fuck are we gonna do?

Better get home, get the kids out of school, fucking fast. Lock the place down tight. I don't care what that fuckwit thinks, with the fucking coppers out of action there's gonna be looters for sure. An' if they come anywhere near me an' mine, I'll blow their *fucking* heads off. *No-one* touches *my* fucking stuff... *no-one*...

Transition – Prime Minister

From *The Age*, 3rd January

State of Emergency: Prime Minister's statement

Below is the full text of the address to the nation by Prime Minister Tony Morrison

As you will know, the international networks are still in disarray, but the news we have been able to obtain from London, New York, Tokyo and Tel Aviv continues to be dire. These are drastic times.

Since midnight last night, all electronic banking, and all financial transactions into and out of the country, have been halted. As a result, all of Australia's banks, stock-markets and other financial systems are effectively closed down, and must remain so until the international situation becomes stable again. This is the only way we can protect our country from being dragged into bankruptcy, as has happened already with some of our international trading partners.

We now know that the political situation is rapidly worsening in many countries. Air-traffic control worldwide is now increasingly uncertain, and all international flights have been cancelled indefinitely. At present, airports will remain open for domestic flights, though we have been advised that cancellations and lengthy delays are likely for many days at least.

If you are a tourist or a foreign national, you should contact your embassy or consulate as soon as you can, for your own sake, and that of your relatives at home. In case of difficulty, any police station or Citizens Advice Bureau will be able to offer help. I do want to assure you, though, that you are safe in this country. You are our honoured guests, and we invite you to continue to be so for the duration of this emergency.

Drastic times demand drastic measures. We have already seen many countries turn to martial law. None of us would like to see the same happen here. Moreover, Australian law requires that in such circumstances the army would be under the personal control of members of the police force, yet with the extent of police crime

74

and corruption recently revealed by the Bannock Commission, we understand that this would be utterly unacceptable to Australians.

History, too, shows that events of this kind have most hurt those who are least equipped to cope – especially the disadvantaged and the poor. Australia has a strong tradition of fairness, a fair go for all: as a government for all Australians, we cannot stand back and let such unfairness happen here.

Unlike many other countries, our laws and traditions do provide us with other options at this time. And we are fortunate in that this emergency has happened at a time when our economy is strong, our nation is strong. Once again, Australia has proved itself the Lucky Country.

Yet we must not delude ourselves. This is indeed an emergency, on a truly unprecedented scale. It is an emergency that affects everyone worldwide, in every way: it may be weeks, or months, or maybe even years, before we see a return to what we thought of just yesterday as normal. In the meantime, life must go on.

Last night, the Federal Emergency Management Council was convened, as required by Australian law. The Council's current chairman is Professor Donald Mercer, whose team at Derwent University has spent decades researching alternatives for extreme events such as these.

The Council has advised us that we have few choices available to us. One is martial law and the rule of the gun, a choice we know we must avoid if at all possible. We have a strong economy, but no normal means to manage transactions, and a high risk of hyperinflation and organised crime, which would destroy us as a nation. We have no time to prepare and introduce a centralised system of rationing, and in the present circumstances, almost no means to control it if we did.

The only viable alternative is to use the system we already have, but using trust and mateship, rather than money, to manage our transactions with each other. It is what we do already, in our homes, and with friends: we now need to find the courage, as a nation, to do the same in everything we do.

The current system works, everyone is fed, everyone is clothed, because everyone plays their part. And we urge you to continue to play your part.

Go to work, exactly as you would have done in ordinary times. If you cannot do your usual work, find what else you could do to help others.

If you go to the shops, do exactly as you would have done in ordinary times. Collect only what you need, and nothing more. Inevitably, in the next few days and weeks, there will be some shortages, but private hoarding will only make those shortages worse. There will be enough for everyone, and there will continue to be enough for everyone, as long as everyone stays calm and respectful of each others' needs.

As the Council has indicated, we can make this work not through a change of system, but through a change of attitude. We need a different understanding of property: what belongs to you, what belongs to me, what belongs to someone else, what belongs to everyone. Our property is ours, but we hold it in trust for everyone. It is not ours to misuse, or to waste according to our whim; it is not ours to withhold from others if they need it.

As consumers, we have become accustomed to think only of what we want; but we must now be more careful to limit our wants, and take and use only what we truly need. As citizens, we have every right, and those rights remain unchanged; but to make this work, we each need a new awareness that we also have every responsibility, not just to ourselves, but to all others, and to the nation as a whole.

We accept the Council's advice that this is the only option for Australia which will avoid the mayhem we already see happening elsewhere. We know that it will not be easy, for anyone, but every alternative would be far, far worse for all Australians.

With the full agreement of both Parliament and Senate, this government has accepted the Council's recommendations, as published this morning. Under Australia's emergency-legislation, those recommendations are now law, and take precedence over all other law, for the duration of this emergency.

Just a few short weeks ago, you placed your trust in us, in all members of Parliament, of all parties, to govern this nation on behalf of all Australians. Today, our world is suddenly very different, and for many, very frightening. Yet we urge you to keep the faith, to continue that trust in us, and in all your fellow Australians, to carry us through these difficult times.

Transition – Paton's

I turn up at work at the usual time, more out of habit than anything else. Not that much surprised at who else has turned up: Malarkey is nowhere to be seen – always was a timewasting little twat – and Minge isn't here but has sent a message that she needs time to calm her kids, but otherwise it's pretty much full-house. All standing outside the locked door, looking bloody silly, on a day when probably everyone else in the whole bloody country is taking the day off.

But we're not the only ones: all round the yard there's people standing outside their works front doors, wondering why the heck they're there too. Habit's a powerful thing.

Mr James comes up in his fancy Range Rover, looking a lot more hassled than usual, and kind of surprised that we're here too. But he doesn't just grunt and open the door, like he's done every day for the past year; he gets out and kind of cringes, like he's as lost as we are but half expecting us to lay into him. Odd, really. No-one says a bloody word for a while, till Hanneko breaks the ice.

"Need to get started, Mr James. Gangers'll be here soon."

That odd cringe again. "I can't pay you, you know."

"No-one can – not today. But we've got a job to do, Mr James. Our customers'll want us to be open – otherwise they can't do their jobs neither. Then nobody's house gets built. So we gotta be here, ha'n't we?"

"Yeah." He kind of breaths a sigh of relief, like surprise that we aren't going to lay into him or something. "Yeah. Yeah. Right. Thanks. Sorry. Sorry to keep you waiting."

And he fumbles in his pocket, pulls out his keys, unlocks the door, pushes it open. And for once steps aside to let us go first.

Fez – foreman to the last – hits the light-switches, and the place comes to life. Funny that – it's like it really *did* come to life, almost. Mr James is still in charge, and we need him to do that part of the job – though I'll bet he's happy to see the end of hassling builders for their unpaid bills. But it's our place now as much as his. Or we're its people, or something. Going to be weird trying to get my head around all that.

A quick check round: the alarm's still quiet, so no looters or anything like that, thank god. Power's still on so the power-workers must be at their jobs too – didn't think of that before. Computer works but the network's down, of course, so it's pretty useless. Oh well, back to paper for the while.

Big roller doors going up in the warehouse bay. We're still here. Paton's Building Supplies is open for business, folks.

Transition – Musician

Whoo-hoo! He's done it! Good on ya, Morrison! "Ya gotta fight / for ya right / ta par-r-r-ty!"

Yeah!

Music *is* work. No more bloody job. No more scraping for the bloody rent. Just get on with the music, an' nothing else. Right!

Okay. Think, guys, think. Whatta we need?

Practice space. Mum'll go spare if we spend any more time there, and Kabba's place is out. Howsabout one of the banks? They won't need their bloody places no more, will they? Nah, you're right, even if they do let us in, some bugger'll complain of the noise if we're right on the high-street.

Warehouse anywhere? Yeah, I guess so, no-money won't make any difference to them, so we won't be able to move in there.

But what about one of them big office-blocks? There's one out on the Walton estate that they've been trying to flog – why don't we just use that one? Once we're in we can prove we're using it, can't we?

But we'll need more to come with us – strength in numbers, the power of the proletariat, that sort of thing. Who's in the same game as us? – the Shackles, the Lazy Dogs, anyone else? Right, we give 'em a call straight after this, get it set up, 'fore someone else thinks of the same idea. Set up some shared gigs, too, so we have proof we're working if some fuckwit government bod comes chasing us.

Gear: reckon we need any more? Don't matter what Morrison says, I'll bet you Manny's'll cling on to their stuff tighter than a cat's bum, and there's no-one else in town with amps or synths. But we can get strings and skins easy enough: if we don't bust anything else we should be fine.

Sleeping-bags and stuff? Those office places have kitchens, but we'll need cooking gear. Food too. Right, make a list, Johnno? Done.

And money, what about money?

Money? Hey, don't need that no more, do we? Whoo-hoo!

Shock-jock

Transcript from Radio 3RZ, 'Bash Bashford' show, 3 January: legal advice obtained.

Identifiers: 'Bash': Graeme Michael 'Bash' Bashford; 'Don': James Donald 'Don' Mercer.

[Note for AM: Channel 3RZ is the only radio-station still operational at present in the Sydney area. It's only a small station, with old equipment, and only runs for a few hours a day, which is probably why it survived the flare. Bashford has a strong following in his own niche audience: he prides himself on being something of a 'shock-jock', to use the media term. Not so much 'no friend of the government' as no friend of any government, or anyone else, for that matter. Letting him loose on Don was probably not a good idea, but unfortunately it was all we had. Suggested response and action, please? – RK.]

[Segment begins 3:23pm]

Bash: So now you know: here we are, Radio 3RZ, the last ones standing. The survivors. The tough guys. Top of the heap, always have been, always will be. I'm Bash Bashford, and I tell it straight, just like it really is: Bash ain't bashful. So now you know. Right. Okay, so now I got a special treat for you, for all o' youse guys who want to know what the hell's going on here. My next guest is the guy who thinks he's our new lord and master, the Emergency Commissioner himself, Prof James Mercer. Your real name's James, right? So why d'you call yourself Don? Think you're the spitting image of old Don Bradman, hey? Or Don Corleone the mafia guy?

Don: Uh, thank you, uh, no, it's, it's my middle name, actually, and…

Bash: So what do you do, Mr Emergency Commissioner? I mean, apart from telling us what to do and how to run our lives and stealing all our money and trying to steal all our property too?

Don: Well, no, it really isn't that at all, I mean, this is a real emergency on a global scale…

Bash: I don't give a damn about a global scale, mate, and neither do none of the folks listening in here. All I wanna know is what the hell you've done with my money, with all of our money, right? Closed the bloody banks so you can steal the lot, hey? That's what I see, and that's what everyone else sees, ain't it, right?

Don: No, no, that isn't right at all...

Bash: What do you mean it isn't right? That's what you've done, isn't it?

Don: No, please, please, let me explain?

Bash: You'd better make it a good one, mate. Or else. You do know what "Or else", means, right?

Don: Yes, I'm, I, I do understand, and I do appreciate people are worried...

Bash: Not worried, mate. Angry. Bloody angry. At you.

Don: Ah. Well, you see, you need to understand that...

Bash: Why?

Don: I'm sorry?

Bash: I don't have to understand anything. It's your job to explain. So explain, right?

Don: As I was... Uh... Well, we are in an international emergency, and...

Bash: You've said that one already. That don't explain anything. Get to the point, okay?

Don: Yes, the, the core of the emergency as far as we're concerned is that the banks have in effect been emptied...

Bash: By you? Yeah, we know that already too. So where's the money gone?

Don: Nowhere. I mean, that's the point. No-one took it. It didn't exist.

Bash: What do you mean it didn't bloody exist? I've got it right here, right in my hand, what do you think this is? It ain't just a bit of plastic, it's money, right, it's real. So where's the money in the bank?

Don: Well, you see...

Bash: No I don't bloody see! Get on with it!

Don: I'm sorry, but you see, what we think of as 'money in the bank' is actually sort of imaginary. It's just a record on a disc somewhere, you see, just a collection of ones and zeros...

Bash: Right now all I'm seeing is a lot of zeroes and no ones, and no-one's happy. No-one's happy at all, and as far as what we can see, it's your bloody fault. We want answers, mate.

Don: I'm sorry, I am trying to explain...

Bash: You're supposed to be a prof, right? Supposed to be a bright guy? But your answers don't make no sense, not to me, not to anyone else. So go to it, right?

Don: What happened was three things happening at once – what you would call a 'triple-whammy', I think?

Bash: Yeah. And so what? Keep going, right?

Don: Uh, yes. The, the, there was a, a, failure of the algorithms that...

Bash: Algo-what? Talk bloody English, will you?

Don: Sorry, the, uh, the computer programs that run the banks' links with the stock-exchange and so on. I suppose we'd have to call it a betting system, so the banks could make money for themselves using everyone else's money, all over the world. And the, the bets, if you like, went wrong. They'd sort of bet against each other, if you like. A very risky bet, all of them. They got into what's called a cascade...

Bash: For gawd's sake, can you please talk in English, not this bloody techno gobbledegook?

Don: Well, I'll have to pass you over to one of the technical experts for that...

Bash: I don't want no bloody technical expert, I'm talking to you. So talk, right? Where's the money?

Don: I'd, I'd have to say that it's gone. It only existed as numbers in the first place. Everyone bet against each other, but they made it into a losing bet, if you like.

Bash: No, I don't bloody like. What, you mean they all bet the farm, and they all lost? C'mon, no-one's that bloody stupid!

Don: I know I'm simplifying it a bit, but yes, I'm afraid they were.

Bash: Sheesh. And you make it out it's nothing to do with you? Or that daft bastard Morrison, right?

Don: No, I do assure you, this was nothing to do with the government. It was entirely outside of our scope of influence.

Bash: Sure. Sure. Thousands might believe you, but I bloody don't, and I don't think anyone else will, either. But keep talking, right?

Don: Well, right at that point someone triggered a computer virus...

Bash: And you reckon this was nothing to do with you either? Sure. Sure.

Don: Well, it was, was, worldwide. We don't yet have the forensics to identify exactly where it started.

Bash: Forensics. More fancy words. Sheesh. Lord and master, right?

Don: Uh, no, it's, it's not like that, I, I, I assure you. What this, this virus did was, was stop the computers from being able to talk with each other. So they couldn't recover from their bad debts, if you like. So everything was stuck at zero. In that sense, no money. And then we were hit by the flare.

Bash: Oh yeah. This magical bloody flare, or whatever you're calling it. Pretty lights bouncing up and down a bit, my phone gets fried and a few other things with it. So what? What difference does that bloody make to anything?

Don: Mr Bashford, I'm sorry, but I, I don't think you quite realise the seriousness of what's happened here? At present we have no banking system, no means to handle any kind of money-transaction other than the cash that's already in people's pockets, much of our electronic equipment and electronic records destroyed, most networks and communications are out of action, we have serious problems in almost every aspect of infrastructure and industry and social governance, and much, much more. And it's everywhere, I do assure you, not just here. So far we have been incredibly lucky in this country, from what we hear, but many thousands of people have died already, and unless we take action straight away, many thousands more will die.

Bash: Who's died? Who's died? Anyone, hey? Anyone who matters? I'm still here, my missis is still here, my mates are still here, that's all that matters to me. Who gives a stuff about anyone else? You? Any of you bloody pollies give a stuff? Yeah, right, don't make me laugh…

Don: I'm, I mean, I'm not a politician, I'm a lawyer, a kind of lawyer…

Bash: Yeah, right, so which one's bloody worse? Lawyer or pollie? Same as makes no bloody difference, all bloody liars, the lot of you. Keep going, mate, you're digging yourself in deeper just nicely.

Don: I mean, if you need an example, you must by now have heard of the crash at Kingsford Smith, two days ago? Two airliners lost all of their avionics on approach, during the peak of the flare? One fell into the sea just short of the runway, the other onto the refinery? I'm sorry to say that more than a thousand people died there just in that pair of incidents alone…

Bash: No. I don't bloody believe you, mate, I think you're just making this up. I haven't heard a bloody dicky-bird. And Bash ain't bashful. I am the news, mate. If I haven't heard of it, it ain't bloody happened.

Don: Oh. Ah. Uh, I do assure you…

Bash: Just get on with it, will you? You're saying that the banks are stuffed, and that it ain't you what did it. And they can't fix it, and that isn't your fault either. And now there's a whole load of people dead, and you didn't make that one up. Right. Sure. I'll believe you, thousands wouldn't. And now you're 'taking action', you say, for this so-called 'national emergency'. What action? From what I hear, you're not satisfied with stealing all of the money, you want to steal everything else as well. Is that right?

Don: No, that really isn't right. No-one's stealing anything, I do assure you. We, we have to create conditions for, the, uh, needs of, for the greatest good of the greatest number. We have no means to do so with money, because it doesn't exist, and we have no means to police it, because as you know, since the Topolski affair, we in essence have no police. The only way we can make this work is if we ask everyone to share. To accept responsibility. To work together. As we would in any family. It's just the same thing, on a much larger scale.

Bash: Who gives a shit? What's mine is mine, and it's gonna stay that way. I ain't going to share bloody anything of mine with some poncy git like you, or some towelhead from the back end of Woop-Woop. Why should I?

Don: Because it's in everyone's interest. I mean, if we are to have any chance to survive this catastrophe, we have no choice but to pull together. Which I know will be hard, but every alternative will be far harder, for everyone. We've looked at every other alternative, believe me.

Bash: You know what? I don't believe you. I think it's just another rort, another way to rip off the little guy, big-time. The biggest rort there's ever been, stealing a whole damn country in one go. My oath you've got some bloody cheek, haven't you? Those last lot, got caught red-handed with their mitts in the drug-money game, they were bad enough, but you're worse. Much worse. You have to be. No-one does anything to help anyone else for nothing, everyone knows that for a fact. Which means the whole lot of youse are the worst thieves this country has ever seen. And that means you're the worst of the worst, Mr Emergency Commissioner.

Don: No, please, please, listen. This is all about making sure that everyone wins. Look, if you can give me any point of reference, I'm sure I can give you an example of how this system of mutual responsibilities will work in practice, in fact works much better in practice than the old money-based system did, better for you, for your family and for everyone else. Please, you do need to give me a chance to explain this. Please.

Bash: No. Why should I? Not interested. No-one's going to win anything off of me, the only one who's gonna win anything here is me, and that's flat. Clear to me that you're just a liar. Just a thief. Fancy label doesn't mean anything to me. Mr Emergency Commissioner, my ass.

Don: Ah... uh...

Bash: Too right. Nothing else to say? No other way to try to pretend you're not stealing from everything from everyone? Yeah, didn't think so. 'Cos that's the real truth, isn't it? That's the real truth.

Don: No, I do assure you, it isn't. But I do accept that you won't believe me, whatever I say. I don't know why not. Good day to you, and to your listeners. Thank you for your time.

Bash: Yup. He's gone. And good riddance. That fuckwit, folks, was the bloke this bloody government has set up as the Emergency Commissioner, Mr Bloody Idiot Mercer. So now you know. He thinks he's special, but I put him in his place, didn't I? Bash ain't bashful: that's me. And that's us: Radio 3RZ, the last ones standing. The survivors. The tough guys. Signing off for the day: I'll see youse all tomorrow.

[Annotation: AM: Poor Don! I'm not surprised you said he was a bit shaken up. He did well, but he's not used to that kind of rough-and-tumble, I guess we'll need to shield him from the press much more from now on. But you're right, if that's the only working station in Sydney, we don't have any other choice. So yes, do it, Bob. Bashford is going to get a nasty shock tomorrow when he realises that the man he had so much fun beating up today has just requisitioned everything that he owns. I can't say I'll feel sorry for him. Perhaps send him the good news via a colonel or two? In a tank?]

Transition – Graphic designer

No more moody faked up pictures of faked up crap food in crap restaurants. No more exciting catalogues of rip-off house-sales. No more pseudo sales-pitches. My god. What are we going to do with our lives now? Might actually get the chance to do something worthwhile for once? Even have some fun?

Ad-agency guys'll go berserk: no fat commissions from stupid clients being sold space they don't need for crap stuff they don't need to sell and that no-one wants. Jesus, they won't know what to do with themselves. Have to wank each other off, I guess. They haven't got anything else that's left.

No more bloody advertising jingles – christ, Minzy'll be happy about that. No more crap "as seen on TV" line-ups. No more slick garbage for the banks and the insurance brokers – they're gone. Good bloody riddance to 'em.

Computer's still working: don't have to go all the way back to pencils and paint, then. Though may do that anyway: too bloody long since I've handled a brush.

Going to take some time to get used to this. But yeah, I think I'm going to *like* getting used to this…

Transition – Golfer

You mean this chap Morrison is serious? No money and all that?

Oh. He is. I see.

Well, I suppose that's good. I was starting to worry a bit about what this mess was doing to my pension fund.

Shouldn't make much difference to me, though, should it? After all, I'm retired now. I don't need to work any more. And I'm not changing that for anyone.

Yes, this is my car. And yes, I do believe just exactly what that sticker says. Work is for people who can't play golf. That's how I got to be where I am. You meet all the right people at golf.

No, of course I don't have anything to do with *those* people! That's why we have gates on this community, to keep that filth out. Lucky to get what we give them, if you ask me. As for the others, well, there's a good reason they're called the undeserving poor, you know. Disgusting. A complete waste of our tax-money.

How should I know? I have an accountant for that. And I tell you, he's not doing his job properly if have to pay any tax, is he?

Oh for heaven's sake! How pathetic. What kind of petty do-gooder planet do you come from? It's only the little people who pay taxes, surely?

Well, you can believe that if you want. I'm not going to. I don't see any reason why I should.

You're joking! You must be. Really? Oh, how stupid! Well, if they're going to be that ridiculous, I'm going to stay right here and work on my golf average and call that my work. Why shouldn't I? I told you, I'm retired now.

I'm forty-two. Why?

That's quite enough of that attitude, thank you. Good day.

Due-diligence

The office for the CEO of a large US multi-national: expansive, expensive, with a view of other vast city tower-blocks. Just visible beyond them is a ring of guard-towers with machine-guns and searchlights: one of the new ghettoes. The CEO is in his 60s, slim, grizzled, with an air of arrogant confidence and manipulative possessiveness. With him is a worried-looking commercial lawyer, holding a stack of papers. Trying to explain the subtle points of international law to a man who's used to believing that his every whim *is* law is not an easy task.

"Chet, I'm telling you, it's all above board. That law's been there for more'n half a century. Way before we bought 'em up. The Aussies'd say we failed due diligence, 'n they'd be right."

"What is this goddamn law?"

"'Emergency Management Act'. Here." The lawyer waves one sheet from the stack of papers. "Quote, 'In a declared emergency the Commissioner may take possession of any property he needs, and offer such compensation as he sees fit.' Unquote. That's it."

"So what's the friggin' deal?"

"They declared an emergency. Covered the whole country."

"Yeah, so did we. So what?"

"They took possession of everything. In the whole damn country. Gave it to the users, not the owners. Called it a 'commonwealth'."

"Shit! They took *everything*? From *everyone*? Including *our* assets?"

"Yeah."

"Without asking anyone? Without asking *us*?"

"Yeah. That law says they can do it. So they did. Real neat trick."

"An' they're offerin' us *nothing*?"

"Valuation on WTO rules at the time they took over, at the bottom of the crash. So yeah, pretty close to nothin'."

"They can't do that! That's *theft*!"

"They can. They have. I'm tellin' you, we're screwed."

"We'll see about that!"

Still glaring angrily at the lawyer, he grabs a telephone and starts dialling.

Transition – Cabinet transcript

From *The Age*

Cabinet response to Troubles revealed

Transcripts of Cabinet meetings released today under the thirty-year rule have sent historians rushing to revise long-held theories and perspectives on the Australian response to the Troubles.

Most critics will concede that Prime Minister Morrison's actions at the time ultimately proved successful, and laid the foundations for much of modern Australian society.

However, possessionist think-tanks such as the Australian Centre for Libertarian Studies have long maintained that Morrison used the emergency to override democracy and instead to introduce and enforce the sustainable-law model. Last week at the History Alliance conference in Melbourne [The Age, Friday], ACLS spokesman Professor David Hamilton asserted "Morrison was a fanatic and ideologue whose one mad dream was to dispossess citizens of all their rights to personal property".

Other detractors have drawn parallels with the Project For The New American Century (PNAC) whose hubris at the end of the last century led the Bush administration in the US to its flawed and ultimately fatal invasion of Iraq.

But the new documents reveal that Morrison's 'free Australia' came about almost by accident, as the last available option for a government facing an unprecedented crisis. And the iconoclastic change in law was first proposed not by Morrison himself, but by the ex-Liberal Party defence minister, right-winger Gary Brussard-Holmes.

The documents also confirm long-held rumours about the crucial role of the armed forces and their then Commander in Chief, General Gordon Cameron.

From Cabinet, 2nd January, 3am. Attending: Prime Minister Anthony Morrison (AM), Home Affairs and Justice Jane Clement (JC), Foreign Affairs and Trade Stavro Sipinski (SS), Defence Gary Brussard-Holmes (GBH), Technology and Innovation Patricia

Corroli (PC). Transcript unedited except for '**' to indicate deleted expletive.

GBH: ...idea if this ** thing works. It's a museum-piece, but it's all we could find with its lights still on.

PC: Press the 'speaker' button, Gary. [loud squeal]

GBH: Ah, right. Okay, Tony.

AM: Right, I know everyone's tired, and it's going to be a long night, but let's give it our best shot. What have we got? Pat, anyone know yet what the heck happened to our information-systems? Are we back to the ark and Simpson's donkey?

PC: Looks like it, pretty much, though ANU's still working on it. Preston says it looks like the algorithmic-trading bots panicked over falling figures at the year-end and ran wild in a cascading downward spiral – a feedback loop like Gary just did with the tape. That was just starting to bottom out, but pretty much as close to zero as makes damn-all difference, when the Kinkaru virus took out the network routers, which meant there was no way to recover except by manual retrieves from the banks' and traders' backups, probably from before the Christmas close. That would have been a big enough fight as it was, but that's when the flare hit us and took out the rest, pretty much exactly the same time. So anything with Zell Effect chips is gone, along with pretty much anything magnetic, even in the deep stores. That's every scrap of IT built in the past five years, pretty much, and pretty much every government record from the last thirty.

JC: Ouch.

PC: The banks'll be worse hit than we are. Nothing left. And that's just the start of it. All the stock exchanges will be wiped, the insurance companies, the forex, the lot, And all that imaginary money sloshing around the globe in leveraged derivatives, none of it was linked to anything real, but it's real enough to take everything else down with it. If the stock exchange tries to open tomorrow, this morning, god what time is it now, there won't be a single cent left. It's that bad, Tony.

AM: Goodbye the economy, then?

PC: Pretty much. And there's a lot more bad news on the tech side. For example, I've checked with Chris, Health says they've lost pretty much all their records too, anything that wasn't on paper, along with almost everyone in intensive care, and probably everyone with embedded electronics.

GBH: What, pacemakers and so on, like Louie has?

JC: He's dead, Gary. Marge called me this evening.

GBH: **, that's hard.

PC: Pretty much the only good news is that the old copper-line network still works for those exchanges that weren't fully upgraded, which with the telcos' greedy penny-pinching these last few years means that's pretty much most of them, in fact. And we still have pretty much all of our power network, for the same reason. The flare did take out some of the controllers and a few of the long-distance lines, but Gayle Hunnicutt says they're repairable, pretty much, though some will be weeks at least.

AM: What about overseas? Are we the only ones to get hit like this, or is everyone else in the same boat?

SS: Is difficult to tell, we have no communications still. Fibre-optics are still there, but as Pat says, controllers are gone. Only communication now is short-wave, see? And flare scrambles much of that.

GBH: Short-wave?

SS: Old ham-radio. Pat knows. So far we hear from embassy stations in Moscow, Addis Ababa, Netherlands, consulate San Francisco and Mumbai, also High Commission in London they are on Morse code only, is all they have. One very old satellite still working, is jammed, too many trying to go through narrow pipe, see? Quick summary, I say they are utterly **, far worse than us, most.

GBH: So it's not just us. Well, that's a blessing of sorts, especially for my boys.

PC: Cameron says military comms is a mess, Tony. They're pulling old stuff out of mothballs as fast as they can, but it'll be days before they can test it all. It could be weeks before they can deploy it, pretty much.

SS: Will be true for everyone elsewhere, almost. Valve will be unaffected, but only ones I know that still use valve for military are Russians, and they have troubles enough at home soon. They not worry us.

GBH: I'd agree, no threat there, you know. The only outside ** I'd worry about are the Indons. They're ripe for another military coup, right on our doorstep, and some of the ** have territorial ambitions, you know. But if they're distracted by civil unrest, and we can perhaps do something about that, they'll run out of hardware ** quick, and if the Yanks are as ** as Stav says, they won't be able to re-equip before we're ready for the ** again. Biggest problem we have right now is avionics is **, so the fighters are ** too till they're fixed, we can't fight a bloody war with cropdusters but we'll do it if we have to.

AM: How is aviation generally? That's one of our lifelines, surely?

PC: In a word, buggered, pretty much, I'd guess. But I don't have many facts as yet. You got anything, Stav?

SS: Is bad, but not as bad as could have been. We know we lose at least four internationals...

JC: Oh god, that's almost two thousand people! If we're lucky!

SS: We be lucky if we lose only hundred times that many. San Francisco consulate say that shooting is already started big-time on streets, with attitude of government they think conservative estimate is million or more dead in first week. Is not good. Though is good Moral America government be too busy to bother anyone else, they are much more of threat to us than Russians or Chinese or even Indonesians. Is heresy, I know, but is true, especially in trade.

GBH: Just ** hang on there, you know?

AM: Please, Gary, Stav, I know what you both feel about this but we don't have time for old fights. We're on our own here, we're up the proverbial without a paddle and the Americans can wait, Moral America or not. Okay? Pat, any more on aviation, or infrastructure generally?

PC: We've had four reports of downed commercials so far, so, yes, sorry, Jane, that's pretty much another thousand casualties there. Fly-by-wire would be the greatest risk, if they were in the air when the flare hit they'd be dead, pretty much. But most of our fleet is fairly old, they'll use some Zell Effect avionics but also dual or triple pre-Zell systems, or even the old inertial nav.

AM: Yes. And there's a lot of good bush-pilots up there who could land on a wing and a prayer if they have to.

PC: Yeah. So if we're lucky we should have most of them on the ground safely by now, pretty much, though we may have lost a few hitting the ground too hard trying to land without ATC or glide-path. We'll know by tomorrow, pretty much. Trains are okay apart from the newest signalling systems, and so far that's just the Sydney-Brisbane. Roads are mostly fine, a few pile-ups reported here and there but not much more than usual. A lot of the upmarket import cars are buggered, Zell Effect chips again, but Holden and Ford and the rest were still clinging on to their investment in the old stuff so the domestic fleet should be pretty much okay. We're lucky there.

AM: The lucky country again?

PC: Only because the last government did nothing to invest in technology. And the government before that.

AM: Okay, understood. Oh, and thanks, that really helped, a lot of work in that. So Stav, how about the shipping fleet? That's our other lifeline.

SS: Is good enough. Most nav tech is down, but they know how to use sextant and chart and lighthouse beacon. We keep foreign ships here, most crews say they want to stay, and all of ours we contact are returning. We are in profit on this!

AM: Thanks, Stav, glad to have any good news at all today. What about you, Jane, do you have anything that isn't bad news?

JC: Not a lot. The police are still demoralised and leaderless, of course, so we can't expect much. The country cops seem to be rallying round, so we're probably all right there, but the factions in the cities mean we're still well and truly stuffed. Since Topolski's murder police reputation generally is down in the depths of the dunny, the polls show the public won't trust them at all, we've even had people refusing to follow police orders over a simple traffic bingle. And Bannock hasn't got enough evidence yet to know who can be trusted in the existing forces and who can't. In short, sorry, but as Gary would put it, we're **. We're pulling the old whistleblowers and known-honest ones back into uniform as fast as we can, but it's a door-knocker job to find them. And that'll be days yet, especially under these conditions.

AM: Do we have days?

JC: No. Sorry. With the cops out of action, the gangs and the syndicates were already moving before yesterday's mess. And there's still enough guns in private hands to fit out anyone's army. Stav's right, it'll be a bloodbath if we don't move soon. And that's everywhere.

AM: Dash it, it looks like we don't have any other option, doesn't it? The states have said they're with us, but we can't do it state by state, it'll have to be the full national emergency, under FEMA rules, all the way to martial law.

GBH: Sorry to be the bearer of more ** bad news, but no can do.

AM: What?

GBH: Cameron's boys won't play. I mean, they'll do anything we ask, he's sure of that, but for FEMA the armed forces are under the civil authority, which means the police. And right now there's no ** way the troops are going to accept orders from any cop when they don't know if the ** is genuinely trying to help or is just in it for his own ** pocket or trying to use them as a private army in his own ** feuds, like we've seen already in so much from Bannock. Cameron's boys won't do that, and they won't be part of any military takeover either, which is what it'd be if we don't do it by FEMA rules. Cameron says he'll have a ** mutiny on his hands if we try to do FEMA by the book, and good on 'em, I say.

AM: I'd agree, but it doesn't help us now. We need their help, ye gods, we need all the help we can get. Jane, is there anything that we can use out of FEMA? What happens next?

JC: We're covered under FEMA section four-sub-one for definition of emergency, it doesn't need to be anything predefined, it's an emergency if we say it is. Section twenty-three says we have to declare the state of emergency and its scope from a broadcasting station, we'll have difficulty with that for today but we can do it via newspapers and flyers if we have to. There's no limit to scope in FEMA, so we can legally make it the whole country in one hit. Twenty-three-sub-six says we have up to twenty-eight days, but we can renew indefinitely if we twist Parliament's arm to let us do so, and twenty-four-sub-two-bee says we can override any law we like, including any and all rights of citizens, for however long we say the emergency lasts. Twenty-four-sub-two-see says we can take possession of anything we need to, up to and including everything in the entire country and any assets we can reach beyond that, while twenty-four-sub-five says it's up to us what we offer in return for those assets, including no payment at all. We've plenty of room for manoeuvre, Tony.

PC: For ** sake, Jane, that bloody thing is a dictator's dream! Is that for real?

GBH: Yeah, it is, and it's been on the ** statute-books for decades too. Cameron's boys knew all about it, you know, that's what they're so ** unhappy about.

SS: And right now we in this room are those dictators, so we better get it right, yes?

AM: Too right, Stav. What about the police problem?

94

JC: Five-sub-two says you're supposed to hand operational control to the Chief Commissioners of Police in each state...

GBH: ...which would be a ** disaster right now...

JC: ...but seven and twenty-one-aich say you can appoint any alternate person or persons as deputy.

GBH: Thank ** for that, that may let us off the hook with Cameron's boys.

JC: Eight-sub-one and eight-sub-two say you also have to convene the Emergency Management Council, but it's been running on a permanent basis since the Black Monday fires, so we don't have to do anything there.

AM: Who's Chair this year?

PC: Please don't say it's Shalbert again. He was a disaster-area desperately waiting for a disaster to prop up his glorified male ego.

JC: It says Professor James Mercer, from Derwent Uni.

GBH: Well ** me, the Don! That *is* good news for once, you know.

SS: Is Don. Is good.

JC: Who is he?

AM: I think you're the only one here who didn't study with him, Jane. You did, didn't you, Pat?

PC: Yeah, part of my postgrad, too many bloody years ago. Quirky old bird, but at least he's got his head screwed on.

SS: Strange ideas, but they make sense over time.

PC: And we'll need some ** strange ideas to get out of this one, too.

GBH: Wait a ** minute, what about SusLaw?

PC: Oh god, that?

SS: No, wait, he's right. Think about it. Responsibility, not rights, that was idea. And it would work, for this.

AM: And we all worked on it, too. I've forgotten half of it now, but it's all there somewhere. And we all know that stuff.

PC: Half of Parliament'd know it, I reckon. Even the Senate.

GBH: And half the ** bureaucrats, too. If they studied at Derwent, and a good half of the ** in my lot did, they would have done the Don's unit on Theory and Philosophy of Law. Which means they know SusLaw. Probably contributed to it themselves as well.

AM: Didn't Cameron say something...

GBH: **, you're right, he did! Got the Don to set up the same kind of course at the Staff College, twenty years back. Which means we should get the ** armed-forces on-side, too. Right!

JC: Sorry, but I don't seem to be part of this frat-party... If Stav and Gary actually agree on something for once, it's above their old party-politics, thank god, but would someone please explain to me what on earth this is about?

AM: Stav's one-line summary, responsibility, not rights. All existing law is based on rights, and what Don said was that that's why we have so much trouble, that it's technically unsustainable, inherently fragile. He's always said that law can only be sustainable if it's based on responsibilities. You would own something because you were responsible for it, not because of some arbitrary made-up right of entitlement. And we all played with these ideas as part of our course-material when we were students at Derwent...

PC: ...and Derwent has always been the uni of choice for anyone going into politics or government...

GBH: ...and the Don's run that course for must be ** thirty years or more...

AM: ...so there's a heck of a lot of people who would know it. Up till now it's always been just theory, a fun game for law-students, because it was so far removed from everyday reality. But to be honest, it's always looked like it would work better than what we think of as the everyday, and the annual SusLaw conferences have shown more and more about how inefficient the normal rights-based economy really is. Anyway, SusLaw always seemed an impossible utopian dream, you know, fun for students, but nothing more. But it still triggers off real questions about what we're doing this for in the first place. True for you, Stav?

SS: More, is why I chose to stay in politics.

GBH: And it's why I changed to politics from law, to prove the old bastard wrong. But in the last few years every ** thing he predicted would ** up has ** happened, including the nice little rorts of my esteemed ** colleagues in the former ** government, so I was the one who was ** wrong all along. Which, now I come to realise it, is why I'm a ** sight more willing to put up with this ** Tony than I would have been even a year ago. SusLaw would work for this. And I'd say Tony's the only one with enough ** to put the Don's ideas into practice. So I say we ** do it.

JC: But what's the point, if it's just some daft utopian thing?

PC: It's not utopian. Not really. It's just different. But it works best when you're right up against something that's completely unsustainable. Like right now, in fact. Up until yesterday, SusLaw made no bloody sense. As of yesterday ** morning, it's probably the only thing that bloody does make sense. Don used to say that it would be so disruptive that you could only bring it in if there was some major calamity, and every other choice was worse. But right now, frankly, what have we got to lose? Every other choice is worse, a lot worse. So I'm with Gary on this. Trust me, Jane, I promise I'll bring you up to speed on this. It doesn't take long, Stav's right, the basic ideas are really straightforward once you get your head round them. It's getting your head round them that's hard first off. And it'll be hard for everyone else, too, but it'll be the only thing that'll work. Trust us.

JC: Okay. I'll go with you on this.

AM: You too, Stav?

SS: Of course.

AM: Me too. Well, I must say I'm feeling a lot more certain that we'll get out of this mess than when we started this meeting. Adjourn for an hour, get some rest if we can? I'll dig out my SusLaw notes, they're around in my office somewhere, we can rough out a plan from that, we'll need to chase up a list of all of Don's students for the past thirty years, and by then it should be close enough to dawn to start chasing other people awake. We'll need them. Oh, yes, and the tape as well.

GBH: Right. If I can find the right ** button… ah, got it…

[ends]

Letter to Mum

telelink::fax-class="letter"
telelink::fax-addressto: Mum
22nd December
Melbourne

Hi Mum!

I did promise I'd write, didn't I? And see, you'll get this before Christmas, too!

I don't know where you got your ideas about everyone being backward with animals running up and down the main street and such, because it looks like just like Manchester or any other big city I've been to back home – cars on the street, but no kangaroos! And I'm sending this by a perfectly ordinary public telelink – in fact this one's in the lobby of the hotel where I'm staying. The only difference is that there's no pay-card scan – it's not no-money here in the Visitor Zone, they use cash-cards just like at home, but the telelink's bundled in with the room, and I'm not being charged for that.

As you can see, I got through the States okay, but I wouldn't want to go there again. Pretty scary, to be honest, but I'll tell you about that some other time. But here it's been real easy, came straight in at the airport and down here to the hotel. Still a bit sleepy with jet-lag, liked they warned us, but otherwise just fine.

I'll try to be going out tonight with a couple of guys from here to take a better look at the town. More later!

Steve

Visitor Zones

From *The New Australia Travel Guide*

Visitor Zones

Visitor Zones are where Australia meets the rest of the world – which is why they look like the rest of the world, too. Australia's famous no-money economy only operates outside of Visitor Zones: inside them, it's money as usual, though usually without the frenetic buy, buy, 'bye of most tourist destinations. That lack of pressure is part of what makes Australia such a great place to relax.

There are Visitor Zones all over the country. You arrive into the country in one, because the international section of an airport is always a Visitor Zone. City centres and popular tourist places such as Surfer's Paradise are entirely set aside as Visitor Zones. The border is marked by a blue line painted on the road (see *"That big blue line"*). As a visitor, you're not supposed to cross the line without an Australian citizen as an escort, though no-one's likely to stop you going for a quiet wander around.

In the larger Visitor Zones you'll see a few places – particularly bars and cafes – showing a crossed-'V' sign: no Visitors. Don't go in unless you're invited: it's where Australians go to get away from money-madness, and they can be unpleasant about having their peace disturbed by some hapless tourist!

Travel isn't a problem, because major highways and popular tourist routes such as Victoria's Great Ocean Road are also classed as Visitor Zones. Roads that are okay for visitors have the usual 'V' mark on the road-sign; likewise visitor-okay service-areas on the roads. Intercity rail stations and domestic airports have areas set aside for visitors – the cabin crew are considered to be your escorts while you're travelling.

Off the beaten track can be more difficult, because in general you're not supposed to be there unless you have an escort or you're on a Workshare visa. If you're genuinely lost, people are usually okay about giving help, but don't push your luck – Australians have had plenty of practice at dealing with would-be freeloading tourists. Anywhere that shows the standard 'V' sign is a local Visitor Zone, though, and you're now allowed to go from point to point as long as you've checked in at each end before doing it. The Tourist Alliance publishes a set of guide-books that list Visitor points throughout the country (see "*Accommodation*"). So it's now possible – and permissible – to 'roll your own' along the back-routes, and it's getting easier every year.

Within Visitor Zones everything you need has to be paid for in the usual way. Australian *currency* is good old dollars and cents. It's all cashless: if you don't have one of the standard transfer cards – Visa, MC, Amex, KA, BBz – you'll need to buy an Australia Card from the Tourist Alliance and top it up from time to time.

Prices are standardised throughout the country. They're based on a complicated system of world averages for equivalent items, and are fixed for a year – so watch out for possible price-changes on June 30. What you actually pay depends on the exchange-rates, so it can seem expensive or cheap according to how your own currency is doing, but by definition it works out fair all round.

A word on haggling: don't. The prices are fixed to make life simpler for everyone. It's assumed you either want the item at that price, or you don't: it's your responsibility, not theirs. Complaints about prices and attempts at bargaining for discounts are often taken as an insult, so don't do it. (See also "*Tipping*".)

Backpacker hotel

The snack area of the backpackers lobby. Steve, looking refreshed, makes an instant coffee whilst chatting to two other guests, Andy Kreuzfeld and Joey Minor. Both men are in their mid to late 20s. Joey is Australian, an athletic type, with tight jeans and t-shirt to emphasise this; Andy is German, tall, bespectacled with long blond hair and carefully-trimmed beard, and wearing pressed tan-coloured slacks and designer-style light jacket.

"Anywhere round here we can go for a drink?" asks Steve. "How do we check in with the cops to get clearance? What time's the curfew?"

Joey laughs, mocking and sarcastic. "What kind of bullshit line they been feedin' you, mate?"

"But I thought…"

Andy intervenes. "Ah. From the States you have just come, yes?"

"Uh, yeah… Is it different here?"

Joey laughs again, though not so sarcastic this time. "My oath it is. No wonder you got such bloody strange ideas. Look, this ain't the States. Ain't even as tight as you Poms. There's no curfew."

"No curfew? *Really?*"

"And no cops, neither, so you don't have to worry 'bout that." Joey pauses for a moment. "Y'know, ain't been no cops here for nigh on thirty year, not since they got busted big-time just afore the Troubles. There's just the good ol' Gee-Ay, and they're fairly harmless s'long as you don't hassle anyone or cross the Blue Line less'n you know what you're doin'."

"Gee-Ay?"

"Guard Alliance", explains Andy. "Also known as the garda. More like your traffic wardens than police. No guns."

"Wow… *That'll* be a change from the States…"

"Same as what your cops used to be afore the Troubles", says Joey. "No gun, you learn to talk your way out o' trouble, not shoot your way out."

Andy nods. "A lot better for everyone."

"Yeah, mate. A lot."

Steve takes a swig of his coffee, winces a moment at the taste, and returns to the conversation. "What's the Blue Line? You said don't cross it."

"Boundary o' the Visitor Zone, where the real Australia starts, 'stead of this faked-up stuff we have to do to keep you vizzies happy!"

He grins. "It's nothin' special – 's just a line on the ground with some 'no vizzie' signs. Andy'll show it to ya?"

He looks to Andy, who nods. Joey continues. "Y'ain't s'posed to go through without an escort, but no-one'll stop you goin' for a quick gander. Just don't hassle anyone or nick anything out there. 'S the one thing the GA do take seriously. No muckin' about with 'no worries' or 'it's your responsibility, mate', they'll kick you out the country faster'n you can blink. Okay?"

"Gotcha. And thanks." Steve breathes in deeply, lets out a sigh of satisfaction, puts down the coffee cup on the sideboard. "Right! No cop-check, no curfew – sounds like it's drinking-time! You coming, guys?"

"Yeah, just a mo'." Joey quietly picks up Steve's discarded mug, moves across to small sink, washes it, rinses it, places it on the drying rack, without a word. "Yup. Let's go. Ain't been out in the old CBD for quite a while."

The three of them move out into the evening air.

That big blue line

From *The New Australia Travel Guide*

That big blue line

It's one country, but there are two entirely different Australias, separated by a bright blue line. On one side – the side you'll see when you first arrive – are the Visitor Zones, the public Australia that's set up for the way people do things in the rest of the world; and on the other side is the real Australia, where people don't have to worry about such crazy notions as money!

The blue line isn't just a metaphor: it's a real line painted on the ground, to mark the boundary of a Visitor Zone. You'll usually see it flanked by road-signs with a crossed-V on them, meaning 'no Visitors'. Out in the country, the opposite applies: service-stations, hotels, restaurants and the like that cater for visitors display a large 'V' sign, and you'll be expected to pay for service in the usual way. Other places won't take payment, but probably won't provide service either – though most people will help you anyway if they think you've a genuine need.

Ordinary visitors such as tourists aren't supposed to cross the line without an escort. That's the law, though in practice most people won't mind, especially close to the line. But don't push your luck: Australians don't use money, but that doesn't mean anything you see on the far side of the line is free for you to take. If anyone complains to the GA (Guard Alliance – see *"Police"*), you'll find yourself sitting in an airport departure-lounge a lot sooner than you intended, and probably with a hefty fine to pay as well.

Think of it as like being in a friend's house. If you're invited in for a visit, you wouldn't expect to be charged for a drink, or a meal; but neither would you walk off with their shopping, or the grandfather clock. If it looked like you're just freeloading, your friend wouldn't be keen to have you around. And if you barged into the house without an invitation, you wouldn't expect your friend to be too pleased about it.

So it's much the same here. That big blue line is like the doorway to a stranger's house. There's no door, no physical barrier: but it is someone else's home. Treat it as such – ask permission, check with people before you do anything – and you won't go far wrong.

Just remember that it's a different world on the other side of that big blue line!

In Melbourne

It's later in the same Melbourne evening. The work-traffic has long since gone homeward; in their place, the night-people are starting to appear. And tourists, of course.

Joey has left to meet up with friends elsewhere, so Steve and Andy are on their own, walking side by side down the evening street in the nightclub district. Things just starting to heat up, with bouncers on duty and lines beginning to form.

"So there's no no-money here, right? We still have to pay for everything?"

"Here, yes, we need the account-card. Drinks are cheaper here than back home in Germany, but not much. I think it will be the same for you."

Nearby, standing in a small shelter at the edge of the pavement, are two people in sort-of uniform with the ubiquitous armbands, this time with the letters 'GA' inside a blue circle. Calm, quiet, yet evidently alert for any trouble. Andy points them out to Steve as they pass, who nods in a 'got it' gesture, then returns to the essential topic of drinking.

"Here just don't seem right, dunno why. Just keep walking a bit, I reckon?"

Andy nods. They walk on for a while, then Steve points to a sign on the closed door of what seems to be a bar, tucked away down the side of an alley. It's like a standard road-sign, circular, with a crossed 'V'.

"What's that one mean, Andy?"

"'No Visitors'. Where ordinary Australians go to get away from money-madness. Best not go in:" – he mimics Joey's voice – "they don' like their peace an' quiet shook up by some stupid bloody tourist!"

"Uh. Right." He grins. "Better keep lookin', I guess?"

The clubs and pubs are thinning now; they pass the looming edifice of an old court-house, an uninspiring concrete office-block left over from the last century, a few closed shops and sandwich-bars which seem more aimed at business-travellers than at the tourist trade. A block or two further, they arrive at a crossing with an almost-deserted main road – and on the far side of that is a blue line painted across the road and pavement, with a crossed-V sign either side of the road.

Steve moves to cross the road, but Andy pulls back, suddenly hesitant and seemingly less confident than before.

"C'mon, Andy, what's the problem? Joey said no-one'd mind if we just wander, right?

Andy nods agreement and, somewhat reluctantly, follows Steve across the road. As they keep walking, Steve glances back: from this side, the road-signs show an uncrossed 'V' and the tag-line 'Visitor Zone'. Nothing visibly different, yet they're in a different world now. Very different.

Everything's quiet – not deserted, empty, lifeless, just quiet. The road curves slightly to the left, opening out onto a shopping area. It looks much the same as the 'money' side, though the shop displays seem more free-form, less focussed on display, and no prices are visible anywhere. A couple walking down the road glance at them, but no-one challenges. And everywhere still that same quiet, the same calm; a living, breathing sense of calm, not stifled or silenced as in the office-block district of Andy's home city of Hamburg. He stops, puzzled.

"Have you noticed what is not here, Steve? There is no graffiti. No litter. No paper blowing down the street."

"Yeah. But not kinda... *laundered*... know what I mean, cleaned-up special for the tourists an' all? 'T'ain't like that. Odd, kinda."

"Yes. Because people want it that way, and for no other reason. Of this I have heard..."

A snatch of music and laughter waft out from a side-street. Gravitating towards the sound, as if on auto-pilot, they come to another bar. No quiet here: this place is a hubbub of activity.

"This is more like it, mate!"

"Steve, we should not be here..."

"Nah, this is right, this is the place."

He walks straight in through the crowded bar, Andy following more cautiously behind him. He leans towards Steve, whispering.

"You heard what Joey said, this is not wise. You know if this were the States, for being here we could be shot?"

"Relax, mate. 'S'all right. Dunno why, but it is. Trust me."

Steve's right: they receive a few nods of acknowledgement, but no challenge. He strides up to the bar, catches the eye of Kara, the barmaid. She's perhaps twenty, slim, with long dark hair. Yeah, definitely his type, he thinks – and then forcefully pushes that idea out of his mind.

"Two beers please, miss – would that be a light for you, Andy?"

As the barmaid places the two glasses on the wooden surface, Steve turns back her with a smile. "What's the damage for that? How much?" A moment later, he realises what he's just said and where he's said it. "Oh gawd…"

Several nearby drinkers spin round to look at them. "You got *another* vizzie, Kara?", laughs one. "Third today, right?"

"You got it, Alan. Beat the yesterday score for you, don't I? What we gonna do with 'em, guys?" she calls out.

More laughter rolls round the bar. Despite its friendly tone, Andy looks around wildly in near-panic, whilst Steve manages to blurt out an apologetic mutter. "Sorry… my mistake… look, we'll just go, all right…?"

The barmaid looks at the two of them with a bright wry grin, and laughs again.

"Hey guys, no worries! Don't panic, we ain't callin' the garda, we're just windin' ya, that's all. An' you're better'n the usual vizzies we get in here, 'cos you offered to pay for it, right? – 's more than most of those buggers do. On the house, okay?" Steve breathes out a sigh of relief; Andy's trapped-rabbit expression eases slowly from his face. "C'mon, just take it, go on, go on, you're welcome!" She stops, head tilted to one side, quizzical. "'Sides, least one of youse is with Workshare, right?"

Steve answers, still a little unsure of himself in these uncertain surroundings. "Uh, yeah. Me."

She leans back with a satisfied smile. "Thought so. Got a different vibe from the usual vizzies, see? 'S right you're here, then, in't it?"

Both men relax at last, as they reach out for the glasses, and start talking.

Time passes.

For Steve, several glasses'-worth of time has passed. He leans against the bar, elbow propped on the counter, watching in happy incomprehension as Andy and Alan toss ideas back and forth in animated conversation. Kara strokes an old ginger cat that sits half-asleep on the corner of the bar, and occasionally throws in a comment of her own.

"...if you were just tourists I'd be telling youse to push off back the Zone, but you'll make it okay. You got it, how it works here."

Andy nods, pushing back his spectacles. "Only three days now I have been in Australia, yet already I see your Professor Mercer is right. It is so different... the economics is real, of the people, not of a government."

Steve interjects, slurred, mildly sarcastic. "Dunno, mate, reckon that's just politics and stuff. Ordinary blokes like us are better off stickin' to our drinkin', yeah?"

Andy shakes his head, with a wry smile, and turns back to Kara. "Herr Professor Mercer, where is he now?"

"The Don? Oh, he's still around. Lives here in the city, out Balwyn way, I think, but he doesn't get out much these days."

Alan nods. "Old man keeps to the self, has done for years. He reckoned the work of him was done after Morrison."

A thoughtful pause. Kara looks at the cat more intently for a moment, then talks to Steve, hesitantly at first, still facing the cat.

"Steve? ...someone been talking to you about a cat and music?"

"Huh?"

"A cat. About a black cat. And music."

"Uh, yeah. Customs guy at the airport. Something about a place called the Black Cat. Said I might get a gig there, summat like that. Dunno what the heck he meant."

Kara laughs. "I do! Alan, you take over here, right? C'mon, you two!"

She dances out from behind the bar, grabs hold of Steve and Andy, pulling them, bemused, out of the door.

Moments later, she bundles them into the passenger seats of a small car parked at nearby roadside. As she skips round to the driver's side, still laughing, Steve turns to Andy.

"Any idea what this is about? Cats bloody psychic or summat?"

Andy shrugs with an "I don't have a clue either" expression.

Apollo Bay

It's late August in Apollo Bay, on the Great Ocean Road. It's fairly windy, and there's a respectable surf: there are a few surfers out in the water, despite the cold and the occasional squall.

I notice two young men in their mid to late twenties, sitting at a table in the window of a cafe-bar, looking out over the beach. One is medium height, medium build, slightly unkempt dark hair, dressed in blue jeans and a nondescript loose t-shirt; he seems almost unremarkable except for a sense of presence and a sense also of searching for something. The other is tall, neatly-dressed, with blond hair and beard. An interesting pair. I pick up a beer at the counter and walk over to them.

"Hi there. Mind if I join you?"

The scruffier of the two heaves out the spare chair and sweeps aside the glasses on the table to make space. "Nah, sure, mate come on in. I'm Steve, by the way, Steve Hallam, from England. We come down 'ere today with a mate from the hostel, Joey, only he's mad enough to be out in the water. An' this here's Andy."

"Andrew Kreutzfeld. From Germany. Hamburg. We have met in Melbourne, two days ago at the hostel – we are both engineers."

Steve grins. "I ain't that good yet – you design things, I just make 'em."

He turns to me. "What about you, mate?"

"Martin Bower. I live up north a bit, the far side of Melbourne."

"Oh right. What's the notepad for – you a journalist or summat?"

"No, just a writer, of sorts. Coming down here to work on some ideas. Which reminds me, you're both Visitors, aren't you? What brought you here?"

Steve answers first. "Dunno... 'seemed like a good idea at the time', maybe? Still tryin' to work that one out – kind of run out of things to do back home, just sort of felt it was worthwhile doin' a bit of travelling, so here I am. Don't really have a reason as such. How 'bout you, Andy?"

"I have wanted to come here since I was fifteen, when about the Don Mercer and his theories of property I read in our underground press. I have been saving for many years, though I had to hide it much – this Australia is not approved back home."

"Why's that?" I asked.

"What you do here is too like the old anarchists. It worries them, they think they will lose control if we see what you do, so they do not want us to travel here. We come anyway, when we can."

"So why did you come? "

"I know it is important for our future – for Germany's future, for the world's future. It is what Die Grunen – the Greens – have tried to tell us, but our government will not let them speak. I have been here only days, and this is the first time I have been outside a Visitor Zone, but already I see that Herr Professor Mercer is right. This works, where our kind of world does not."

"How so?"

"The difference is in the people. I know it is true that everything has its price here, just as at home. But no-one here tries to sell me anything: it is there if I want it, but not if I do not. Here I am free to be who I am – not what someone wants me to buy to pretend to be, so that they can sell me more and more of what I do not need. And poison our world and our lives in the process."

Steve cuts in. "I dunno 'bout any o' that guff, really. 'S all theory-stuff to me, the kind of stuff me Mum talks about all the time, though she never does anything about it other than talk."

He points out the window at the surfers. "But that there's the life, innit? Or it would be if it was summer – they must be bloody crazy to be out there in this weather. Me, I think I'll stick to me beer for now! You get us another one, Andy? – this one's almost done."

Andy nods, rises, and turns briefly to me.

"My shout, I think you Australians call it?"

"Yes, a light beer would be good, thanks."

Andy moves off to the bar. Whilst being served, he strikes up a conversation I can't quite hear, with a young woman sitting there. Steve and I continue without him for the while..

"Steve, you said you'd "run out of things to do back home". What kind of things were you doing there?"

"Bit o' welding, that sort of stuff. Construction, heavy machinery, one-off specials, anything that's different. Don't like doing the production-line stuff – course I can do it if I have to, but it bores me shitless in minutes, an' I get sloppy. Hate doing that – I like to get things right, otherwise it's not worth doing at all."

"How'd you get started in that?"

"Me Dad, really. We was still down in Dagenham then, and Dad was running one of the big repair shops at Ford's. Didn't have a clue what I wanted to do after school, though me Mum nagged me enough about it. Might have been the reason I didn't, p'raps." He gives a brief wry grin. "Anyway, Dad got me started in the Ford's training course after school nights. But I was still at school when we moved up to Bolton – you know where that is?"

"It's northwest, near Manchester, right?"

"Yeah, 'sright. Dad took over teaching fitters at Bolton Tech, Mum picked up another English job at a secondary school in Bury, and I finished off me apprenticeship and fitter's Cert at a firm called Hobart's, mostly doing heavy gear for refineries and chemicals places. Good money, but I didn't really fit in there. As usual."

"Was there anywhere where you reckoned you did fit?"

"Not really. Always kind of looking for that – I s'pose that's part of why I'm here. We'd moved about a fair bit when I was a kid, following Dad's work, so I've always been kind of on the edges, really. Not into sport, which shuts me out from a lot, but I've never been able to see the point. Mum and Dad are in different worlds, too: Dad's always been a fitter and a foreman, straight union and the rest, while Mum's lot are all university, and she's a fair bit that way herself. So I'm kind of torn every which way – 'specially with Mum naggin' at me all the time to 'better meself' an' all that crap! Only thing which is really mine is music, and I ain't been able to do even much of that since we moved up north. Which is why I sold all me gear for this trip – I just wasn't using it any more. Be nice to get back to it if I can, though."

Andy returns from the bar with two beers.

"My apologies for taking so long. Anneka, that woman I have been talking to, she is from Bremen, knows friends of mine in Die Grunen. If you don't mind, I must go back to her."

"No, sure, go to it."

"Thank you."

Leaving the drinks on the table, he heads back to the bar, and his animated conversation in German. Steve picks up his glass, stops, then slowly puts it down again, with a kind of blank gaze looking more inward than out. His voice becomes pensive, reflective.

"Yeah, you're right, though. I actually don't know why I'm here, and I need to. Almost like something's calling me, except that's just plain daft. Gonna have to think about that a bit..."

A brief pause.

"Andy's right, too. I hadn't thought about that before. So much bloody pressure back home to buy crap we don't need – don't even use most of the time – so that we have to stay in shit jobs to pay for 'em, and other people have to stay in shit jobs to make 'em, and so on. And no-one gets a chance to get off the bloody treadmill, 'cept perhaps for the rich, and from what I can see even they don't get much of a life either. What's the bloody point?"

Another brief pause. Steve shakes his head, and waves his hand out at the panorama with a cynical smile.

"But is it really any better here, mate? Joey and those other blokes in the water must be bloody crazy to be out there right now, but do they really get to swim as long as they want? Really? Or is this 'Free Australia' stuff just another bloody fiction, like everywhere else?"

It takes me a while to search for the right words for an answer.

"Yes and no, I guess. There's always some drudgery, wherever you are, whatever you do, but there's probably a lot less of it here than most other places. We're not carrying the overhead of the rich, for a start. Pretty well everyone can see that side of it. But we're also not carrying the huge overhead of the money economy and its 'double-entry life-keeping'. And that's a far, far larger overhead than 'the rich', but probably much less visible to you overseas, because it's the sea in which you swim – it underpins the entire economy and social system in which you live."

Steve barks a sarcastic laugh. "C'mon, mate, you don't get owt for nowt anywhere in this world – even here."

"No, you don't – you're right there. To use the terms you would, it's still true that everyone has to pay the way somehow. There's still the equivalent of taxes, in the form of sharing out the work that otherwise no-one much wants to do. That's part of what Workshare's about. But it doesn't eat up a third of your life, as taxes you have do in practice. And whilst just about everyone does some kind of equivalent of paid work, there's a lot more room for choice about what you might do, because it's focused on playing a part in the society as a whole, rather than forced to fit into the limitations of the money-economy. For example, we don't have the crazy situation you have back in Britain, where parents are classed as working if they look after kids of other people, but not if they're only looking after kids of themselves."

Steve is flatly incredulous. "You're kiddin' me, right? You mean, Joey just goes swimming if he wants to, summat like that? That's called *work*, is it?

"Depends – of course. Those guys probably do Workshare of them working flat out for a couple of months on the farms somewhere, and spend the rest of the year down here. Quite a few of the serious surfers do that. Or if they're doing the kind of work you do, they might do a couple of days a week, or perhaps a block of a few solid weeks or months on some project, as a lot of work-crews do – or interweave it with the projects of self in some way, as most people manage to do somehow. Some of those guys may teach surfing at a Visitor Zone up north, or may even be working the way up to the level of world-class competitors: that's all 'work' as far as Workshare's concerned. The real currency here is respect, backed up by responsibility, and through Workshare it's easy enough to find out if someone's been doing the part in it or not."

"So if I was living here, like, I could do pretty much whatever I want?"

"Yes, pretty much. Don't try it first off, of course. But as long as you can show that you're being responsible in how you do it, and that it contributes in some way to 'the Commonwealth', and also that you're doing the part in the general Workshare, pretty much anything goes.

Steve looks reflective. A brief pause, in which he starts to speak, and stops, several times. "Interestin'. And kinda scary, too: dunno why. Actually, I *do* know why, come to think of it. Back home, everyone's tryin' to push you into being something you're not. The birds are always doin' it, an' I don't like it, which is prob'ly why I ain't had much luck in that department. But here, from what you're sayin', no-one's tryin' to push you into anythin' – you gotta work it out for yourself. And that's hard. That's *hard*. A lot easier to just go along with what people are pushing, and put up with the crap that goes with it. Hmm..."

He stops, looks upward, clearly lost in thought, in a private world.

After a few moments I clear my throat to attract his attention and bring him back to the conversation. "You said the birds were always pushing you, and it kind of got in the way of things. Do you have a girlfriend at the moment?"

"Nah. Had a few flings, but nothing's ever lasted. Part of it's that they're always pushing, sure. And most of them seem to want a slice of you, and ain't too keen to give nothing in return. An' I don't just mean sex, neither. Seen too many of my mates trashed that way, and I'm not all that interested, to tell the truth. 'S like sport, I just don't see the point, on its own, if it ain't going anywhere else. Know what I mean?"

"Not quite..."

Steve grins. "I ain't a total nutter, y'know. Sex an' such is nice enough in its way, but there's no point unless it's part of the real thing, the sharing an' all that. And I ain't never really felt that with any bird I've known. 'Cept one."

It's clear there are painful memories there, though he doesn't volunteer any more comments about it. Instead, he returns to the thread of women in general.

"The birds, y'know, always felt like they just wanted me as something they could own, a possession, something they could show off like a piece of jewellery or summat. A toy they could play with for a while and then throw away soon's they got bored with it. Never really felt any of 'em was interested at all in what I felt. Never felt any of 'em wanted me as *me*."

The bitterness in his voice is all too evident. "Possession can go several ways, you know", I say, quietly. "Any possession also possesses you: that's the real problem with possession. And you can be as much possessed as much by what you don't have as by what you do. Or possessed by the longing for someone you don't have, too."

Steve looks up sharply at this point, questioningly, but makes no comment, so I continue. "If you're running away from the memory of someone, someone you care for deeply, you're still possessed by that longing. And you can't be free – and perhaps she can't be free either – until you let go of that possession. But you can't just throw it away, either – anti-possession is as strong as possession. You have to get the balance right, respecting the feeling yet without possession either way. As we say here, non-attachment is also non-detachment. I don't know if that makes sense, but I hope it does?"

From Steve, a thoughtful pause for a brief while. "Yeah, you're right. An' to be honest, I guess it's more me than them. Always felt an outsider; never know how to talk to 'em, for starters. Sure, I know some of the reasons: we was always movin' on when I was

114

a kid, because Dad had to keep quiet about his union stuff and so on. And it didn't help that Mum was teachin' in the girls' schools – that was a real turn-off for 'em when they found out! But yeah, those are just reasons. Short answer is that, yeah, sure, I'd've liked it to've worked out with some bird – yeah, with her especially – but it just ain't 'appened so far. Might be one reason why I've found meself here, ain't it? Who knows, perhaps I might find the perfect bird here, mightn't I?"

He grins, and continues. "Yeah, I know – it ain't exactly likely, is it? But I may as well have some fun pretendin' to meself that it's possible. In the meantime, I'll just stick to what I know, and see what happens."

He stops, looks around, sees Joey coming back from the beach with wetsuit under one arm and surfboard under the other. He starts to get up from the table. "And what I do know is that right now I want another beer! You want one, mate?"

"Thanks, but no – think it's time I headed off."

"Right you are, mate – see you 'round. And looks like I'd better get a crowbar between Andy and this girl he's yabberin' with, or we'll never get 'ome tonight!"

"Thanks – good luck in the travels."

Steve waves and heads over to the bar as I head out of the door.

An interesting young man indeed. A sense we'll all see more of him some day, too. Hmm...

Put it to the vote

Interview transcript: Ossie Corrigan, Campbell's Home Perfection store, Werribee

What, go back to money, right? Or keep Morrison and Mercer's no-money system like what we have right now? Okay, here's what I think, for me, anyway.

I've got to run the store, like – it's what I do, in't it. An' I'd have to say it was sort of easier in the old days, of course. All we had to do was get new boxes in through the back door, shove 'em out the front door, and collect the money. That was it, pretty much. Okay, you had all the fuss about how to lay out your store to get the punters to find the expensive stuff before they got to the cheap an' all that, and – what? yeah, you're right, bloody security was a nightmare, making sure people didn't nick things and closing up the shutters and viewing all the camera tapes and clearing the cash tills and banking and all that crap, jesus, I'd forgotten about all that. But the straight paperwork's no better now, not really, p'raps more, if anything, know what I mean?

Yeah, sure, it's different, and Workshare does make it a heck of a lot easier than it was, but we got to check things in and out both ways, it ain't just a one-way flow through the store no more. In fact it's more like about six different bloody ways, all-up. Sure, we do still get some new stuff, and yeah, it's bloody good, well made an' all that, it does last, unlike so much of the old crap we used to sell, so that's just like the old in-and-out, 'cept we have to check it off our books and put it on the taker's record an' all, which is a hassle but not like credit cards was, I s'pose. But we also get all the old stuff coming back in when people don't need it no more, an' we have to check that in, and put a bar-code on it or whatever, an' I tell you, those hidden UV bar-codes for antiques and fancy stuff that's all on show are a bugger to find if there is one and a bugger to put on if there isn't, and then check who's around who can check it out and fix it up if it's worn or whatever. So we have to book it out to them, and then we have to book it back in when they've done, or write it if off it's buggered, an' all that crap, y'know? And when it goes out again, it's either out to a taker, which means we got to book it to their record, just as if it was new stuff, like, or it goes off to another store or to the regional rep or whatever, for that we gotta book it out the back door instead, with all *their* codes and such. Bloody nightmare sometimes, 'specially if we're busy.

Not that we get busy like in the old days, like at Christmas and sales-time and so on. And jesus, the buggerising around we had to do for sales, you wouldn't believe, all the price tags coming off, rethinking all the bloody price-tags for that matter, everything going back on, all the sign-boards, the crap decoration, and the absolute crap we had from vendors that they wanted us to put up in our store, an' all the vendors bickering about who gets front-ranking an' all that, jesus wept, what a mess. Stock-taking was no better, neither, and it was always a real frightener seeing how much stuff had been pinched despite all the security-cams and so on. When we did catch 'em, it was usually just kids buggering about for a dare and such, and I know I did that too when I was a nipper so I just give 'em a thick ear and told 'em to bugger off, no matter what the coppers and the social workers said I should report 'em an' such, or else it was welfare wobblers, you know, single-mums an' all that, an' it damn near broke the missis' heart seeing them stuck with buying crap instead of decent stuff 'cos it was all they could afford, but we weren't running a bloody charity an' they had to stick with it just like we did. But that's all changed, and all gone now, an' I can't say I miss it.

Do I miss doing the taxes? No I bloody don't, you're right there! Didn't do it meself that often, it was mostly the missis, but she used to do her bloody crust every time it come tax-time. Every bloody quarter, it was, an' she was that effin' and blindin' about it you wouldn't believe. Paperwork coming out of her ears, I don't blame her, every friggin' night for weeks it was. An' there was always something that didn't bloody add up, and the tax-people down on us like a ton o' bricks if it didn't, bastards even did a full audit on us once, an' that was no fun, I can tell you, we had to do a full bloody stock-take just for them, every bloody item in the whole bloody store. Jesus I hated them bastards. But they're all gone now too, and good riddance to the whole bloody lot of them. And the banks. And the insurance bastards. And the rest of them bloody parasites, like the stock-exchange an' all that. Morrison's right, we're well out of that, if you ask me.

Would I want it back the way it was? Doubt it, not now, not really. It was easier in some ways, like I said, there was only the one way things went through the shop, and there's different hassles now, but grass is always greener, in't it? We don't get nothing like as much new stuff as we did in the old days, and it was always kind of special, opening a new box an' all that, and seeing what the vendors got new for us and so on, so yeah, I do miss that. But all that buggerising around with money, tryin' to find out if there's enough in the till for the kids' school uniforms an' all, and then finding the bank's hit us for new charges without telling us and the tax-man's taken the whole bloody lot anyway, no, I wouldn't want to go back to that. 'S good seein' the missis not tearing her hair out over the bills, an' I see more of her these days, too, which is nice.

But it's just different now, that's all. We always was in the middle, like, so it don't make all that much difference to us. It's made a lot of difference to the welfare wobblers, I know that, an' you ask around, there's a lot less fights an' such, an' a lot less kiddies getting damaged an' all that, which is good. And a lot less of the fat cats poncing around and pretending they're better'n everyone 'cos they've nicked more than anyone else has, an' I'll tell you I'm glad to see the back end of them bastards.

So yeah, it's different, but I'd say it's better. Yeah. Better than it was.

So yeah, I'd say we keep it this way, yeah?

Letter to Mum

BY AIR
28th January
Castlemaine, VIC 3450

Hi Mum!

Like I said last time, I reckoned it was time to move on and get down to some work. (Yeah, I know I'm supposed to be on holiday, but the only way of getting to know people here is to work, and anyway it's what I <u>feel</u> like doing – though I don't know why, really. Odd.) So around lunchtime I'm sitting next to this bloke in the Workshare office in Flinders Street, who's asking me all sorts of questions about what Manchester is like and how long I've been playing music and which soccer team I follow – 'barrack for', he called it – and so on. A lot more friendly than the DHSS back home! Nothing about rates of pay or anything like that, either, which felt pretty odd, too.

All the time he's clicking away on his computer, and muttering to himself. Then he picks one screen, and says, "Best I can suggest is this one: alliance up at Castlemaine need a welder skill. Repair and rebuild, not production – that's what you said you want, isn't it? Country town: think you'll like it. Bit cold up there this time, but probably no different from home, yes? Sound like kind of people for you, and they know visitors: shouldn't have any problems there. Suit you for now?" So I said yes, and he took me through to another area where I had to hand over my money and passport – "Won't need that for now, it's safer with us", they said, and I reckon I didn't have any choice but to believe them. I've got a telelink address for when I need it back, so I don't think it'll be a problem. They told me which train to catch, and then asked "Need escort?", which I reckoned I didn't, though I'll admit it did all feel pretty strange.

About an hour later I got on the train, which they said was going to somewhere called Bendigo – I haven't been there yet, but it's a small city a bit further north from here. The line went through the usual city suburbs, with a lot of signs in foreign languages – Vietnamese was one, I think? Lots of houses with paintings on, for

119

some reason. But it took me ages to realise what was missing: all the adverts. No-one's trying to sell anything: and believe me, Mum, that still feels weird...

It took about an hour to get up to Castlemaine, over a long flat plain and then up through the hills. A bit surprised, it's actually higher here than up on the top of the Moors, and the big hill I went past about halfway to here – Mt Macedon, someone said – is apparently higher than anywhere in England, but it doesn't look it at all! The trees out here are more grey than green, and look kind of fluffy, like a sea of grey-green cotton-wool in places. Didn't see any kangaroos, though! – but there were lots of little farmlets scattered all over the place, with sheep and cattle in the fields and so on.

As I got off the train here, this bloke called me over – I think the Workshare place must have sent him my photo. He said his name was Mike – Mike Howard – and that he was 'source' for the foundry alliance, which is where I'm starting work tomorrow. They said something about this 'source' thing at the Workshare office, but I still don't understand it yet: I suppose Mike is the boss, because he's the one who decides what we do and when, but apparently it doesn't quite work in the same way as back at home.

We got into a little two-seater van, took my pack to a hostel just down the road from the station, and went on to the foundry. It's an old place that went out of business just before the Troubles, and we're supposed to be repairing all the old equipment ready to bring it back on line. Most of the foundry gear is pretty ancient, but I reckon it's no worse than what we had at Hobart's. What isn't ancient is the repair gear we're to use: most of it's brand new, and some of it I just don't recognise at all. I guess I'll find out all about that tomorrow.

Anyway, Mike introduced me to most of the members of the 'alliance' – it's what they call work-crews here – and took me off to a tea-room for 'a bit of a chat', as he called it. He's about ten years older than me – about the same as Dave Hodge at Hobart's. He said that he'd been warned that this was my first Workshare job, and told me flat that he expected me to make plenty of mistakes at first – not with my welding but with other people, and just with everyday living – and that he'd do his best to get others in the crew and the town to put up with it. He gave me an armband with a big double-'V' on it – means 'Workshare visitor', apparently – and told me to wear it – I'm wearing it now, in fact – to warn others, he said, that I'd be likely to get things wrong and would need help. A funny comment he made about it, too: "Be careful with that band", he said, "it's important, so make a point of remembering to put it on, every day. When you do forget it, you'll know that you're here." Don't know what he meant by that: no doubt I'll find out.

He gave me the rest of today off, to wander round the town and get my bearings, which is why I'm sitting in a cafe writing to you. I tried using the telelink – Mike said there's a public terminal in the library – but the place was closed. So I went to the post office to buy an air-letter, remembered I didn't have any money, and was about to walk away and give up when a girl from behind the counter called, and said "You're looking lost – are you needing to write a letter home?" So I said yes, and she gave me a pen and this aerogramme, and showed me where the post-box was, and so on. No charge – and I hadn't noticed before that there's no price on the printed stamp either. I still haven't got used to this idea of no-money yet, but it seems to work – did there, anyway! They said you can write back to me at Post Office, Castlemaine, 3450 – the same sort of deal as in Melbourne – and that I can pick it up from here. I'll check up about the telelink in the next couple of days, too.

The next thing I needed was somewhere to write, and round the corner from the post office is this cafe, where I now have a mug of tea – it's a bit too early for drinking! – and a wad of cake. So that'll do for now!

But since I left the Visitor Zone, no-one's asked me for any money, for anything: and that still feels really weird...

More later, anyway!

Much love

Steve

Tipping

From *The New Australia Travel Guide*

Tipping

Don't. Even in Visitor Zones, tipping is often regarded as an insult. Remember that respect, not money, is the real 'currency' for people who live here. So if you want to show appreciation for good service – in your hotel, for example – say so in person, or ask someone to pass the message on.

Negotiations with Ausam

telelink::mailto: bill.gough@calesta.com
telelink::mailfrom: geoff.allen@calesta.com
telelink::mailvia: public.net.au
telelink::subject: **Negotiations with Ausam**
telelink::autodictate-start

Bill,

Well, so far I'd say it was worth coming over here, though you were right to warn me they're canny bastards. They may not use money at home, but they certainly know how to price! To give you an idea, the best I can get out of them for their KGH-20 carb adaptor is dollars four hundred forty three twenty FOB in quantities of hundred up. That's about twenty percent more than Nikkei were quoting us for their equivalent, but the test results Ausam gave me claim theirs is a far better product, and I'd reckon to believe them. More than just reckon: Nikkei's quoted best was four eight mpg, but here they're getting nearly a <u>hundred</u> mpg out of a four eight four vee eight! And that <u>is</u> for real: it's not just paper figures, I've seen it in action myself. Apparently they've been using it for years over here, but no-one believed 'em – or wanted to believe them, I guess. Mobil & Co. sure aren't going to like it, and might try to kick up a stink with the feds, but what the heck, this is <u>business</u>!

You'd know better than me on this, but we should still be able to make good dough on Ausam's price in the US, probably Canada too, though we'd need to pick our wholesalers carefully or keep it strictly to direct retail. Someone else already has Europe, and Brazil too – won't let me even start to cut a deal on those – but they might talk turkey on CentrAm or the Russian states: do you want me to try for those, and if so, what starting price?

This <u>is</u> a weird place, though. From what you'd said about trading with the communists, years ago, I'd expected it all to be gray and gloomy, with everyone drunk and frightened to talk. It isn't like that at all, though it's real hard to describe what it <u>is</u>.

For example, they certainly drink enough, but I wouldn't describe the place as gray – if anything, there's too <u>much</u> color everywhere. Although there's some kind of central exchange system called 'workshare', they only handle the money side, and there's no compulsory import-export agency like you said the Soviets used to use, so we can deal with Ausam direct.

And Ausam isn't a regular company, like Miras Engineering or Nikkei or Palo Auto: it's called an 'alliance', and I still can't work out whether everyone's a shareholder, or no-one is, or what. Andrew Macilvoy, who you spoke to, is described as the 'source', which is kind of like company chairman, but different in ways I still don't get. Someone said his main job was 'to hold the vision for the alliance', whatever that's supposed to mean. And Doug Hutton's job title is 'Liar' – that's what they call their salesmen, for God's sake! – it seems to be some kind of impenetrable Aussie joke, but I don't think it's in very good taste.

He took me to their equivalent of a businessmen's club, over near Tulla, which quite a few of the engineering firms use: there may be some useful contacts for us there, but I didn't get all the guys' names – I'll try again later. I tried to buy a round of drinks, and of course they all just laughed at me: I still can't get used to their crazy system. They had a full bar there – even had a Jim Beam, which I hadn't expected. And the food was damn good, too – as good as at the Hilton, which I'll admit surprised me.

While we were there another of Ausam's so-called 'liars', Jane Marshall, explained to me how their import system works – which is, as you'd expect, kind of strange. What happens is a company like Ausam gets a set of specs from someone like us, with delivery schedules and price-breakdowns. (They're <u>real</u> fussy about specs, and proof of conformance to those specs. They won't even look at it if we can't prove it, which may be a problem with some of Palo Auto's cheaper stuff.) Then they put it up on some national net that I haven't seen yet, but which is supposedly available to any 'alliance' who wants to see it – though one bit I <u>have</u> seen is some output from a really neat spec-comparison search-engine, so I reckon I understand how they do their buying. If people like our specs, they place a preliminary order; Ausam checks if the dollars are available from central workshare, and if they are, places the order with us, and handles all the follow-on shipping.

They don't get anything for doing all this, they don't make any kind of profit from the deal, which strikes me as just plain crazy. Marshall's been around the tracks enough to see that it didn't make any sense to me, but she just said it was part of their job 'for the commonwealth', as she put it, and suggested I leave it at that. Certainly couldn't work back in the States: anyone stupid enough

124

to try would be out of business in a matter of weeks, and I said so – and they all howled with laughter, like I'd made some kind of great joke, and called for another round of drinks. Weird people...

I followed up your hint, by the way, and had a good look at the cars around the place. All the ones in the Hilton parking-lot were electric: there's no key as such – anyone can use them – but I had to use my room-card to start it, so there's some kind of interlock. I couldn't work out at all how they're recharged, there's no socket on the thing, and no fuel cap for a hydrogen cell. There were others parked throughout the Visitor Zone, the guy at the Guide Alliance said they're supposed to be parked only in marked bays, so perhaps there's some kind of aerial. I've never seen anything like it elsewhere.

Most of the people at Ausam seem to use public transport, even Andrew Macilvoy. Fair enough, the transport network is good, from what I saw of it, and most of the staff seem to live nearby anyway. Doug Hutton had his own car, though – sorry, 'the car that he uses', as he insisted I put it – and there were plenty of others around, many of which were obviously personalised and generally done up. One guy got real touchy when I started to have a look at his car, so they do have some kind of concept of private property, though whatever it is it's a pretty weird one.

Nice gear, though, all of it: didn't see a junk-heap anywhere, other than one which I'd guess was halfway through a rebuild. And they know their engineering, too, I'd guess the quality at Ausam and elsewhere was among the best I've seen, and that includes Japan. I'll have to admit it, we'd be hard put to sell anything from Palo Auto here, though Miras might be worth a try.

Oh yeah, one other thing. While we were over at Tulla I had a chance to see what was going in and out the old airport. There were the usual commuter planes, of course, and some medium-sized transports, most of which seemed to have foreign markings. There was also some kind of dirigible, which they apparently use for heavy lifting, a bit like the forestry blimps up in Oregon, but a heck of a lot bigger. But what really caught my eye was a small aircraft, shaped kind of like a slightly streamlined brick, but about the size of a medium truck, like a standard cargo container – I couldn't make it out at the distance. Whatever it was, I couldn't see any wings, or tail, or rotor or even an engine, but it lifted straight up without using the runway, damn near silent, and moved off _fast_ but in a kind of crazy zigzag, with a flickering that sort of hurt the eyes, like it was kind of there and not there at the same time. Weird. I asked Doug Hutton about it, but he made some comment about it being a 'cargo bootstrap', then said briskly 'it's not for export', and told me to forget it. Any idea what the hell it was?

I've attached the full details of Ausam's current offer. Let me know ASAP what you think about this, I'm due to see Doug again in the morning.

Talk to you later.

Geoff

telelink::autodictate-end

Letter to Dave

telelink::fax-class="letter"
telelink::fax-addressto: Dave G
18th February
Castlemaine VIC 3450

Hi Dave!

Great to hear from you, mate! Say 'thank you' to Mum for me, will you? And tell her I <u>will</u> be writing soon – honest!

Sorry to hear you've split up with Trish, but that's life, innit? I'm the same: I still can't make head or tail of what the birds want, most of the time, so we're both in the same boat, aren't we?

Tell you what, though, it's odd having so many birds in the work crew. (And yeah, they do still call 'em 'sheilas' here!) They're good, though – have to grant them that. There's a big hefty broad here called Robyn, a real master with a Mig welder: real education watching her, I can tell you. Almost makes the thing get up and dance! Don't think the old guys at Hobart's would believe it, but it's true.

Part of it's this no-money thing, I guess. People are in the crew because they want to be, not because the money's good, because there isn't any. I'm still kipping at the hostel, but I don't have to go looking for food, or trying to rustle up a tin of baked beans or something to save money – I just wander down to one of the cafes. They like cooking, I like eating: it works! If I go back for more, and they reckon there's not enough left for others, they just tell me to piss off, which seems fair enough.

The only time I've had a fight about it was when I got pissed on the first weekend. I wanted another beer, and another, and the barman finally wouldn't give me any – he said I'd had too much already. I took a swing at him, but then everyone just piled in on top of me: said that if I didn't shut up, Deano – the guy who runs the bar – would smash the bottles, and then <u>no-one</u> could get pissed. He's done it before, apparently. So I shut up after that, and anyway, the crew took me back to the hostel, where we found a bit more booze, and I went to bed, absolutely ratted.

Mike Howard, the boss or foreman or whatever at the foundry, had been there at the pub, keeping an eye on me as promised, he said. So we had another one of our 'little chats', as he calls 'em, in the tearoom when I got in on Monday morning. Said he didn't mind me getting pissed – "that's your choice, mate", he said, and sounded like he meant it – but if I came to work ratted more than once or twice the rest of the crew would kick me out. It wasn't up to him, he said, it was up to the whole crew. "We work as a crew", he said. "Sometimes we get pissed together as a crew, but we work together as a crew, too. And we can't work as a crew if some of us are too rat's-arsed to pick up a bloody spanner, can we?"

Mike's okay, though. He can be a bit of a prick at times, but I do like the guy: doesn't talk down to you like those wanker engineers at Hobart's.

We've got a lot to do here, so we're working straight weeks at the moment, Monday to Friday, seven to three. Feels too bloody early in the morning, but that's what the Aussies have always done, apparently, and I'll get used to it. And I do like getting off work when it's still light – it's getting on to autumn here, of course, and bloody cold at times.

It's a bit of a funny way of working they do here, but it seems to work. It's a bit like those blokes from Volvo talked about, you remember? We seem to do a lot of talking, but then we split off into little groups, like the Volvo crews did, and just do it. They're real fussy about getting it done right, but there's no-one breathing down our necks, and no-one yells at you if you screw up: you just sit down to work out how to fix the screw-up, and fix it. Once everyone's done, we take a break – a 'smoko', they call it, though there aren't that many puffing away on the old fags – and then check back in with Mike or whoever about what the next bit of work is. I like it: actually get a sense I've <u>done</u> something by the end of the day.

Some of the gear we're using here has to be pretty weird: I don't understand how some of it works, and they haven't bothered to tell me yet. At the moment I'm mainly using a straight arc welder and a gas torch, and I'm sticking to what I know until they ask me to do something else.

But I haven't a bloody clue how they're doing some of it, specially the heavy lifts. Back on Wednesday we had to get one of the feed-hoppers up over the top of the main furnace, and the bloody thing must have weighed ten tons. The roof crane's been downrated to five till the wall-track's fixed, and the only mobile we've got is only a lightweight job.

So Mike said we needed a lifter crew, and I reckoned we'd have a week up-front to take half the roof off first to get the crane in over the top. But we did nothing about it, even though I asked, and next day what we got was these two birds who turned up with some kind of computer gear on a trolley. They said they couldn't 'get sync' while I was there, so Mike told me to piss off to the tea-room for half an hour. When I came back, the birds had gone off somewhere, but the bloody thing was up there – God only knows how they did it! I must have looked bloody stupid, gawking at it. I said "How'd they do that? Get the pixies to lift it for 'em?", and someone said "Yep!" and they all laughed at me. I like being here, but some of the Aussies have a weird sense of humour...

It's strange here, all right, but it's been pretty good so far. Doesn't feel so... dunno... pinched or squeezed or something, as it did back in Bolton. Certainly makes a difference not always struggling to work out where the next quid's coming from – or where the last one went!

Reckon you might like it here, too. You've got a Class 2 Cert., haven't you? If you really are done with Trish, and she's screwed your job with McClure's, you could do worse than giving the consulate a call. The workshare interview's a bit of a sod to get through, but you know what you're doing with work, and you can prove it. You'd have to get the money together to get out here, but Trish hasn't ripped you off all that much, has she? Give it a try, anyway.

The beer here's okay, but it isn't the same as Cooper's... tell the other buggers at the Monmouth to get properly pissed for me, will you?

Steve

Don't drink and drive

Seen on a freeway billboard

If you drink
then drive
you're a bloody idiot.

(Transport Accident Commission, Victoria)

Mishie

Baz,

U know i said this course was just a trick that Overseas uses to make it difficult to get a passport? Gods is that true or what! This bloody stuff cant be real, u would not <u>believe</u> the crap they make up about what the vizzies are supposed go through for resources – even the most <u>basic</u> everyday stuff!

They made us all sit through the most boringly stupid bloody lecture this morning, about what they called 'the economics of money'. It made no sense at all: how u have to have credit or this actual money stuff – paper and coins and so on – before ure allowed to take anything, or use anything, or <u>do</u> anything, really. And if u live there u can only get the money by working for someone else, and <u>they</u> have to get it by working for someone else, and so on. If thats real, gods only knows how parents would survive, or kids, or the old, or the sick. Perhaps Overseas think they dont? though apparently theres something called 'welfare' which we wont get anyway. They said something about how all that works, with something called 'taxes' that everyone hates, and that we would have to give them even though we dont get any benefits, but it was all so bloody complicated i just gave up. I mean, who gives a shit? the headcases get into that stuff, but i just want to get on the road, dont i?

I guess they must be making it look worse than it is just to keep us on our toes and all that. They keep on saying stuff that the money has to do a two-way balance, to the dot, in everything – but everyone <u>knows</u> u cant get that in real-world systems, I mean, thats basic system-symmetry stuff from primary school, isnt it? And then they say that the more u have – the 'richer' u are – not only does that get u to more stuff and better stuff, but they give u more money as well, just because uve got the money in the first place. So theres no way it can balance anyway. I really dont get it. I mean, <u>no-one</u> could design something that stupid.

We had a go at it this afternoon, but gods its crazy! Theyve got this place laid out like a store street, like in a country town they said, but all the store windows are these bloody great sheets of glass and everythings on display and all really pretty and stuff.

Everythings got prices on, money-labels, except for a couple of real fancy stores where there werent any prices, they said the idea was that if u have to ask the price it means u cant afford it, which apparently makes it better or something, but i cant see the point. And the prices are all different for the same thing in different stores and u have to go backwards and forwards and backwards and forwards to work out which ones less, they called it the 'cheapest', in each place and get each thing in turn from each one and it takes ages to do it and noone would do it for real anyway so obviously its just another Overseas fake.

Theyve got actors and stuff to pretend to be storekeeps and so on. So they gave us this stupid moneyfold thing, which the girls are supposed call a 'purse' and the boys a 'wallet' even though its exactly the same thing, and got us to sit down in a cafe place and pretend to be prissy ladies and gentlemen from some poncy old pommy flick, drinking afternoon tea and all that kind of crap. And were supposed to look at the menu thing and check all the prices and look at the folds we each have and each count all the coins and paper in the fold and make sure we have enough to match the price of everything we ask for, then the biz takes the order and brings it all back and we have the dainty tea and she brings back a single bill and we all have to work out who ordered what and put it all in the middle and it never adds up because noone has the right coins and stuff, and the biz adds it all up again and makes sure weve given her enough and then e takes it away and brings back the extra – the 'change' – and we have to check es given us back the right amount and then were supposed to divvy that up and it doesnt balance either so were supposed to argue about that till its fair somehow, and then we have to work out an extra bit called a tip that goes to the biz and we have to argue about who pays what of that too and we put that on the table and then we can finally walk out the door. Overseas must be making all this stuff up to be stupid, of course, i mean, its like the prices thing, would <u>anyone</u> do all of that kind of petty crap for real?

So they took us next to a store and told one of the boys that the travel-pack e uses is bust and e has to get a new one. So e goes looking for a return bin to put the existing pack in for repair but e cant find one so e leaves it by the door to the back storeroom, then e goes to the rack and e picks out one thats the right sort of size and fitout, even waves at the storekeep to let en know es checking it out, and e goes to an unused scanner and e scans it and heads out. U know, just like anyone else would do? But no, Overseas want to make it all complicated just for the hell of it. Alarms go off as soon as e gets near the door, some lump of a guy in a black and white uniform thing comes out of nowhere and grabs en and yanks the arm of en up the back and other people come running up and call en a thief and the rest, and all other sorts of crap.

Its all play-acting of course but the Overseas instructors look smug and say they did it to show us what happens if we get it wrong like that. What es supposed to do is <u>really</u> stupid, even worse than that fart-arsing around we did in the cafe. First thing is – get this – there <u>isnt</u> a return-bin, in fact if e leaves the pack by the back door for repair itd be called littering, es supposed to just throw it away someplace else so it <u>doesnt</u> get repaired or reused. This is 'good for the economy' apparently though id say its totally bloody mental. Then e goes to the rack and theyre all different prices with long-use ones more price than short-life ones, which again is stupid because everyone knows the short-lifes are more wasteful. Then e has to look in the fold e uses and see if e has enough money for the pack e chooses and if e hasnt then to use the credit instead and if e hasnt enough in credit e has to forget it or pick out a crappy short-life or something, and i asked the instructors how es supposed to know if e has enough credit or not and they said e has to know the 'balance' for him at all times even without a telelink, which again must be just them being petty for the sake of it. Then when e thinks es got the right pack and the right money e has to go find a queue for a scanner that one of the storekeeps is using and wait in line for that and then the storekeep scans the pack and asks for the money and e has to give the coins and paper or the credit and the storekeep then checks all of that and gives back the change if es used coins but this time there isnt any tip, and the storekeep clears something in the scan because when thats all done the alarm doesnt go off and es allowed to go out of the door without being attacked by the thug in the white shirt. It all takes about twice as long as the ordinary way and ties up about twice as many people and its really <u>really</u> stupid. So i think Overseas are just making it all up to try to put us off. Well it hasnt worked for me – Im still going.

There was more of that crap for the rest of the afternoon but i couldnt be bothered, i just went to the cafe instead with some of the others. And we didnt play their stupid money games, we had drinks and tucker in the normal way just like we should.

This evening there was another stupid lecture about how its sposed to be easier if we stick together as a crew and use someone

133

whos been before as a kind of guide. Well im stuffed if ill do that, im nineteen years old for gods sakes and i know how to look after the self and i don't need a bloody nursemaid, thank you Overseas!

Just two more days of this crap to put up with and then ill have the passport so i can at last get the hell out of this stupid back-water of a country for a while at least, until they drag me back or something. Ive managed to scrib a flight slot on Monday week, so see u again in a few months time!

Mishie

— — —

Baz

Im in the pound at the consulate. Theyve booked me on the next flight home, so Ill probably see you tomorrow.

I lasted <u>one day</u>, Baz. Just <u>one</u> fucking day. Thats it.

One fucking <u>awful</u> day.

I got in from the port, dumped the packs at the hostel, went out for a drink, like anyone would. Its real pretty out there, lots happening, lots of girls, the rest. Went through a couple of glasses, pints they said, and had a few laughs with the girls in the bar and the mates with them and all, and they said that i was paying for it all, which was fine, its just a drink, right? that's what u do, isnt it? Well, not there, apparently, the barkeep said that was most of the money for the week for me gone in one hit. I was just about trying to make sense of that when i went out for a piss, left the fold on the counter, came back and the fold wasnt there any more and the barkeep said e didnt know anything about it and it was the fault of me anyway for not looking after it and told me to piss off because i didnt have any money left.

So fair enough, id had enough to drink so I left and went to a cafe down the road for a feed. All smiles and such, and nice tucker, too. So id finished and i got up to go to the door, like u do, and this biz whod brought me the meal comes running up and says i havent paid. So i says, yeah, i dont have any money with me any more, someones walked off with the fold, so whats the problem, all this money stuff its all some stupid bloody game isnt it? And e gets real pissed off at this, and this big hefty security guy comes up and starts being snarky at me so now <u>im</u> getting pissed off at the lot of them, so i just walk out the door of course. Then the

134

stupid bugger comes after me and tries to grab me, and ive had a couple of drinks and im half out my skull from the jetlag so i think were back in Defence so i flip en onto the floor and leave en there and keep walking.

Next thing i know theres a couple of GA cars come screaming up and they all jump out and they push guns at me – the fucking garda have <u>guns</u> here, Baz! – and they mustve thrown a vomit-comet because thats it, its like someones hit me with a sledge-hammer and im on the ground puking the guts out. They pick me up and slam me against the wagon and turn me round and tie the hands behind the back, but as soon as i open the mouth to ask what the fuck theyre playing at, someone says something like, shit, its a jaffa, means just another fucking aussie apparently, and they stop playing quite so bloody rough and just turn sarky instead, which i guess was kind of them but it didnt bloody feel it. And then they do an iris-and-retina and they cant find a match of course and they ask questions and more questions and <u>more</u> bloody questions and they bundle me into the back of the wagon and take me back to the hostel.

So we get to the hostel and at least the doorkeep says es seen me check in before so they ease off a bit at that. But they want to see the ID for me because i havent registered at the GA yet and they keep saying there will be charges but i dont whether they mean money or court or both, and we get to the dorm and the packs arent there which means the passport isnt there and noone knows where theyve gone. So im up shit creek apparently.

They bundle me back in the wagon again and we turn up at the consulate and the sergeant says to the counterkeep im making out im 'one of your fucking lot' and that if e can show a match for me e can keep me and theyll hit the consulate with the bill, otherwise theyll take me to the cleaners and the rest of it. So thank the gods for the consulate and for bloody auto-DNA or i really would have been fucked i reckon.

The guys here have been pretty good about it really, specially after i said it was the first day and all. They said i was bloody stupid to try to go it alone as a first-timer, but that was about it: u arent the first and u wont be the last, someone said. So now i got a bunk for the night and a change of clothes and some proper tucker this time, and ill be off in the morning.

They even said i can have another passport and another go if i do the course again and come over with a crew next time, but i dont think ill bother. They are <u>mad</u> here, Baz – fucking <u>insane</u>. And they can keep it. Ive had my adventure – "true journey is to return", wasnt it, in that book we did in Year Nine? So i reckon im staying home from now on. Isnt so bad after all.

See u soon

Mishie

Letter to Mum

telelink::fax-class="letter"
telelink::fax-addressto: Mum
24th February
Castlemaine again

Hi Mum!

Did promise I'd write again soon, didn't I? Thanks for telling me about Dad – glad he's okay now – and thanks too for telling Dave where to write, I had a letter from him last week.

I've been here nearly a month now, but I'm not in any great hurry to move on. The work's okay, and I've got plenty of time to myself, just to look around, or go out drinking with the crew from the foundry. I just want to settle in with the way they do things here before wandering on a bit. The no-money thing still feels pretty strange, but doesn't actually make all that much difference, especially as there's nothing much to spend money on anyway. I tried working it all out the other day, and I reckon I'm actually living about the same as I would if I'd still been at Hobart's, except there's a lot less hassle all round.

Most of the time, anyway – I managed to get a few people pretty annoyed with me this Sunday! Miros, one of the scaffolders at the foundry, told me about this music-exchange place – sort of like a music shop – just off Mostyn Street, in what used to be the old shopping area. He said they might have a keyboard there that I could use. And they did: a DX7, one of the old originals from way back when. So it's now back in my room at the hostel – a bit ancient, but it works well enough. So did the amp I picked up with it: it doesn't now... thanks to Old Tim and his temper. I got a bit carried away with playing the DX – after all, I haven't had a keyboard of my own for a fair while, since I sold the Roland to pay for this trip – and Old Tim got a bit raved up and he came in and shouted at me, and then kicked the speaker in.

He's a bit of a nutter – always going on about 'mine, mine' when nobody else seems to say anything's theirs at all... apparently he thinks he owns the quiet or something. Couldn't call the cops, of course – there aren't any – but a couple of hefty blokes from upstairs came and leaned on him a bit till he quietened down. The speaker's had it, but the shop – sorry, the <u>alliance</u>, everything's an 'alliance' here – said they should be able to get hold of another one fairly soon. In the meantime, I'll have to make do with head-phones – which might be a better idea for now anyway! It's funny, though: that's the second time someone's broken something, or threatened to break it, to stop me using it. Some people are just like that, I guess.

Old Tim's not the only nutter round here – sometimes I reckon the whole place is pretty crazy, even some of en down at the foundry, though we all get on pretty okay. A couple of nights ago, though, Mike asked several of us to come back in to help Kieren, another of the techies, to set up some kind of collector ready for the night. That's what she called it, anyway: it's part of one of the weirder bits of their welding gear that I haven't had a chance to use yet. Why it had to be that just night, I don't know – moon-phase or something, Mike said – but she was ranting and raving the following morning about the sky clouding over just as the moon rose and wrecking whatever it was they were trying to collect. Sounds loony to me, but Mike seemed to take her seriously. That gear really <u>is</u> weird, though: it doesn't use an arc or a gas bottle or anything I've seen before, it just puts out a very thin thread that becomes part of the metal itself. It seems a bit more like the buttonhole thing on your sewing machine than a proper welder, but it obviously works. They use it for some of the trickier joins in the main pipework at the foundry.

There's quite a lot about here that's strange, but I reckon it's the shopping that'd throw you the most, Mum. It's not just the no-money thing, it's the whole way they do it. That keyboard I bought on Saturday – well, that's the way we'd describe it back home, isn't it? – I didn't pay anything for it, but it's legally mine. They registered it in the workshare system, and apparently I really will have to pay for it if I want to take it with me when I leave, but right now it's mine because it was spare, and because I want to use it. And that's all there is to it. Food shopping's easy enough, too – though I don't bother with it that much because it's easier to eat in the cafes – but if I want something like an apple to eat at work, I go to the old shopping area and ask for it, and if they've got it, they just hand it over. (About the only thing I really miss in the way of food things is Mars bars! – plenty of other sweets and the like, but they don't have that one. Don't know why.) It seems to work pretty well, but it doesn't always work out right: some of en at the foundry keep complaining that the storekeeps hide things away to give to people they like, which isn't exactly fair. I suppose it's the same sort of thing as what your Gran said happened with rationing back in the war days.

Shopping for clothes is simple enough, too. It's much the same as with food: there are quite a few places in the old shopping area that are like clothes shops, and they've got all the usual things there. The big difference from home is that they keep asking what you need. Last week I had to go and get some new overalls for work, and replace some of the socks and stuff that I've worn out in travelling. I got those okay, and then the girl asked me again what I needed – whether I needed anything else. And she was right: I walked out of there with a pair of jeans, a new jacket and a couple of shirts which I've been wearing when I go out in the evening. They're a bit weird like that, sort of knowing what you actually want, but I suppose it's not that much different from the salespeople in the shops back home. Except that they're not trying to sell anything, in fact often trying to not give stuff away: there was another bloke there at the same time who said he wanted this, and said he wanted that, and in the end he went away with nothing because they said they reckoned, from what he said, that he didn't actually need it. I can see how some people can get pretty cross about it, but as Mike said, the stuff's got to be shared round one way or another, and this way does seem to work without needing all the hassles about money and so on.

The big difference is with trying to get hold of other stuff, like tools, or a car, or a place to live: they make quite a big deal about "what do you need?' and so on. Tools are like with the DX7: if they're there and no-one's using them, you can take them and register them as yours, and if you really need tools they haven't got, there are people who've made it their job to find them – the same sort of job as a salesman, I guess, except they're not paid to rip you off! There's less stuff around, and it's not as easy to get hold of as just walking into a shop at home. But as Mike says, it's sort of 'quality rather than quantity': what there is is a lot better made than most of the stuff at home, and doesn't just fall apart in a heap as soon as you use it.

Houses are a bit harder again. Okay, I couldn't afford a place of my own back home anyway, but here you've got to show that you need it. Which at the moment, fair enough, I suppose I don't – I'm going to be travelling on soon enough, I guess, and having my own room at the hostel is fine for now (as long as Old Tim doesn't take it into his head to come barging in again!) – but I reckon it'd be nice sometime to have a place I could call 'home'. What's good is that getting hold of one is exactly the same as with getting clothes: if I really do want a place, and there's one available, it's mine. I don't have to go through any of those nightmares like fighting the bank for a mortgage: I just have to show that I need it. There is a catch, though, Mike told me: if I do get a house of my own, I have to maintain it myself, or get other people to do it with me, and show that I'm keeping it in good nick, or else I can lose it in something called a 'challenge' – sort of like a housing survey or something. So for now I'm probably best off where I am.

It's almost harder getting hold of a car or a van: there aren't all that many around, so I'd have to prove that I really need one before they'll bother trying to find one for me. Fuel's a bit scarce, too: most of the cars round here are electric, which means they can't go all that far from home. Apparently it wouldn't be too hard to get a van if I wanted to set up on my own, travelling around welding, but there doesn't seem much point at the moment: I'm doing okay working at the foundry. It's easy enough to get around, if I want, because people are good about giving lifts, and there are buses and things. And I can get into Melbourne or Bendigo or wherever on the train pretty quick, too. But up till now I haven't bothered, because I get on well enough with the crew from work, and we don't really need to leave town, even in the evenings – the drinking's good enough here!

Anyway, I'd better stop there for now. Thanks for telling me what's going on back home – I do miss it sometimes. I'll post this off in the morning, but right now I need to get to bed!

Love

Steve

Police

From *The New Australia Travel Guide*

Police (GA)

There is no distinct police-force in Australia. Instead, the police role is taken up by the *GA*, or *Guard Alliance*. If you need police assistance, or any kind of emergency assistance, look for a GA station, or anyone with a 'GA' armband.

The GA system covers all emergency services, including police, ambulance, fire and rescue. Its full title is the 'Guard, Accident, Rescue and Disaster Assistance Alliance', hence usually shortened to 'GA' or *'garda'*.

As with many uniquely Australian institutions, the GA arose out of the turmoil of the Troubles and also, in this case, the political upheavals immediately preceding it. Since their inception as 'the Rum Corps' in the late 18th century, corruption and criminality amongst Australian police had been so endemic that they were sometimes more of a threat to public order than they were a means of improving it. In the wake of the Topolski affair, in which police and government alike were caught red-handed in large-scale drug trafficking (see *Topolskigate*), the Bannock Commission took the extreme step of disarming and disbanding all police forces throughout the country, as essential for public safety. Not all police gave up their weapons willingly: in New South Wales they eventually had to be disarmed by the army (see *Sydney Street Siege*).

But in any case, the simplicity of the SusLaw framework, and the effective disappearance of theft and most other property-related crimes, had largely removed the need for a separate, permanently-armed police force. Within a month after the start of the Troubles, all Australian states had merged former police, ambulance, fire and other statewide emergency-services into a single combined corps under the new 'alliance' structure. Most Australian states also include equivalents of traffic-wardens and citizens-advice under the GA umbrella – West Australia and North Australia are the only exceptions. There is also strong coordination with the

Australian Defence Force, which provides armed-response units on the rare occasions where these may be needed.

All GA members are authorised for and trained in the use of night-sticks, tranks and vomit-comets, and even the ambulance crews are not averse to using the latter on obstreperous drunken tourists – be warned! And whatever you do, don't call them 'cops': given the history, it's not far off an insult, and they don't like it. But in general the GA will beat even the Brit police for politeness, and are regarded as amongst the friendliest and most helpful police in the world.

GA vehicles all use the world-standard checkered-stripe colour-codes: blue for guard, green for ambulance, red for fire, orange for general emergency services. Most places have road-signs pointing the way to the nearest GA station.

Emergency contact via telelink:

- *dial*: **000**, or the European *112* or US *911* emergency-numbers
- *addr*: **ga** or **garda**, or the world-standard *MAYDAY*

Cutting gorse

A nondescript section of dirt road, with open forest to one side and dense gorse on the other. A heavy tractor-mounted slasher and a light tractor and trailer are parked to one side; a middle-aged man stands next to a light four-wheel-drive van behind them. He lights a cigarette, stamping his feet and rubbing his hands. Early-morning half-light on a cold autumn day.

A minibus comes up the road and pulls to a halt. Mike Howard, Robyn, Miros, Kyle and the others climb out, with Steve Hallam one of the last to leave. He's again wearing his 'vizzie' armband.

As they spread out down the road, Mike calls. "Robyn, you're source on this one, yes? You know what to do here, I don't."

"Okay."

The others start to gather round her; they move off to the four-wheel-drive, where she and the man confer inaudibly, then start handing out gloves and rakes and other equipment from the back of the van. Mike turns to Steve.

"Steve, a quick chat?" Steve nods, and Mike continues. "Think of this as income tax. Gorse like this is one hell of a fire hazard, but clearing it is a sod of a job: no-one wants to do it. So we share it out, and other jobs like it, so they do get done. Some people do their bit solo, but we've always done ours as a crew – gets it done faster that way!" He grins. "It's recorded in Workshare – a couple of days here, and you won't have to do it again for at least a couple of months."

"Workshare?"

"Yes. Same as the work you've done with us. You're due for some time off if you want. Let us know when."

"Oh." He looks a little lost and dreamy. Something in the land-scape, perhaps.

Mike cuts in: "Steve?" He returns, perhaps a little disoriented, to the everyday world. Mike finishes his instructions. "Robyn's source here – the boss, if you like. Join her and the others?"

"Yeah, okay."

A few minutes later, the crew starts work, following the slasher carving through the gorse. Miros drives the tractor; others use spot-sprays to poison the stumps; the rest, with Steve amongst them, use long rakes to load the cut branches onto the trailer. Robyn moves round from one person to another, checking up and giving instructions.

"Careful, Steve, don't shake the branches. Bloody stuff germinates if you tread it in."

"Okay. I'm stuffed, I'll take a break."

He stops, resting on the handle of the rake. Across the way, in the semi-open paddock, are a mob of about thirty kangaroos. As he watches them watching him, the sound of the slasher, the tractor and work-crew fade away, first replaced by bird-sound – magpies warbling, cockatoos squarking, tiny chirrups from the smaller birds – then another sound, a continuous drone like a didgeridoo, mixed with random syllables in a regular ta-ka-ta kind of pattern. This grows steadily louder and clearer; to Steve, the landscape colours shift and change, becoming hyper-real. After about ten seconds, Robyn's voice breaks through the pattern, faint at first.

"Steve?"

Louder: "Steve?"

Definitely louder: "Steve!"

Steve wakes up, looking at his hands holding the rake handle. The kangaroos have vanished.

"Jeez, mate, thought you'd gone to sleep there." She sees his face, steps back a moment. "You all right, mate?"

"Yeah. Yeah. Sorry." He shakes his head, as if to wake up. "Did you hear that? Like a weird kind of music? Sort of pattern stuff?"

"Nah. But there's all kinds o' weird shit around here, from the goldfield days an' way back. Gives me the willies sometimes."

"I wasn't just imagining?"

"Nah, it's real. Sort of. Different people get it different ways. You're a muso, ain't ya? Stands to reason you'd get it as music."

Steve looks a bit blank.

"C'mon, Steve. You ain't crazy. Get your arse into gear and get movin', that's th' best way to clear it. No worries, okay?"

"Yeah. Thanks."

They walk up the road to join the rest of the crew, who've already moved on some way. As they walk, Steve looks back at the stretch of road, then turns to face the work ahead.

144

Letter to Mum

telelink::fax-class="letter"
telelink::fax-addressto: Mum

3rd March

Castlemaine

Hi Mum!

Thanks for writing! Glad to hear Nick and Jo's baby arrived okay: say hello to them for me, will you? Marina, they've called her – nice name. And no, really, Mum, I don't think I'll be doing that for quite a while... come on, gimme a chance, I haven't even found a girl I like yet! (Just teasing!)

But yes, sorry, Mum, you're right, I hadn't noticed I'm picking up bits of Aussie-speak already. People round here tend to say 'e' or 'en' when they mean 'he or she, and it doesn't matter which' – sort of like 'e went to the station', if you see what I mean. There's a few other funny things they do, too. One is that they keep sticking 'e' on the end of words, so that a bloke on a motorbike isn't a biker, he's a bikie. I'm often called a 'vizzie', which means a visitor, on a workshare visa, and so on. And they tend to stick an 'o' on the end of other words, especially names – so Dean, at the bar, is 'Deano', and they'd call Kieren, one of the technicians at the foundry, a 'techo' – or a 'techie', sometimes. The other one they do which I still can't get my head round is that they usually don't say 'mine' or 'yours' or things like that – they talk about how someone <u>uses</u> something, and so on. So my keyboard isn't mine, for example, it's 'the keyboard I use', and my clothes are 'the clothes I wear'. They wouldn't even say 'Nick and Jo's baby': they'd say 'the baby of Nick and Jo', or even 'the baby they parent'. It's a bit odd, but I suppose it all comes from the idea that no-one really <u>owns</u> or <u>possesses</u> anything. It does sort of make sense like that, anyway.

Work's going fine, but this week's been a bit different. Mike Howard (I've told you about him, he's effectively the boss at the foundry) said that we were a bit ahead of schedule, and badly behind on something he said was 'the alliance's general work-share commitment'. So instead of our usual building work, we've been spending part of the week cutting down some gorse and clearing and repairing an old road out the far side of the forest south of the town. And it's been a lot of fun, too – that old phrase about 'a change is as good as a rest'? Though some of the gorse was pretty vicious – even worse than on the hills above Bolton!

I'm still trying to understand how this workshare thing works. It's kind of like a job agency, the social security, a swap-meet and a bank all rolled into one, because it passes information around about where to get hold of tools and work-materials and so on – what Mike calls 'resources' – and keeps track of who has what, like me and my keyboard. It's big, it's all over the country, with links in every town and village, apparently. And Miros told me that there's a kind of work-history for everyone in there as well, which alliances and so on can look at if they want, but which we can look at too, and also add to and comment on if we want – not like the dear old DHSS, hey? I haven't checked up on mine yet: must do it sometime, though, if only to see what's in it.

From what Mike said, another thing that workshare does is keep track of the jobs that no-one really wants to do but have to be done somehow, and shares them out. So everyone does their bit – and if you don't, it goes on your workshare record, and among other things you find your name in the local paper with a nasty comment about you! That's how we ended up cutting the gorse this week: it's a big job that can really only be done at this time of year, so they have to get as many people onto it as they can. I remember you saying something like this about the long summer holiday at school – that the reason it was when it was, and as long as it was, back last century, was so that the kids could help getting the harvest in. That's what you told me, wasn't it? This seems to be same kind of idea, but with <u>everything</u>, not just the harvest.

It was funny, too, to see how all the jobs changed – and how no-one seemed to put up a fight about who was 'boss'. Even Mike backed off, and handed over to big Robyn because, as he said, she was the one who knew what was what out there, and how to get it done. And we all just got on with whatever she told us to do. So Miros, who's only a general labourer at the foundry, was the one who drove the heavy tractor, to haul out the branches as we cut them down, and Mike and Kieren and the other techs – who admitted that they weren't up to much in the way of heavy hacking! – ended up following us around to put weedkiller on the stumps as we cleared them. Now we're back at the foundry it's 'all change' again: and it all feels okay to do it, just as it was before. Funny how it works out sometimes, isn't it?

It was good to get out of the town, though, and do something different. Especially out in the country, and the forest. It's... I don't know... quieter, somehow... time to slow down, in a way, even though we were working pretty hard. The trees are quite different here: they don't shed their leaves in the winter, they sort of do it all the time, bit by bit. And the forest is much more alive than the pine plantations back home: here there are birds everywhere, squawking and screeching, and there's one that's called a magpie – even though it's lot bigger than the ones back home – that's always warbling away like an old tape-player that's gone badly wrong. I even saw my first kangaroos! – a whole mob of them, thirty or more, grazing close to the edge of the forest as it started getting dusky.

But there was something else out there that I just couldn't place... dunno how to describe it... Like a kind of music, I suppose: it had a kind of rhythm to it, or a flow, or something. A little bit like casso, the kind of of music I usually play – but obviously there was no-one playing a tune or something like that! It was more sort of <u>in</u> the place itself, <u>of</u> the place – does that make sense? At one point when we were working out there on the road the music, or sound, or whatever it was, seemed so clearly <u>there</u> that I asked big Robyn about it, asked her if she heard it too. She said she didn't, but then said "you're a muso, so you would, wouldn't you?" – 'muso' meaning 'musician', I guess. So apparently other people do hear it too: it wasn't just me going crazy! Odd. Felt good, though... felt <u>right</u>, if you know what I mean?

My own music's going pretty well, too. I still haven't been able to get hold of another amp after Old Tim busted the first one, but I've been getting a bit of practice down in the evenings, before meeting up with the rest of the crew down at the pub. Some of the others in the crew play music: for example, there's Miros, who found the keyboard for me – he plays guitar, but it's all folk-music, which isn't my scene. He's lining up some possible people for me to play with, which is kind of him, though he said he won't be able to set up a meet with them till next week. So you'll have to wait till the next letter before I can tell you more!

Thanks again for telling me about Nick and Jo. And I'll write again soon.

Love

Steve

Workshare

From *The New Australia Travel Guide*

Workshare – the Great Australian Monolith

If you're visiting Australia as anything other than a tourist, you're going to come across Workshare. It's the nervous system of the Australian economy: in some ways it *is* the Australian economy, because it's the means by which jobs and resources are shared out and the foreign transactions handled.

Functionally, it's a huge computer network, most of it firewalled off from the rest of the world, but accessible everywhere in Australia. Every alliance (company) uses it to register jobs and search for materials; every hostel uses it to publish vacant rooms; and Workshare itself uses it to find appropriate work for you and to keep track of who's done what, and when – which is how they know whether you're up to date on your 'working tourist' visa.

It's also the public record system. If you're on anything other than a Tourist visa, you'll have your own public file, which includes your complete work and accommodation history. Ask someone to show you how to find your file: you can't delete anything, but you *are* allowed to add your own comments, which can be important if someone somewhere you've worked or stayed with has posted disparaging remarks about you. If you know your record is unfair or wrong, go to a Workshare office: they're the only people who can edit or delete anything from the records part of the system.

Workshare also handles the **Workshare commitment**, which is the Australian equivalent of income tax. The mundane work that most people don't want to do gets shared out so that everyone does their bit. And they're strict about it: even the chairman of BHP has to do a stint of litter-picking or night security from time to time. Most work on a basic Workshare visa is in this class, so you usually don't have to worry about it. If you're on a full Workshare visa or Academic or Business visa, it'll usually be organised for you – most alliances do their workshare commitment as a group – but you'll need to check anyway. In most places it averages out at around one day a month, so it's not a lot – but not doing it can cost you your visa, so make sure you don't miss it!

Letter to Dave

telelink::fax-class="letter"
telelink::fax-addressto: Dave G
28th February
Castlemaine VIC 3450
Hi Dave

I'm sorry you took it that way, because it just wasn't what I meant. I wasn't slagging you off, or Trish for that matter: I only suggested you try coming out here because I thought it would help, and that's all. Okay?

And I don't think you've been exactly fair to me, either, especially if you <u>have</u> been telling all the lads that since I've come out here I've started believing in the fairies at the bottom of the garden. I'm telling you it really <u>did</u> happen like I said: the birds <u>did</u> move that bloody feed-hopper, and they did it without a crane. If you don't want to believe me, fine: but you know bloody well I was never daft, and I ain't started now. So don't slag me off around the place, okay?

Anyway, it wasn't just the once now. The two birds came back again a couple of days ago, for the other feed-hopper, and this time they didn't mind my being around, so I <u>did</u> see en do the lift. It's bloody difficult to describe, though... Sod it, I'll try, though you probably still won't believe me!

The two birds – Jenny and I've forgotten the other one's name – spent ages going through all the drawings, and getting <u>us</u> to look at all the drawings, and at some doctored photos on the screen that showed the hopper in place. They told us to keep looking at the photos till we could see them with our eyes shut, if you see what I mean. While we were doing this they were winding up their clockwork – I've seen plenty of computer gear, but nothing like this, though the headsets were a bit like the VR screens those Army techs used, remember? – and I started to feel a bit woozy, which they'd warned us about.

Then they told us something like "shut your eyes, and keep 'em shut, but keep that picture of the hopper in place in your mind". God only knows what they did then, because it suddenly felt like I was pissed out of my brain – more pissed than I've ever been in my life – and one of them yelled at me to keep my eyes shut and concentrate on the picture in my head. Then they said it was okay to relax and wake up, and sure enough, it was up there, just as in the picture.

What was odd was it felt like it had always been up there: I had to rack the old brain cells a fair old bit to remember that it hadn't, and it felt pretty weird when I <u>did</u> remember it. But christ, I was bloody exhausted then, and by the look of it so was everyone else. It felt like we'd lifted the bloody thing up there ourselves, hauling away on a block and tackle or something, which we couldn't have, of course, because it was too far up and way too awkward an angle and we'd probably have pulled the bloody roof down anyway, but that's what it felt like.

Mike said we could call it quits after that – it was near knock-off time anyway – and we all trooped down to the pub. Big Robyn said something to me about it being important to get some liquid and "a shitload of starch" back into the system after a big lift. Lunch at the pub with plenty of booze is as good a way as any of doing it, she said, and I wasn't going to complain! Funny, though: never used to think much of stout – which is what Deano dished out for all of us instead of the usual beer – but just then it felt like just what the doctor ordered, I can tell you!

I got to talking a bit with that Jenny about it. She says the gear's called a 'bender' – or rather, that isn't its proper name, but that's what everyone calls it, anyway. I don't understand the half of what she was saying, but it seems it doesn't actually do the lift at all. She was saying that it really <u>is</u> that <u>we</u> do the lift – sort-of, anyway – which is why we all felt so splatted afterwards. It all has to balance out, or something like that, she said: the effort has to come from somewhere, and the only place it can come from is us, or through us, or something. She can do small stuff on her own, she said – said she's been doing it since she was a kid, even without the bender, which is why she got picked out for the job in the first place – but not the really big stuff like that feed-hopper. "It's been done", she said, "but it'd probably kill me if I tried".

What the bender does, she was saying, is help sort of bend things a bit so that the lift sort of happens by itself, sort of like the world changes, but it doesn't change, because there's nothing to change, but it changes anyway – something like that, anyway. Apparently that's why the pictures stuff is important, because if the world's changing it needs to know where it's supposed to end up. And no,

I still haven't a clue what she meant by all that – like I said, she was talking technical half the time, as if I knew what she was talking about, which I don't.

Anyway, I asked her why we had to go through all this weird stuff – why we didn't just use a crane, like anyone else would. And she told me what should have been bloody obvious if only I'd thought about it: we can't get hold of one that'd do the job. We'd have to take half the roof off, and half the cross-members with it; and with the angle and all the buildings round it, we'd need a long-reach hundred-tonner at least. The nearest one that size is in Melbourne; it'd cost a fortune in fuel alone to get it here, and it'd be a bugger to get round the site anyway. And it'd take us a week at least to get the roof off and put it back on again – if we didn't bring the whole place down on us while we were at it, because the building is bloody ancient! While this way, as she says, it's just two birds from down the road a bit with a barrow-full of gear, half an hour of everyone's time, and a few pints at the pub – which is a hell of a lot cheaper all round. So yeah, it's weird, but I take her point: that bit at least does make sense, even if nothing much else does.

She said something funny about me, too. Said I'd changed, or something: "last time we were here we couldn't get sync at all with you around", she said, "but this time it was dead easy". She was asking me a lot about what I'd been doing in the past few weeks: seemed to think it was important that I play music, for some reason. And when I told her about that sort of music-like sound I was kind of hearing when we were out cutting gorse for firebreaks – oh, that's right, you probably won't know about that, I only told Mum about it a couple of days ago – she seemed real interested about that. Dunno why.

She's a nice bint, though, that girl: real nice. Seems she quite likes me, too, because she got us to swop numbers and said she's probably coming in to town again come Friday night and that it'd be nice to meet up then. Have to wait and see, won't I? Wish me luck, perhaps?

But you be careful with Trish, all right? And enjoy yourself, okay?

I'm sorry I got a bit pissed off with you up there. Oh well: I'm like that, and you know that, anyway. Write again!

Steve

Lifter crew

Extract from Gerald Moore's report to the Royal Society of Arts Manufactures and Commerce, London, July

It was in Chewton, on the outskirts of Castlemaine, immediately after my interview with the industrial alchemist James Dawkins (see 'Courton Alchemy'), that I finally met up with one of the rumoured 'lifter crews'. I had noticed a van with the sign 'Bendigo Industrial Lift' parked with its rear doors open outside a small ironworks. I stopped on the off-chance of a meeting, and was fortunate in that I did not have long to wait.

Two young women came out of the works. One was pushing a standard industrial rack-mount electronics trolley; the other carried a helmet/visor combination and some kind of harness with what appeared to be a pair of brace-mounted joysticks cabled to the helmet. As will be seen from the transcript below, these appear to be the so-called 'bender' and its control-system in its configuration for industrial levitation.

As usual, I introduced myself as a journalist from The Age, using the business cards provided for this role. One of the women expressed some doubt at this, with a jocular comment on the lines of "what are you, some kind of Pommy spy?". Although I believe this was from a combination of intuition and my own demeanour rather than from intentional telepathic inquiry (see 'Indications of remote scanning at Australian Customs'), it was disconcerting nonetheless, and further evidence of the difficulty of maintaining objectivity during this assignment. However, the potential risk was bypassed, without threat of exposure, and I was able to initiate conversation.

As will be seen from the transcript, the two women, who gave me their names as Jeni Silver and Kim Vasic, work as a team, with clearly-defined roles. Jeni was thin, wiry, fairly tall, fair-haired, wire-rimmed glasses. All her movements seemed bird-like, cat-like, buzzing with energy, barely contained. Kim was much more 'laid back', with a heavier peasant-stock build and an easy smile and laugh. Both were dressed in purple industrial overalls, and appeared to be in their early to mid twenties, though Kim seemed the older by perhaps one or two years.

As far as practicable I have transcribed the conversation from my embedded recorder, verbatim and in vernacular, with additional comments to explain some of the interactions between the two women, and key incidents during the conversation. As in other transcripts, I have used the present-tense to convey some of the immediacy of the conversation.

I began by asking for some background, in other words how the women had started in their business. Jeni replied first, turning to the other woman for confirmation.

"Goes back a while, doesn't it, Kim? We were always best mates at school, and Kim was always great at keeping the other kids from hassling me, particularly when I got on the program."

Me: "Why did they hassle you?"

Jeni: "Dunno – just thought I was odd, or something, didn't they, Kim?"

Kim grins. "Well, you was, were'ncha?"

Jeni sticks out her tongue, then laughs. "S'pose so! I was a bookish kid in a school that wasn't; you can guess that it wasn't easy. I couldn't take the teasing, so I was always getting into fights."

Kim cuts in. "The girls was worst, they just wouldn't leave off. I was a fat kid in them days, so they'd tried to have a go at me too. But if I thumped 'em they stayed thumped, so they soon learned to piss off an' leave me alone. Then they thought they'd pick on Jen here as an easier target, so I thumped 'em for that too. So they learned to leave us both alone – most of the time, anyway."

Since this seemed to contradict the Australian propaganda about responsibility-based education improving self-discipline within schools, I asked whether 'Plan, Do, Review' and the like were supposed to prevent this kind of behaviour. Jeni replies for Kim.

"It does, sort of. Slowly. But kids learn from the parents of them, don't they? And they learnt it from the parents before, and so on. From what I've read, we're a lot better off than they are in Europe, let alone the States, but it'll take more than one generation for a big change like that to come through. In the meantime..." She shrugs. "...We're human, aren't we? There's still fights, kids propping themselves up by putting others down. Lots of them."

I asked where this school had been.

"Out Broadie way – Broadmeadows to you."

Kim agrees. "That's right. And then there was that time when you was, what, twelve, thirteen, right? Just startin' to push the tits out?

An' they thought they'd have a real go at you about that, calling you a titless slag an' all. Well, you must've got a bit pissed off, 'cos when I got there they'd run off screaming and you was all hunched up in a corner, with broken plates everywhere. Must've chucked half the canteen at 'em, didn't you, darls? And that was from a good twenty metres away, on the far side of the canteen door. Huh. Lucky for them it weren't knives, eh, darl?"

This description seemed to make no sense – apart from being surprisingly personal, it was clear there was key information missing – so I asked for more detail about what had happened. What followed was startling – a clear indication that the reported skills are real.

Jeni's terse 'explanation' was "PK. Or TK, rather. Sorry – psycho-kinesis, and telekinesis. It's what I do."

She stops for a moment, reaches out, slightly dreamily, slightly sad. A spanner in the back of the van drifts upward into her open hand; rests there for a moment, as she looks at it; then rises gently to eye-height before drifting back to the ground. She watches it as it falls, again slightly wistful and sad, and then returns to the conversation.

"Was the first time I knew I did it for real. I knew it could happen, and I'd sort of guessed it might be me, 'cos things had tended to happen around me when I got angry with Mum at home. But at school I'd really taken on the 'Plan, Do, Review' stuff, so I knew that trying to fight back wouldn't work. They were just going on and on at me, and I didn't know what to do. I felt like I was going crazy, tearing apart inside, and then something sort of burst through. There was a lot of noise, and next thing I knew Kim was helping me up and everyone just staring at me."

Kim: "Mr Hobbs sorted it out for you, didn't he?"

Jeni: "Yes. I thought I was going to get into a lot of trouble, but instead he took me straight away across the city to see the PK crew at CCAT. He was great, and so was Amber. That's when I got on the program."

The school-teacher is probably of no relevance, but 'CCAT' would appear to be the Caulfield College of Applied Technology, and 'Amber' would therefore be Amber Inigrou, head of the 'intuitive technologies' development unit at the college. Although we do already have some considerable information on the history and apparent role of this unit, I feigned lack of knowledge and asked Jeni what this program was.

154

"PK development program. It's not really a training program, it's more like learning to manage what's already in you. Amber says anyone can do it, but it's actually harder for people like me who do it naturally 'cos it starts off feeling like it's a raging beast that's out of control. It's worse for us girls, the boys have it easier – the main trick with them is to stop getting lost in the electronics."

This reference to gender-differences appears to be new, so I asked Jeni to expand.

"Sure. There's a few boys who do PK, but mostly it's us girls. I was probably doing it a bit even when I was small, but for most of us it starts in puberty…"

Kim interrupts, with a bright grin. "Raging hormones, innit!"

Jeni: "Yeah! And it usually fades away again quite quickly if the energy can find another outlet."

Kim: "Like boys!"

Jeni gives Kim a bright shove on the shoulder, with an affectionate yet rueful smile. "Easy enough for you, you slag! I must just frighten 'em off, I guess."

"You frighten everyone, darl."

"'Cept you."

"'Cept me." Kim grins. "An' I love you for it, don't I, darl?"

"You do. And to go back to where we were before I was so rudely interrupted…" Jeni smiles. "…Amber's training helps us to not shut it down but keep it going, channel it, hone it so it becomes an everyday skill like walking or riding a bicycle."

"An' you're a fish without a bicycle, ain't you, darl?"

"Get off it!"

Behind Jeni, the spanner spins into the air. It drops with a clang; Jeni turns round to look at it.

"Oops. Sorry." She grins, weakly. "Don't wind me too much, Kim girl, hey?"

Kim grins; it is evident there is a lot of affection there. Jeni continues.

"Anyway, it tends to be the quiet boys that get into Marko's side of the program, not the noisy ones. It's mostly boys, though a few girls do it too. They're the ones who disappear into books, or into machines and the like. The ones who really disappear, leaving only their body behind – you know, the kind of "lights out, nobody home" disappear, because it's easier than dealing with people?"

I indicated that this was familiar to me. The 'Marko' referred to here would appear to be Marko Ivetic, the chief engineer on Inigrou's team at CCAT.

Jeni: "Marko shows 'em how to come back but still able to go deep into kind of being the machine or whatever. Calls it 'telempathy' – 'far-feeling'? They learn to change things from the inside out, whereas I kind of change things on the outside going in."

This seemed to indicate that the skills were essentially internal to the operator, so I asked Jeni about the equipment and its role.

"Oh, that's the bender. 'Category Four Ivetic Amplifier' – one of Marko's lovely toys. Doesn't actually do anything by itself, but makes the lifts a heck of a lot easier. Helps us focus and direct the PK. On my own I usually can't lift much more than that spanner, but with the bender we can sync everyone else in to help with a big lift like in there today, or the ten-tonner we did yesterday. Kim here is usually about as psychic as a brick, but even she can get things moving when the bender's running."

Kim: "Only when you're around, darls – still can't do it on me own."

Jeni: "Not yet, but we're working on it, aren't we?"

Kim: "Yup!"

Although the term 'sync' remains unexplained, this exchange seemed to indicate that lifter ability is not a 'gift' limited to a small group of rarities, but a generic learnable and transferable skill – a key concern if it is to be usable as a consistent technology. I will admit that I was most excited at this, but was careful not to interrupt Jeni here.

"Cat Fours are the main ones we use here – they're projection standalones. Cat Twos are hardwired, for tuning things like car computers. Cat Threes are scanners – the boys use them for remote debugging of circuits and the like, stuff that frankly scares the shit out of me. Oh. Sorry. Cat Fives and Sixes are kind of freaky Cat Threes that the defence people use. I don't think any-one uses Cat Ones any more, other than for practice, but they're good to start on."

It seems that further investigation would be advisable to clarify this system of categories and the respective capabilities of each type, especially as there do appear to be military implications. With the intent of eliciting further expansion, I indicated a bewilderment which I admit I was in fact feeling in earnest here, but unfortunately Jeni took this for a lack of interest.

"Doesn't matter – the bender's just the bender. I know a fair bit about the physics now – the virtual solutions to the Maxwell electromagnetics, recursive tuning of the null, the link between the null-field and living tissue, that sort of thing. And the psych stuff, like Batcheldor witness-inhibition and ownership-resistance. But you'll have to ask Marko for the rest. Or Josh or Helena or Piotr, or any of the others on the design team."

I indicated assent here. Initial research on the theoretical background points to an unusual application of the complex-maths equations in Maxwell, specifically the imaginary-axis solutions symmetrical to the more commonly-used real-axis solutions. The core of the device appears to be an electromagnet that cancels its own field, which makes no sense in our current physics but does technically conform to the specified mathematics; the term 'null' would seem to refer to this auto-cancellation. The reference to living tissue is at present unexplained, but other research (see 'Health – alternative medical frameworks') suggests it may perhaps have its roots in non-European models of medicine. Since no further information seemed to be forthcoming on this, I drew the conversation back to Jeni's previous comment about trouble at school after she joined 'the program'.

Jeni: "Yes. I think they were all scared of me after the canteen incident, so they didn't say much to my face, but I heard a lot of snarky whispers about 'the Monster'. A lot. I wanted to change schools, but Amber wouldn't let me – said it wouldn't be any better anywhere else, and that I just had to learn to deal with it. I can see now why she said that, but it wasn't much fun at the time. The teachers helped a bit, but there wasn't that much they could do. The only one who really stuck with me was Kim."

Kim: "An' I've stuck with you ever since, ain't I, darl?"

Jeni: "You have. The boyfriends come and go with wild abandon, but Kimmie-love is always there!" Her grin fades sharply. "Poor Andy: wasn't till later I realised he'd been a classic telempath, but the bullying at school got to him too much, and he killed the self. So I was lucky Amber and Marko got to me first."

A reflective pause, then she continues with an angry tone in her voice. "But I don't want anyone to have to go through what we went through. I'm no bloody freak! Sorry. Anyway, I reckon I know most of the signs by now: spikiness in the girls, that sort of 'which world am I in?' look in the boys, the way so many of them hide in music. Outsiders, all of us – we never manage to fit in.

Which is why so many of us get bullied. The same's true of many of the bugs, the vizzies – it's why they come here in the first place, to get away from there."

The intensity of this young woman was startling, and quite disturbing: it is easy to understand how she would be regarded as a 'freak' in British culture. It is interesting, too, to see how this excess of energy has been channelled to a more constructive end, rather than the more likely prognosis here of self-destructiveness, and even to suicide, as in her comment above about the fate of her fellow student. But to distract her from what seemed a possibly dangerous train of thought – especially considering her barely-controlled interaction with the spanner – I asked her about these two terms 'bugs' and 'vizzies'.

"Oh, sorry. It's just slang. Workshare Visitors, otherwise known as vee-double-yous, or beetles, or bugs."

Me: "I understand. So, that was at school – what happened after school?"

Jeni: "I went on to study full-time with the crew at CCAT. At least I felt normal there!"

Kim: "An' I went to learn catering at William Angliss, an' hated it. So when Jen finished and needed someone to back her up on the road, I jumped at the chance."

Jeni: "And the chance to ogle all those nice muscular lads with their shirts off at the sites we go to has just nothing to do with it, does it, Kimmie?"

They share a happy grin, as Kim shows what I would best describe as an obvious 'oops, I've been spotted' expression. Jeni continues.

"Marko pulled some strings and wangled us the van, or else we'd never have got started. But we've proved our worth. The small lifts don't save much other than hassle, of course. But we do plenty of big stuff too these days: in there it was holding all the bits of a five-tonne assembly in place while they fixed it together. Jobs like that probably save a week or more of work-days each, and several hundred litres of fuel for a crane. If they can get a crane in there at all, which they couldn't have done for yesterday's job. So yeah, it's a lot, and our regulars know it. Just wish we could do more, but a lot of the older people don't trust us. They must know by now that it's just straight physics, but they still don't believe us!"

Behind her, the spanner starts to rise again, then settles back down as Jeni subsides. I notice this with real concern, but Kim seems unworried, watching it with a wry expression – it seems likely she's seen this happen often. Jeni continues.

"But then the crew did warn us about this: it's just Batcheldor psych again, people afraid of anything they don't understand. Which is fair enough, I suppose, though it means a lot of extra work when we have to weed out the people who can't get in sync."

Kim: "'S all part of the job, darlin'."

Jeni: "I know, I know! I just wish it wasn't, that's all."

Kim: "Anyway, girl, we gotta get movin' – s'posed to be over the new cannery at Heathcote by four."

Jeni: "...so you can be chasing after that Dylan you fancy by five? Honestly, Kim, you're more transparent than a sheet of glass sometimes... Yeah, okay, okay, we'd better go."

At this, they picked up the trolley to put in the van, and climbed into the cab. Other than parting pleasantries, the interview was effectively over.

I was able later to confirm that this two-woman 'crew' have been able to lift and manipulate the large masses as stated, for example a ten-tonne feed-hopper for a furnace at the nearby Thompsons works.

The comment about 'Batcheldor' earlier, and in that exchange above, appears to refer to a booklet entitled "Manual of Advanced Psychokinetic Procedures" by psychologist Kenneth Batcheldor and engineer Colin Brookes-Smith, first published by the British Society for Psychical Research in the 1960s. This purports to provide instructions on development of psychokinetic capability as a group-learnable skill, using instrumented feedback and some ingenious psychological ploys to bypass issues around fear and self-doubt. Unlikely as this claim seems, the records do indicate some genuine success, both for their own groups and those coordinated on the same model by Isaacs in the 1980s. If real, this would appear to be a key component to developing similar capabilities in Britain, and perhaps also justifiably claimed as a British invention. We should note, though there may well be legal concerns about threats to crane-operators' livelihoods and the like, and even on incitement to theft, if we consider 'lift' in a more colloquial sense.

As with other interview subjects, what struck me most was the blasé, routine manner in which these personable young women described their extraordinary capabilities and activities, ones which most scientists here would dismiss as impossible. In the United States, of course, any reference to any such supposedly 'supernatural' matters can be grounds for ghetto-incarceration, whilst purported demonstration is a capital offence. Once again, we will need to use extreme care in introducing the results of this study to our US partners.

At the Cannon

It's early on an autumn Friday evening at the Cannon. It's a pub that's popular with the younger set: it offers a mixture of loud music, serious drinking and quiet spaces to talk. The band are setting up for the evening's music.

As Steve enters the door, he meets Robyn and Miros from the foundry-crew coming out. Steve is unusually well-dressed, in clean slacks, open shirt and light jacket, with the now-inevitable armband. He looks slightly embarrassed to see them.

"Oh... hi", he says.

Robyn nudges him playfully in the ribs. "G'day, Steve! Bit dressed up, hey? 'Specting someone, are ya?"

Steve winces – her 'playfulness' is a lot rougher than she thinks it is. "Uh... Jenny, from the lifter crew."

"*That* one? Got a strange taste in women, 's'all I can say." She grins. "'Ave fun – go for your life!"

"Uh... right..."

To Steve's relief, they leave. His confidence visibly collapsing, he heads into the quieter middle bar. He picks up a beer from the counter, nods a greeting to the bar-keep, sits down at a table, his expression a mixture of slightly worried and slightly hopeful. His face is towards that doorway when Jeni appears through the other doorway behind him, accompanied by an Aboriginal man in his mid-30s. He's medium-framed, but with a presence that makes him seem larger than he actually is. His appearance suggests he spends most of his time outdoors, yet his movement and stance imply a university education. A strange mix.

"Hi Steve", says Jeni. "Thanks for coming." Steve spins round to see them. "Thought you two should meet. Brian – sorry – the Wirinun, this is Steve, the vizzie I told you about."

"Pleased to meet you", says the newcomer. He glances to Jeni. "Drink?"

"Something simple? – lemon lime and bitters? – thanks."

As the man moves off to the bar, it's bitters for Steve as well, it seems. He's visibly disappointed: this isn't the way he'd hoped his evening would go. He leans toward Jeni.

"Who's the black guy? Your boyfriend?"

"Huh? Good god no! – I've a lot more respect for him than that. No, an elder with the Land Council. Important."

From the bar-keep's shaking of the head, Jeni's 'simple' drink will take a little longer than expected. The Wirinun looks back at them with a wry shrug. Steve disappointment shifts to barely-concealed sarcasm.

"*Important*. Is that why the fuss about the name, huh? Why not call him Brian like you started, hey?"

"Can't. Death in the family. Same name. Shouldn't say name till the mourning's over, so for now we use the work-title."

Embarrassment sets in immediately. "Oh. Uh... sorry." Quick change of subject, then. "So what does 'Wirinun' mean, anyway?"

The man returns to the table with the drinks, and smiles at Steve's question. "In English, it means 'sorcerer'."

"Huh??"

The Wirinun grins. "Yep. Almost on a par with 'the Dreamtime' as the world's worst translation. Don't worry, not what you Anglos think of as sorcery – though I might try that if you mess up Jeni here!" A glance passes between them, a flicker of a smile that betrays a deep connection – yet one that is more professional than personal, the love of mentor and student. A glance that's all too easy for others to misinterpret, though.

Jeni leans forward, hands open, explaining. "We're on the lands of the Djadjawurrung, the long-time people. The Wirinun represents the people to the land. That includes the knannugeetch, the step-brothers, and step-sisters – the whites here, like you and me."

Steve pulls back a little in his chair, defensive, wary, almost hostile. "What's that supposed to mean? What's it to do with me?"

The Wirinun nods, moves into university-lecturer mode. "You'd think of land as someone's possession. To us it's more the other way round: the land owns us, and we're responsible to it. When people and place interact, the place has choices too. So that's the job I do – to listen to the land, understand those choices, and help people find the best response to each choice."

"So?"

'University-mode' may not have been a good choice: Steve's ironic tone is more like the drawing up of battle-lines. Jeni takes over, to make it more personal.

"Most vizzies get it eventually – or give up and go back to their homelands, what's left of 'em. But I've never seen a vizzie change as fast as you. A month ago I couldn't get sync within fifty metres of you. This week you were the easiest of the lot."

"That's good, is it?" Openly sarcastic now.

The Wirinun misjudges the moment. "Impressive, certainly. And I've been picking up hints that someone like you was around. Mainly from the forest in the Ranges, but elsewhere too."

Steve flares into anger. "How the hell d'you know where I've been? Everyone round here bloody spies or summat? An' what the hell you mean by 'someone like me'?"

Jeni holds up her hands, urgently placating: "Steve, Steve, it's not like that!"

The Wirinun joins in: "No, it's not. Honest."

"Then what the fuck *do* you mean?", Steve seethes.

"Steve, calm down", says Jeni, still placating.

"All right", says Steve, firmly. It's clear he's still just one step short of exploding. "But you better start tellin' me what's goin' on here, or I'm gonna deck someone – an' right now I don't give a shit about what happens after that, okay?"

A dangerous moment: Jeni and the Wirinun glance at each other; a quick decision reached. "Okay, I'd better go first", says Jeni. "Steve, we don't know much about this ourselves as yet. We were hoping you'd be able to tell us." A pause for breath, as the tension eases a little. "What I can tell you is you're unusual. A month ago you were just a typical new vizzie. A walking nuisance, mostly."

Not a good choice of words: Steve tenses his fists in anger.

"Cool it, please, cool it – that's not a put-down. *Every* vizzie starts out like that. But most take years to get it together, while you seem to've done it in weeks. We guess it's linked to the music you heard out in the ranges" – Steve flicks up his head in renewed suspicion – "look, you told me that yourself in the pub after the last lift, remember?"

The Wirinun cuts in. "There's a connection, but we don't know what it is. Something's changed in the Dreaming here, and you may be the only one who knows which way it's moving."

Steve looks at each of them in turn, then slumps back into his chair, anger deflating like a punctured balloon. When he does speak again, the tone is defeated, bitter, sarcastic.

"Great. Just fuckin' great."

"I'm sorry?" The Wirinun is clearly confused by this sudden change.

"All my bloody life I've 'ad people tryin' to tell me who I am an' what I 'should' do. Came here to get away from that crap. An' now you're doin' it. Great."

"Oh." An awkward pause, in which Steve seems to slump further from sarcasm into self-pity, then pulls himself together.

"I'm sorry, Steve", says Jeni, gently.

"Ah, sod it. I'm screwin' you around. Screwin' me around too." He manages a wry grin. "Best tell me what you want, an' I can work it from there, can't I?"

A sense of everyone releasing held breath.

"Thanks", says the Wirinun. "There's not much more we can say right now. Whatever you're doing, you *are* doing it right" – another wry smile from Steve – "even if it doesn't seem like it!" He grins. "Okay, man?"

"Yeah."

"Just if you hear the music again, or anything like that, you let me know, right?" He holds out a business-card. "Or Jeni. You've a number for her?"

Both Steve and Jeni nod. The Wirinun glances up as a large man in work-overalls passes the table. "Oh, excuse a jiff." He rises, calls after the man: "Ricko? Some news for you about the Chandler house." He turns momentarily to Steve and Jeni. "Excuse me."

As the Wirinun leaves the table and follows the man into the back bar, Steve looks down at his drink, then glances up at Jeni with an embarrassed expression.

"Sorry I lost it back there."

"It's okay. Do understand."

"'S real, though. So many damn people tryin' to tell me what I 'should' do that I don' know who the hell I really am."

Jeni nods. "Perhaps you're trying too hard to find out?" Her expression turns bitter for a brief moment, somewhat self-deprecating. "Know I did. Still am." She gestures at the Wirinun, just visible out in the back bar. "Says the only one who can tell you who you are is you. Perhaps that's what you're doing, with the music and stuff? And coming to Oz?"

"Yeah. Dunno. P'raps." Steve lowers his eyes, then looks at her with another embarrassed expression. "Uh. Dunno that I *am* doin' it right, whatever he says. Looks like I got the wrong end of the stick here, anyways."

"Sorry?", says a puzzled Jeni.

"I, uh, thought you were coming tonight to see me."

"Huh?" The bewilderment is plain on Jeni's face.

"Y'know, see *me*?" Steve sighs. "Got that wrong, didn't I? Sorry."

"Oh." A moment's pause. "Oh." Jeni looks at him as if for the first time, her face suddenly a welter of confused emotions. "I... I..."

Steve smiles, a flick of understanding. "You thought I was just a specimen, didn't you? For your science class?"

"I..." An embarrassed pause from Jeni. "You're right. I did."

Steve grins. "An' I ain't. I'm Steve. I'm me." A wry smile. "Whatever that is."

She breathes out, puts on a weak embarrassed grin. "I'm sorry."

"S'okay. You's you, too. Whatever *you* is." Gentler; the flicker of a smile. "S'okay." He stops for a moment. "Well, guess that's about it, innit." A wry, slightly sad pause; the end of hope, perhaps. "Want another drink afore you go?"

"Uh... No... No thanks..." She makes no move to leave – she's staring at him, bemused and a bit lost. He looks at her with a new confidence.

"You know what? Don't think I do either. But that music's sounding good. Fancy a dance?"

He gets up and holds out his hand. She looks at it, almost blankly; looks at him; tentatively puts out her own hand. He takes hold, gently pulls her to her feet; holding her hand, he leads her towards the front bar, where flashing lights and a noisy crowd can be seen through the frosted glass door. As they move through and into the crowd, she looks around in confused wonderment, as if finding herself in a new and different world.

Who are you?

A small bedroom in a stone-built miner's cottage. Ghost-gums and wattle-bushes are visible through the window, in the first hint of dawn; light curtains the colour of red wine billow in the gentle breeze. The only sounds that can be heard a magpie warbling in the distance, and the faint gentle murmur of breathing within the room itself.

Looking round, there's a bedside table, with a light and a small pile of technical reference manuals and science books: Rupert Sheldrake's 'Seven Experiments That Could Change The World' and F David Peat's 'Blackfoot Physics' are some of the titles that can be seen. Another well-thumbed notebook, headed "PK Best Practices: Procedures for Large-Mass Moving Objects", lies open on the floor, handwritten annotations across every page.

There's a chest of drawers, a small wardrobe, a chair with a clutter of clothing and an old-teddy-bear resting on top. Well-worn work-boots off to one side. A few decorations here and there. A room that one person – one rather studious young woman, we would guess – would call home.

And a bed, quiet, restful, with two people in it.

Steve is asleep, facing away from Jeni. She's awake, resting gently against his back, stroking his hair, looking at him with the same slightly bemused expression.

Jeni whispers, ""Who *are* you, Steve Hallam?"

She closes her eyes and snuggles closer into his back.

Pretty scary

A warm quiet early morning. Steve and Jeni sit next to each other on the retaining bank of a farm dam, the old miner's cottage visible in the background. Beside her is a fishing net on a short pole. Steve looks around in bemused wonderment. Jeni idly tosses pebbles into the brown waters of the dam; the stone she's just thrown stops in mid-air, holds still for a moment, then falls vertically into the water with a splash.

She smiles. "I'm glad we didn't – you know."

Steve grins in return. He reaches out across her back to squeeze in a gentle hug. "Might have been nice, but didn't seem right."

Jeni smiles, and nods, leaning into his embrace. "I'm afraid."

Steve looks at her in surprise.

"Not of you", she says, her face quietly serious. "Of losing it. But it's still there."

Steve grins at the unintended double-entendre; she realises what she's said, laughs, punches him gently on the arm.

"That too! But I meant the PK. It's been my life. It *is* my life."

She grins, then throws three large pebbles up in the air, one after the other. She juggles them for a moment, then pulls her hands away, laughing. The pebbles continue in the juggle-pattern for a few seconds, then fall to the ground as she turns to Steve.

"Always afraid a man would take that away from me. Afraid the energy'd vanish if it found another outlet. But it hasn't! Thank you!"

She throws her arms round Steve's neck, pulls him in and kisses the side of his head. Steve is staring at the ground and doesn't much respond; Jeni leans back.

"Steve, what's up?"

It's true – he does look more than a little worried, searching within himself for the appropriate words. "You ain't the only one who's afraid, y'know. What you do is pretty bloody scary. I know you say it's just physics, but it ain't any physics I've ever known." He points to the fallen pebbles. "I know I'll get used to it, but right now it still scares me shitless, seein' you do stuff like that."

Jeni looks crestfallen, lost – like a child about to have her toy taken away as punishment for some unknown offence.

"I'm sorry…"

"Jeni, s'okay. It's okay. I *want* to get used to it. You're the first bird in years I've felt safe with – that you weren't goin' to screw me over an' all. Just give me a bit of time, right?"

He reaches over and kisses her, much as she did, on the side of the head. She sighs, relaxes, leans against his shoulder, as they both stare contentedly out over the water.

At the airport

In the fading orange light of a Canberra dusk, Don Mercer and Tony Morrison stand side by side on the windswept tarmac beside a medium-sized aircraft – the Prime Minister's jet. The older man breaks the companionable silence with a sigh, and then reaches out to shake the other's hand. Time to go.

"I'll wish you good luck for all of us in Geneva. God knows we'll need it."

Tony nods in grim agreement. "You're probably right. We've had a free run this past year, but we have to face the music sometime."

"Be careful what music you face, Tony. This is a small country. Most of them could crush us without even trying. Everything we've done is legal, by their own rules, but they still won't like it." He shakes his head. "We're like yabbies in an old farm dam, never knowing if someone's about to pull us out and have us for lunch."

"Then we'll have to be a bit *more* like yabbies, won't we? He grins. "Surprise 'em with our pincers – and move off sideways when they're not expecting it!"

He turns toward the press corps by the aircraft steps, and calls back a last aside to Don. "You're the one who taught me to do that. So keep thinking sideways for us – and keep 'em busy while I'm gone!"

He walks toward the steps in a blizzard of camera-flashes. Yet another tense day in the politicians' world.

Yabbies

Gum-leaves and small pieces of bark float on the surface down by the waterline of the dam. Steve leans back on the slope of the dam wall. Jeni is on her knees with the net in the water.

"Got one! Come and see."

Steve gets up and comes over, as Jeni pulls up the net, containing a yabby clinging onto a fragment of meat.

Jeni smiles. "Yabbies. Funny little things. Some people eat them, but I'd rather let them be. All in their own little world at the bottom of the dam."

Steve nods, in quiet amusement. "A bit like us, ain't they."

She looks at him in some surprise.

"Can't see a thing for all the mud in the water, see? Bits and pieces drift down, in any old order, all out of sequence. An' we have to make sense of them as best we can." A wry, happy laugh. "Story of my life, really."

She grins at him. "What sense do you *want* to make of it, Steve? What would *you* like?

He grins in return. "Dunno yet. Gettin' there. But summat with you in it, I guess?"

She drops the net, and pulls his head down to kiss it. As she does so, the yabby takes advantage of the distraction, working its way free of the net and back into the water, still holding the prized piece of meat.

Crazy scientists

Part of transcript from *Channel 6 News*, Tuesday

Max Amon (presenter): The annual meeting of the British Association for the Advancement of Science descended into farce today when Australian scientist Cory Osmer, from Derwent University in Melbourne, claimed the country's economic system makes people psychic. Claire Hamill has the details.

Claire Hammill: Yes, Max, we had sober scientists heckling and jeering as she gave her talk. Two even climbed to the podium with a straitjacket and offered to tie Osmer up in it.
Osmer herself had this to say when I spoke to her earlier.

Cory Osmer: We've tracked a steep increase of capability for intuitive technologies in Australia over the past five years. So-called 'psychic' skills like remote sensing, telepathy and telekinesis.

Claire Hammill: Are you saying these things are real?

Cory Osmer: Of course. There has never been any reason for any real scientist to doubt this.

Claire Hammill: Okay, if you say so. So, how does this link to economics?

Cory Osmer: Self-responsibility. The responsibility framework is the core of our economic system and educational model. It's the only factor that differs from the rest of the world, where these skills are still as rare as before.

Claire Hammill: And do you think this is something new, something specifically Australian?

Cory Osmer: Not at all. These skills have always been available to anyone. The psychology, physics and physiology of this have all been known for decades. And much of the key research work was done here in Britain, back in the last century, though sadly most of those studies seem to have been forgotten now. Really all that we've done is confirm them.

Claire Hammill: Were you surprised by the response at the conference?

Cory Osmer: I was disappointed, but not surprised. After all, scientists as prone as anyone else to the effects of Gooch's Paradox.

Claire Hammill: What paradox is that?

Cory Osmer: Seeing is believing, but believing defines seeing. Most people find it hard to see past their beliefs about truth when they face contrary fact. Some facts are unpalatable. But as scientists we do have responsibilities to report what we find.

Claire Hammill: Back to you, Max.

Max Amon: Well, there you have it. Australia the crazy country. Crazy economics and crazy scientists too.

Next up, Bob Frankland's prediction for tomorrow's weather.

Witness-inhibition

A warm evening back at the miner's cottage. Out on the back verandah, with its rusted canopy and clutter of boots and work-gear, Jeni, Steve, Kim and Kyle are sitting in pairs on worn-out sofas, drinks in hand. Four or five empty beer-bottles each at Kim and Kyle's feet; just one at Steve's; Jeni still holds her first bottle of soft drink.

"So how *does* the lift work, Jeni?" asks Steve. "I mean, what's this stuff about 'getting in sync' an' so on?"

"Sync is what links everyone together to give the energy for the lift", she replies. "But it can be blocked by witness-inhibition and ownership-resistance."

Kim rolls her eyes. "Translation for normal people: 'this isn't happenin', and if it is, it ain't me what's doin' it'."

Jeni grins. "Yeah. Ownership-resistance isn't the big problem, because people think it's the lift crew or the bender doing it. Not true, in practice – as you saw at the foundry, most of the energy really comes from you. But it feels that way."

Kim makes yawning gestures; she and Kyle start giggling, which Steve carefully ignores.

"Yeah, okay. But what's 'witness inhibition' then?"

Kim interrupts. "C'mon, Kyle, they're gonna be at it all night. You know what 'at it' I want – all sync, no witness, no inhibition!"

She jumps up, pulls Kyle out of the sofa, and drags him bodily towards the back door of the house. He looks back toward Steve and Jeni with a silly 'she's the boss' expression. As they disappear, giggling, Jeni gets up from her sofa with a grin.

"We'd best get out of here, Steve. Going to get noisy in a minute, won't be able to hear the selves of us think. It'll be quieter up in the trees."

She starts walking as Steve gets up out of the sofa, remembers, comes back and holds him by the waist. They walk up into the woods, arms around each other. It's open forest here, with leaf-litter and boulders and traces of mine-workings all around.

"Witness-inhibition is what most blocks sync", she continues. "It's a bit more than 'this isn't happening', though. What we're really doing in a lift is bending reality a bit."

"That's why you call that gizmo a 'bender'?"

"Uh-huh. And anyone who holds too tight to *their* reality'll block it. Any fixed view of the world will do it. Even too much desire for what you can't have will block it. 'S why it rarely works out where you come from, or in the States and the like: too possessive, too fixed a view of what's real and what's not. Same for most vizzies." She looks up at him in a brief thoughtful pause. "Doesn't explain why it's worked with you, though. You're a puzzle."

She grins, then suddenly but gently pushes him to one side. "Hey, careful, that's a mineshaft."

"Where?"

She points to a slight depression in the ground, which they're now walking past. "There. Whole forest's full of 'em. Supposed to be capped, but after two hundred years none of them are safe, and capping just makes them harder to see." A bitter laugh. "Gold-miners. Huh! Worst example of waste ever: a few grams per ton of pay-dirt, and the rest is somebody else's problem. Talk about lack of responsibility!"

Steve returns to the previous topic. "How come it can work easier here? The bender, I mean."

"'S funny: it's straight out of the responsibility framework, though I doubt the Don ever planned it that way. Self-responsibility plus boundaries equals self-definition. If you've got that, you're okay when reality changes around you, because you'll always have something to hold. If you haven't, you daren't let it change."

"Yeah. Seeing you do your stuff is still pretty scary – even if I know it's 'just physics'."

She grins and pulls him closer. "Doing pretty well so far!" But it's clear Steve is distracted. "Steve?"

He's stopped, listening to something; he holds up a hand. "Ssh..." A pause, then "Nah. It's gone. Weird. That pattern again, only different – sort of 'yan-in-em-booka' this time."

"'S odd", says Jeni. "Sounds aboriginal, though. Could talk to the Wirinun about this. Perhaps we go back where it started?"

Steve nods. He's still a bit withdrawn. "Yeah..." He returns slowly to the present. "Best head back afore it gets dark?"

Jeni nods, kisses him lightly, and then leads him to a more visible path homeward. Steve looks thoughtful. "Hmm. I know you can lift things. Can you lift people?"

"Not often. Pushes witness-inhibition too much. They freak, and it blocks the flow."

"But *you're* okay about it, surely? Can't you lift yourself?"

"Not really. That's the other side of it: it pushes ownership-resistance too much – too visible to us, see? Besides, it'd be like lifting the selves of us by the bootstraps."

Steve's expression shows he's suddenly deep in thought. "Uh... You can lift any amount of metal, stuff like that?"

"Depends on how many people we have in sync. Up to ten tons is usually okay, wouldn't ever want to go above twenty, though."

"And the bender – how much power does it need?"

"Not much: runs on a car battery. Only sets up the null-field, y'see, not the actual lift." She looks at Steve, puzzled. "Why?"

"Just workin' on an idea. Bootstraps..."

Arriving at the slope above the house, they walk down the slope, arm in arm, Jeni leaning on Steve's shoulder.

Letter to Dave

telelink::fax-class="letter"
telelink::fax-addressto: Dave G
8th March

Castlemaine VIC 3450

Dave

I'm <u>not</u> away with the bloody fairies over here, whatever you bloody well think – and neither is Jeni, so for Christ's sake leave off about it, will you?

And I've said it before: I'm <u>not</u> slagging you, and I'm <u>not</u> slagging Trish. From what you've said, it sounds like it's bloody obvious to everyone – it's certainly bloody obvious to me – that it ain't going to work for you with Trish. It ain't helping you, or her, or anyone: best thing you can do is just drop it. And I mean that, mate: I really mean it.

Really wish you <u>would</u> get your arse into gear and get yourself out here, mate: I know you think everyone here's off their trolley, and me with 'em, but it'd open your eyes a bit, it really would. Can't you see that you can't <u>buy</u> Trish? And even if you could, she wouldn't be worth having, <u>because</u> you could? Doesn't matter what you earn, money ain't going to make any difference: she ain't for sale – <u>no-one</u> is. But if you think she thinks she is, you've got one hell of a problem. Can't you see that? Can't you <u>see</u> that?

Oh, sod it. You've been one of my best mates all along: I don't like it, seeing you getting yourself all trashed like this. But it sounds like I'm just making it worse, so I'd better shut me trap. Sorry.

Good luck or something

Steve

Deathday

From *The Age*

Deathday of Maria Keanes

Over 300 well-wishers were present yesterday for the deathday of Maria Keanes, at St Andrews Hospice, Hawthorn.

Thanks and tears alike flowed as Ms Keanes gave the farewell to family and to former students and colleagues from the faculty of history at Derwent University.

Ms Keanes worked at Derwent for most of the long career of her as an academic. She resigned the post as head of faculty last June on grounds of ill-health.

She will be especially remembered for the pioneering work of her on the geo-socio-history of relationships between aboriginal and coloniser women in the early 19th century.

Ms Keanes was suffering from inoperable liver cancer. The funeral for her will take place on Wednesday at St Winfred's Chapel, Carisbrooke.

Lines in the landscape

Out in the forest ranges, at the roadside verge where the foundry crew did their gorse-clearing. Steve and Jeni stand beside her van, holding each other close; another bright, cold early morning, with raincloud in the distance.

"How much time you reckon we got?" asks Steve.

"All day, if you need it." A brief flicker of bright amusement. "Kim won't want the van – she's not going anywhere if she's got a warm bed and Kyle in it."

Steve grins in return. "Well, no bed, but I can keep you warm anyway, can't I?"

As they hug, a battered double-cab ute comes up the dusty road. The Wirinun climbs out, with a grin of excitement.

"G'day!" He claps his hands and rubs them together in bright anticipation. "So what have you got for me?"

Steve points along the lie of the road. "This is where I got it last time. Still get it. But it's fussy 'bout where I am. Like here…" – he moves to one side of the road, closer to the trees – "…if I stay still, it starts off same kind of pattern, that 'ta-ka-te'. But soon's I start movin', it goes to summat different. Here it's sort of 'tar-rak-yeh-rip'. And over here…" – he moves to the more open side of the road – "…if I stay still, there's that 'ta-ka-te' again. But if I move, the pattern's different: sort of 'nor-nor-bull-bull'. An' there's sort of over-patterns that come and go: one like 'mo-ro-nah' a while back. It's like that all round here: 'ta-ka-ta' if I stay still, all kinda patterns if I move." He waves up and down the road. "But further up an' down there's nothin' at all. Make any sense?"

The Wirinun nods, reflectively. "A lot of sense. The guess of Jeni was right – most of those sounds are like words we use for trees, animals, birds. That 'mo-ro-nah', was there a rainbow earlier?"

"Yes, there was", says Jeni. "A real beauty, like coloured fire!"

The Wirinun nods. "Yeah. Sounds right. To the Djadjawurrung, the people I belong, a rainbow is 'moronga'."

Steve is completely perplexed. "Huh? That don't make no sense at all. How can I know the language?"

"You don't", says the Wirinun. "You don't need to, because the land does. Or rather, the language is linked with, part of, drawn from the land. It's not the language itself you're hearing, but its source. One of the sources."

He pauses, trying to find the right words to explain. "We call these patterns 'songlines'. They're lines in the landscape – which is why you hear it here…" – he points to the ground, then up the road – "…and not there."

Another pause for the right words. "People and place interact, remember? Some of the lines are 'people-stuff': clan boundaries, routes to camp-sites and so on. But others, like this one, really are part of the landscape. Some even go right across the country. But they all have the song of them in the Dreaming. Follow the song, the changes in pattern, and you could go anywhere."

"So what should I do about it?" asks Steve.

"Nothing, as yet. Or 'no-thing', rather. There are no 'shoulds' in this game: only is or is not, do or do not. Just you and your own 'response-ability'." He laughs. "'Do what you will, but be very sure that you will it!' – that's one of the old Anglo sorcerers, isn't it?" He pauses, with a smile. "I'll do some research, see what I can turn up. If nothing else, we still need to make sense of why it's you that's finding this."

Steve's expression shows an odd mixture of worry and something closer to fear. The Wirinun moves to reassure him. "Don't worry, man, you're doing fine. Better than you realise." He grins. "Things do work out if you let them – and if you only let things go the way you expect, you're limiting your chances! Reckon there'll be a few more twists in this, but you're getting there."

Steve too grins at last. "Wherever 'there' is, hey?"

They laugh; Jeni pulls Steve in for a closer hug.

What's the project?

The cluttered planning office at the foundry. A large flat table is covered with plans and engineering drawings, a drawing-board and large-format printer behind. Mike Howard sits at a desk, working on a drawing on a computer, as Steve leans in through the door.

"Mike. Some help for a mo', if you could?"

"Sure, come in. What do you need?"

Steve comes forward and stands in front of the desk, like a worried schoolboy. Mike waves him to a seat beside him: this is a relationship of equals, not 'boss' and 'worker'. Steve sits, one hand resting on the desk, the other on his knee, not sure how to start.

"Uh... you said I was due some time off, right? A few days?"

"Yes, sure. No worries. We're ahead, we can re-schedule easy."

"Only... I was hopin'... could I use some of the gear here?"

Mike looks at Steve, quizzically. He grins. "I know that look. This isn't time-off at all. What's the project?"

Steve is taken aback. He expected this to be harder. "Uh... dunno what to call it yet... 's just an idea... an experiment..."

"Whatever it is, you're working at it, and working hard." Mike pauses to find the simplest explanation. "Look, this isn't back home. You don't have to explain it to me, or prove it, or make out a business case or commercial risk assessment or any of that nonsense. Here we know that most ideas go nowhere – and that the best ones usually come from places we don't expect."

He pauses again, leans back in his chair. "Call it engineering, or science or art, you're still contributing. It isn't time-off: you're working. All anyone here cares about is that you do whatever-it-is in a disciplined way, and are responsible in the way you do it. But it's up to you to find that discipline. Which you are. You have."

Steve is still somewhat bewildered at this: he'd geared himself up for a struggle, and there isn't one. At least, not in the outer world: he's now struggling with his own assumptions and expectations. Mike grins again. "Yeah, I know. Isn't easy to get the head round it. But it always comes back to that one principle: 'what do you need?'. It really *is* as simple as that."

Steve nods, silently, struggling to understand this clash of world-views: the one he's known since childhood, and the one he's in now – a clash that's not yet resolved. Amused yet respectful of the struggle, Mike points to the screen.

"Come on. Let's show you how to register the project of you in Workshare. I'll do the 'verify' part, verify the project's real and so on." He grins. "That's all the 'paperwork' you need to get you started. The rest is up to you."

The view pulls back as Steve leans in toward Mike and the computer screen.

Later, inside the foundry building, Robin and Kyle can be seen setting up for a weld on a large frame, with Miros holding it still with the tractor hoist. As Steve comes in through the side-door, Robyn waves.

"Steve. G'day."

"Hi all."

He walks over to Miros, leans against the tractor. A brief pause, as if gathering courage.

"Can you help me a bit? Want to build a frame, like a mini pickup – sorry, a ute. Light 'n strong, take the weight of a couple of people. Any chance of some ally tube, 'bout hundred mill, say twenty metres all up? Structural grade? And some thin sheet, for a floor and for a box about yay big?" He gestures with his hands, showing a shape about half a metre each way.

"Yeah, sure, no worries!" says Miros. "Sheet's in stock at Abbott's, there's some old dural scaffold at Peterford."

Steve looks relieved, though he's still following his hidden train of thought. "Any ideas for a couple of truck seats? Y'know, the ones with the long-travel shock-mounts?"

"Easy. There's a write-off at Five Flags. Get 'em here this arvo." He points to an empty area. "Set you up over there. See Mike about the ally welder, we aren't using it this week."

"Great! Thanks."

His face again shows he's surprised it's been this easy – and perhaps waiting for the world to collapse around him. In the meantime, Kyle wanders over. "What's this about, Steve?"

"Workin' on an idea for Jeni. She don't know 'bout it yet." He pauses, grins. "How's Kim?"

Kyle's expression instantly turns dark. "Drivin' me bloody *crazy*, mate." Steve looks surprised: it's not the answer he was expecting. "She's bloody *on* at me the whole time. Pesterin' for attention. 'S like she thinks she owns me or somethin'. But still chasin' after every other bloke she sees."

Still somewhat shocked at this turn of events, Steve struggles to find suitable sympathy. "Oh. Sorry to hear…"

Kyle returns a sardonic grin. "Nah. Bloody sheilas all crazy, ain't they? Too bloody possessive."

A twitch of the mouth from Steve. "They'd prob'ly say the same 'bout us, wouldn't they?"

"Yeah, right!" Kyle laughs. "Anyway, I better get back to it, mate, brickies are here at last, we don' wanna hold 'em up."

He waves and walks back to join Robyn at the welding frame.

More'n enough rope

Over the next few days, Steve wanders around his little corner of the foundry, drawing, measuring, cutting, welding or, from time to time, just standing and thinking.

Out of this blur of activity a structure slowly starts to form. It looks like the skeleton of a tiny ute, without wheels or engine. Roughly in the middle are a pair of truck-seats, mounted side-by-side, facing forward, with what looks like a cage for an instrument-rack between and forward of them. The right-hand 'driver-side' seat has a strange mount at the end of each armrest, as if to take some kind of control-handle. The frame extends a short distance behind the seats to counterbalance the legroom forward and provide a brace for the roll-cage. Simple skids run the length of the frame, to keep the base off the ground. It's just small enough to fit on top of a standard six-by-four trailer.

Finally, with a last coat of a striking purple paint over the aluminium tubing, it all seems to be complete, Steve signals for position as Miros lifts the frame on a sling from the tractor hoist, lowering it onto a trailer hitched to the foundry van. Miros helps Steve rope the frame onto the trailer.

"Thanks, mate!" says Steve. "But more'n enough bloody rope here. You sure you can spare all this?"

Miros nods. "Uh-huh. Just bring it back in one piece when you're done. Or else you'll find someone else'll need it. She'll be right, mate, no worries."

Steve grins at the classic Australianisms, then pauses as he climbs into the driver's seat of the van. "Where's Kyle got to, by the way? Ain't seen him around this last while."

Miros shrugs. "Buggered off somewhere. Gone south with some sheila from the city, last I heard. Reckon they won't be back, neither."

A wave of concern crosses Steve's face. "Uh-oh... Kim won't be pleased 'bout that..."

Looking somewhat worried, he closes the door and drives off, exchanging a wave with Miros as he goes.

Bootstraps

Jeni comes out of the back of the miner's cottage to find Steve sliding the bright purple frame from the trailer to the ground. She leans against the door-jamb looking both puzzled and amused.

"You been getting into sculpture, Steve? Or what?" She shakes her head in happy incomprehension. "What *is* it?"

Steve makes a proud sweeping bow. "Your bootstrap."

"My what?"

"Bootstrap. You said you needed a bootstrap to lift yourself with, so here it is." A wide grin. "Thought I'd add another seat so I could come too."

She stares at him for a moment; stares at the frame; bends forward, hand over mouth in delighted shock; runs across the yard, laughing, and gives him a wild, crazy hug.

"You're mad! Brilliant!" She laughs. "Probably both!" A brief pause for thought, then "Wait here, I'll get the bender."

She lets go, turns and runs back across the yard.

A few minutes later, Steve is kneeling inside the frame of the bootstrap, mounting the bender into its cage. Wires trail off about twenty metres or so, to where the harness is resting on the ground. Jeni leans against the frame, grinning.

"Don't break it, Steve! But no disaster if you do, it's only the spare. Works okay, though – tested it last week." She leans in, checks one of the dials. "Yep. Working now. We got sync." She looks again, a little more closely. "A *lot*. More than I'd expect. Hmm…"

Steve plugs in the harness cable and looks up, the assembly complete. "You can run this on your own?"

Jeni nods.

"Where *is* Kim, anyway?" Steve asks.

"Inside. In the room for her. You heard about Kyle?"

"Yeah. Took it bad, did she?"

"Uh-huh. Cried the eyes out the past two days. Gone through every bottle in the house. Poor Kim." She glances back at the house, looking pensive. "Hope she gets the act together soon, though. Good job we've no bookings till Wednesday." But she brightens up. "C'mon, you mad thing, let's try this out!"

Steve fits the last anchor-panel in place, and they move across the yard to the harness. Jeni pulls on the helmet with practiced ease, clips on the harness straps, sets the joystick control-rests under her wrists, and switches on. Within moments the bootstrap drifts upwards and settles, floating about two metres up in the air, silently, the air flickering around it. The 'ta-ka-te' sound-pattern can be heard faintly over the hum of the bender.

"Well, that works", says Jeni, now very definitely the professional. "Should do, of course, but it's the first time anyone's bootstrapped a bender. Wasn't sure the cables'd take it."

"What do the controls do?"

"Not so much controls, more a focus. A bit like dowsing, if you've done that. Displays what should happen, so I can guide the PK. Sort of feed-forward rather than feed-back?"

"Yeah, I get you."

"Right's movement: forward, back, left, right, up, down." She moves her hand slightly on the right-hand joystick of the harness as she gives each direction; the hovering bootstrap moves briefly in each direction. "Left's rotation: left, right, up, down, roll left, roll right." Again the bootstrap echoes her movements. "All relative to self." She grins. "I'm self-centred, y'see!"

She turns to kiss him, forgetting that the mask is in the way. In the confusion the bootstrap crashes to the ground.

"Oops…"

"Women drivers…"

Both burst out laughing, then Jeni returns to 'professional mode' again. "A lot easier than I expected. Almost no load. You feel anything?"

"Not much. Like I've lifted a heavy pack or summat, not the whole frame."

"Odd. No idea where the extra power's coming from, but some lifts are like that. Hmm."

Steve gives her a playful nudge. "C'mon, you can analyse later, it's playtime now! My turn!" He runs off toward the grounded bootstrap.

Jeni is uncertain. "You sure you want to do this?"

"Yup!" He vaults into the 'passenger seat'.

"Ready?"

Grinning wildly, Steve nods.

"Okay – rolling!"

The bootstrap moves smoothly into the air, the faint 'ta-ka-te' pattern again audible over the hum of the bender.

Steve, it's clear, is having the time of his life. "Woo-hoo!!"

Jeni tweaks the controls, moving the bootstrap a little each way, as before, then smoothly to the ground again. Steve barely waits till the flickering stops before jumping out and running over. He can hardly contain his excitement. "See, oh grand master? Witness-inhibition fixed for us poor slobs? C'mon, let's nail ownership-resistance!"

He pulls her, with some resistance, to the 'driver's seat'. "Your carriage awaits, mam'selle!"

He mimes opening a car door, bows, ushers her into the seat. The harness fits neatly into the seat recess, the controls facing forwards as if there's a steering-wheel between them. He closes the imaginary door, re-opens it, tucks in the harness cable that had been trailing on the ground, closes the 'door' again.

"Oops. Can't leave your skirt hanging out, can we?" He runs round to the other side of the frame. "Wait for me!"

He jumps into the 'passenger seat', stops, puts his hands in his lap, looks straight forward with a silly grin on his face, then side to side in a parody of a tourist. He turns to look at Jeni, wearing her harness and helmet. "Nice crash-helmet you got. Racin' bootstraps, the latest sport." A brief pause for another parody of a rubberneck tourist, then "Well, are we goin'? Are we there yet, Mum?"

Jeni splutters with laughter, shakes her head. "Mad. Totally mad."

Both convulse with laughter. Jeni struggles to resume her 'professional' face, and promptly loses it. "Do you have *any* idea how stupid this looks? A couple of overgrown kids sitting in a play-cart? "She collapses with laughter again, and pulls herself together by parodying a take-off check. "Sync? Check. Engines? Check. Brakes? Oops, can't find 'em."

"Tower to Bootstrap One, you are cleared for take-off", says Steve, in a parody voice of air-traffic control.

"Bootstrap One", replies 'pilot' Jeni. "Thank you, Tower. Rolling!"

At "rolling", the bender hum cuts in, the 'ta-ka-ta' pattern clearly audible behind it. Seen from over Steve and Jeni's shoulders, the view flickers between the normal and the hyper-real as the bootstrap rises. Both yell in excitement as Jeni tweaks the harness controls, twisting the bootstrap around from about two metres up.

After about ten seconds the bender hum fades out rapidly, followed by the sound-pattern. The flickering vanishes. Like a cartoon character running over a cliff, the bootstrap hangs in the air for a moment, then crashes to the ground.

"Oof!" laughs Steve. "'What goes up must come down', hey? Good thing I did use the sprung truck-seats!"

Both again convulse with laughter, turn round and hug each other. Jeni checks the bender's controls. "It's out", she says "Still running, but no sync. Not surprised after that beating. Wow, what a ride!"

They climb out of the now slightly distorted frame. Jeni pulls off the helmet and harness, drops them to the ground, runs to Steve and throws her arms round his neck. "Didn't know that was impossible, did you? But you did it! Brilliant! Brilliant!"

They turn towards the house, to discover that Kim is leaning limply against the frame of the open door. Her eyes are bloodshot, her hair disheveled; frankly, she's a mess.

"Nice to see *someone's* havin' fun…", she says, in a bitter, sarcastic, self-pitying voice.

"Oh, Kimmie-love, you poor thing…" Jeni walks toward her, with Steve close behind. The two women hug, then all three move into the house.

The deep-stories

Steve walks across the floor of the quiet bar in the Cannon pub, holding a beer in one hand and Jeni's drink in the other. He arrives at a table, where Jeni and the Wirinun already sit, the Wirinun with a half-full beer-glass in front of him. Steve passes Jeni her glass; she looks up with a smile.

"Thanks."

Steve sits down next to her.

"You're on to something here, Steve", says the Wirinun. "The Dreaming changes all the time. Mostly it's little changes, people-stuff like tracks and boundaries. Sometimes it's big, when a volcano or an ice-age changes the whole landscape. We have fellas can go back two Dreamings like that, even three. But sometimes it's as if something in the land itself wakes up. Looks like that kind of change that's happening here."

Whilst he says this, Steve takes a sip of his beer; grimaces; looks at the beer-glass; puts it down. "'Scuse a mo'", he mutters. He gets up and heads towards the bar, taking the glass with him. The Wirinun continues talking to Jeni.

"Glad Steve put me onto this. Spent all of last week in the library stacks at the University. Opened my eyes to a whole lot new about you whitefellas. More like us than I'd thought."

Steve returns from the bar with a clear glass of soda-water, as the Wirinun continues. "Seems every culture has its own version of the Dreaming. Not blackfella stories, of course, but the deep part where people meet the land itself." He pauses, leans back, eyes upward, then returns. "Some are pretty close to us. Bushmen. Inca huacas. Hopi dance. Then there's Indian vastushastra, Chinese ch'i and sha. But there's a lot in the Anglo tradition, too."

Jeni looks at him in surprise. "Didn't think we had any…"

The Wirinun grins. "You probably wouldn't unless you know where to look! I had to weed my way through a whole load of rubbish about ley-lines and the like. But it's all there. Spirit of place. The deep-stories. The crucial difference between sacred sites and power-points. The core's the same."

"So where do I fit in?" asks Steve. "How come me?"

"Music's one part of it. I've heard casso, Steve: the rhythm and patterns are close to natural resonance. And you've had a strong connection with country, I'd guess?"

"Yeah. Was usually stuck in towns, but got out whenever I could. The old places. A stone circle called the Nine Maidens was best."

"Yes. The old places. Exactly." The Wirinun nods, and turns to Jeni. "There's energy, there, Jeni. A *lot*. But it depends on place, and people's relation with place."

Jeni also nods, analysis coming to the fore. "Explains why some lifts are much easier than others. Extra's coming from *place*, not people."

"If you can connect to it, there's more than enough to lift the bootstrap, and follow the songs to wherever you need to go. Like magic. An older kind of magic."

Expressions are more of awe than excitement on everyone's face as the Wirinun continues. "*Need* may be the key here. A beautiful quote in one of the books, a children's story: 'the Old Magic is a magic of the heart, not the head; when it awakes, it will answer to your need but not to your command'." He pauses, leans back again, and nods with a smile. "Looks like you blokes are in for an interesting time."

Steve and Jeni glance towards each other, excitement finally breaking through.

You've got to go

Steve stands in the dirt road at the edge of the forest, as if listening to something. It's a warm day: he's dressed in shirtsleeves, still with the 'Workshare Visitor' armband. Jeni leans against the van, arms crossed, an amused expression on her face. Behind the van is a trailer, carrying the bootstrap, covered with a tarpaulin tied down with an excessive amount of rope. Kim is just visible in the middle seat of the van. She doesn't look happy.

"Yeah, this is right, this is the place", says Steve. "Pattern's here. Strong."

Jeni grins. "Let's get Baby Bootstrap unwrapped and ready for her travels!" She leans into the car. "Kim, girl, give us a hand, you're better here than moping at home."

If anything, Kims slumps further into the seat. Grumpily she mumbles "Kyle should be doin' this, not me."

Jeni is frankly irritated. "Well, he's not here, and you are, so come *on*, please?"

Kim gets out, slumps down against the side of the van, does nothing more. Jeni gives a snort of annoyance, then turns to help Steve unravel the rope around the frame. "Why so much rope, for heaven's sake?" she says.

"Was all of a piece. Didn't want to split it. Waste, that."

Jeni nods in agreement. They pull out the last of the rope, haul off the tarpaulin. The bender control-harness and helmet are resting between the seats. She climbs up to the frame to switch on the bender. There's no hum.

"Odd", says Jeni. "It's on, but no sync. Not a squeak. Drop must have busted it. Oh well, can always use the main."

She jumps down, opens the back door of the van, leans round the door to call to Kim, who's still slumped by the side. "Come on, Kim, do help us with this."

"My Kyle should be 'ere wi' me..."

Jeni glances toward Steve with pursed lips and a shake of her head, then turns to the electronics rack in the back of the van. She turns back a moment later. "Steve! What have you *done*!"

Steve lifts his arms with a 'huh?' expression. "Ain't done nothin'. What's up?"

"No sync! Not even on the main! *Nothing!*"

Steve looks puzzled. "It ain't me. Can't be. Can still hear the pattern loud 'n clear."

"You're the vizzie here, it *must* be you. Or the way you're interacting with that music, or pattern, or whatever it is." Conflicting emotions pass across her face, then she seems to come to a decision. "Either way, I can't have this happening to me. I *can't.*" A bleak pause. "I'm sorry, Steve, I can't have you near me. You've got to go."

Steve stands still for a moment, silent, his face sombre, then nods briefly. He moves towards the trailer, starts pulling the tarpaulin back over the now-useless bootstrap.

Love beyond reason

From *Love Beyond Reason – the personal papers of Don Mercer*, edited by Elisabeth Mercer Kellner

My dearest Mary

Happy Anniversary! Our silver wedding, this, for I still feel your presence with me every day, and I thank you so much for that gift.

Yet it is a slightly sad anniversary for me, too, since this is the first year we have been apart for longer than we were together.

We miss your company, of course. But George still knows when you are here: he jumps out of the chair by the fire and pads into your studio, looking around and meowing, with his head to one side.

And we are an odd couple, are we not, you and I? Year by year, always growing more and more comfortable with each other – comfortable as an old coat, as my grandfather would say. Our friends are kind enough to put up with our quirks, our little eccentricities! And that there is just one of us now to do what two once did together makes little difference.

Our family of students is growing well, and I feel an uncle's pride in their achievements. Your Nick Apostopolou, for example, has taken over the SusLaw conference this year, and is doing a better job of it than I ever did! And young Tony Morrison – I always think of him as 'young Tony', though he must be almost in his forties now! – won his re-election to Parliament only last week. He and his Blaise now have another son, too, their Jez, who was born in October. I am too old-fashioned for these new-fangled names!

But I suppose I always had the makings of a crusty old man, didn't I? Even in the days when we first met? You showed me so much about how to let go, to let things be, to let them emerge as they will.

And you still show me so much. I know I will never have your touch for fabrics, your feel for colour. And yet when I falter in some piece for a tapestry or a quilt, I feel your guiding hand, leading me to the perfect choice for each place. I know because you know, not because I think it so in my so-honed mind of reason, of analysis and calculation. And the wonder of that, the mystery of it, never ceases to astound me.

You have taught me so much about possession – that we may love each other, 'to have and to hold', yet we cannot possess each other, cannot possess anything at all. And yet we still have always this greater truth, this greater being, that we both share. Non-attachment is also non-detachment.

I love you, my dearest. I love you beyond thought, beyond reason. And beyond death.

Your husband for always

Don

Music of the lost

Steve sits alone in his hostel room, playing the keyboard. He's wearing headphones, so there's no sound other than his fingers on the keys, but from this and his listlessness it's clear he's playing a slow, sad tune.

The clock beside his bed shows three in the morning. There's a kettle and a coffee-mug close by; also an unopened beer-bottle. He stops playing, pushes back the headphones, sighs, reaches for the beer-bottle, picks it up.

"No. That'd just make it worse."

He puts the bottle down, sighs, pulls on the headphones, starts playing again. A cycle that's been played through many times this night.

A convenient untruth

From *The Independent*, Tuesday

Australian PM died of heart-attack

As the body of the Australian Prime Minister Anthony Morrison returned to Melbourne yesterday, the Australian government have acted quickly to quell 'unfounded rumours' about the cause of his death. The autopsy report provided by sources in Canberra confirmed that he had died from natural causes, in a heart-attack. Mr Morrison is believed to have had a history of heart-complaints.

Morrison was found dead in his hotel in Geneva on Saturday, just hours after completing the final round of controversial asset-settlement negotiations arbitrated by the International Court. The Court ratified the binding agreements with foreign investors who had claimed compensation for loss of assets from nationalisation during and after the Troubles. The precise circumstances of his death still remain unclear, however, fuelling suspicions of an assassination plot.

His body was cremated yesterday afternoon at a private ceremony for family and friends.

A state funeral is expected to take place on Sunday. His long-time colleague, trade minister Stavro Sipinski, said that all Australia will mourn the loss of the man who masterminded the country's smooth transition through the Troubles. "He will always be remembered as the father of a free Australia", he said.

Nothin's no good

The foundry office, much the same as before: the usual clutter, Mike Howard sitting at his desk, the computer showing the current drawing. Steve again leans in, but his expression and hangdog movement show he's given up hope. For the first time, his 'Workshare Visitor' armband is missing.

"Mike. Some help, if you would?"

"Sure. Come in. What do you need?"

Mike again waves to the seat beside him, but this time Steve won't sit down: he places himself in the 'failed worker' position, standing in front of the desk.

"It don't work", he mutters. "Nothin's no good." A long pause; Steve shuffles his feet listlessly. "Was gonna ask if I could work here to pay off me dues, then best push off back to England."

Mike runs his hand through his hair, not sure what to say. "Well, sure, no worries. If you're sure that *is* what you want to do?" Then he notices that Steve's armband is missing. "Where's the armband, by the way?"

"Dunno. Couldn't find it no more." Steve sighs. "Just summat else that says I ain't s'posed to be 'ere."

Mike gives a wry grin. "More like it means that you are." He leans forward. "If you really do want to leave, we'll help any we can, but don't rush it, okay?"

He pauses for a moment. "You're fond of Jeni, aren't you? From the lifter crew?"

Steve looks embarrassed, but nods. "Yeah…" Muttered, cautious.

"Reckon she needs the help from you right now."

Steve's alarm betrays all the feelings he's suppressed. "What's up? What's 'appened?"

"Nothing serious, as such. But the lift here this morning failed. Couldn't get sync at all. She was pretty upset about it."

"She would be – oh gawd, she would, an' all…" Concern for Jeni pulls Steve out of his dejected apathy. "D'you know where she's gone?"

"Back home, I think."

"Please, can I use the van? Gotta get out there, an' fast…"

Mike grins. "Key's in it. Go for your life, mate!"

Steve blurts out a thanks as he rushes out of the door.

A gift from the land

Sound of a van skidding into the yard, then a car door slams. Steve bursts through the back door of the cottage, almost tripping over the spilled stack of empty bottles sprawled across the floor. Another slab of beer sits on the kitchen table, most of the bottles empty.

"Jeni? Jeni, where are you?" he calls.

The only answer is Kim's slurred voice from the next room. "Hi cutie. She ain't here."

Kim appears through the doorway, looking decidedly disheveled, her hair shower-wet. She's wearing a bathroom wrap, only partly tied, showing dark red knickers and nothing else. She's also very drunk. "Thought you was my Kyle. Wan' 'im back. Nothin' bin right since th' bloody bimbo pinched 'im from me."

Steve tries gently to penetrate the wall of self-pity. "Where's Jeni?"

"Dunno, cutie. Wen' out. C'n wait 'ere 'f y'wan'."

Steve sits in the sofa, tense, though worried more at Jeni's absence than by Kim's state. Kim drops awkwardly into a chair beside the table and picks up another bottle. "Ya wanna beer?"

"No thanks."

"Wassup wi' ya? Kyle said you was good on the piss. Jeni curin' you a good habits?"

Steve shakes his head, says nothing. Kim opens the bottle, takes another swig. "Kyle." She shouts to the air: "'E's mine, ya bitch, I fuckin' wan' 'im back!"

She turns her bloodshot eyes to Steve. "I'd give anythin' t'ave 'im back. Fuckin' *anythin'*." She wobbles against the table, muttering sadly to herself, "I'd give 'im fuckin' anythin', I would. Anythin' 'e wanted."

"Kim, you can't buy him, y'know", says Steve, in a gentle voice. "An' even if you could, it still wouldn't work, *because* you could." "Huh?"

"Doesn't matter what you try to give 'im, ain't gonna make no difference. Ain't no-one's for sale – you *know* that. But if you think he is, or he thinks he is, you'll both be in the shit, big-time. Can't you see that?"

"You sound like fuckin' Jen..."

At Kim's bitter tone Steve quickly pulls back. "Sorry. Ain't helpin'. Better shut me trap."

An awkward silence, broken by Kim's sudden shout, "Where the fuck are you, Kyle? I wan' a root!"

Automatically, if unconsciously, she opens her legs wide in the chair, leaning forward, arms between her legs, holding the chair-seat. She returns to her bitter muttering. "That fuckin' bimbo. Stealin' my root. *My* root. Kyle's best bloody root I 'ad."

Following that train of thought, though with no particular intent, she looks appraisingly at Steve. "Huh. You'd be good root. You doin' it yet?"

Steve is carefully non-committal.

"'F you an' Jen ain't doin' it, she don' know what she's missin'." She picks up another bottle, levers herself up from the chair, wobbles erratically over to the sofa. "C'mon, 'ave a drink, keep me comp'ny."

Steve says nothing, gently shakes his head. She collapses, giggling, onto the sofa beside him, dropping the unopened bottle onto the floor. "You wanna root, cutie? Ya do, don' ya. All blokes wan' a root. Allus wan' a root."

Steve's pulling-back suggests this assertion just might not apply. Kim, however, doesn't notice, but burbles on in blurry pride. "I'm *good* root. Be better root than Jen, wouldn'I?"

She slumps across him, reaches up, fumbling with his buttons. As Steve gently tries to fend her off, the back door opens, and Jeni walks in on this awkward scene.

"Shit!"

Kim blurrily turns round, with a pleased-with-herself grin. "Just warmin' 'im up for ya, darls!"

This doesn't improve matters for Jeni, as she takes in more detail – but not enough detail – of what's going on. "Oh shit! Steve! Not you as well!

"Jeni!" Steve gets no chance to say anything else: Jeni rushes out, slamming the door. He struggles to lift Kim off without dislodging her robe; she's so drunk as to be nearly a dead weight.

Kim finally realises there's a problem here. "Ah fuck it. Nothin' bloody workin'. Kyle gone. Jen pissed off wi' me. Bloody bender stops workin' soon's I go near it. An' you don' wan' me neither. Fuckin' nothin'."

Steve barely notices the stream of words as he struggles up from the sofa, letting Kim sprawl back again. A moment later, a single phrase catches up. "Did you say the *bender*?"

"Yeah. Even the fuckin' bender don't like me no more."

She slumps into self-pity, but Steve lights up, all worry erased. "Jee-zus! 'Too possessive'...!"

"Wha...?"

Steve's shout starts to wake Kim from her drunken stupor. He turns to her, shakes her brightly by the shoulders. "S'all right, Kim! It's all right! I know why the lifts don't work! Come on, Kim, wake up, get some bloody clothes on, we gotta find Jeni!"

He pulls her up from the sofa, hugs her briefly in delight and relief, then runs out of the door into the evening half-light.

Kim stares blankly at the now closed door, and shrugs her shoulders. A happier smile crosses her face. She holds up her hand, index finger pointing upward, as if giving instructions to herself. "Clothes. Right." She shrugs off the robe; stands there not quite naked for a moment; then walks off toward her room with a more determined air.

In the meantime, Jeni sits on a log in the quiet of the forest, wearing her work-overalls. She's slumped over, head in hands.

In the distance Steve can be heard, crashing through the leaf-litter on the path. "Jeni! Jeni, where are you?"

"Go 'way!" Jeni's voice wavers between lost dejection and bitter hatred.

Steve arrives, but stays at a respectful distance, squatting on his heels. Jeni doesn't move or change her posture.

"Damn you, Steve, she was all over you like a rash."

"Jeni, it's all right. It's not what you think. Silly bint was pissed out of her brain, I couldn't fend her off."

"It's *not* all right! You were just the last straw, is all." She turns toward him, her face streaked with tears. "I've lost it, Steve! I've lost it! It's gone. I can't do it any more." A bitter pause. "You've no idea how stupid I felt when that last lift failed. Couldn't lift a thing. Not *a thing*." The tears mutate into anger. "Always afraid a man'd take it from me, and you have." Her voice turns venomous. "No good for anything now but a suburban housewife. Is that what you want me to be, Steve? A suburban housewife?"

Despite her fury, Steve grins. "Ain't up to me what you choose. An' you ain't lost nothin', neither." He scoops up a palm-sized chunk of quartz and tosses it towards her head. "Here, catch!"

Startled, on reflex, she holds up her hands to protect her face. The rock stops in mid-air about half a metre away. Open-mouthed, she lowers her hands, looks at the rock, then looks at Steve. The rock slowly drifts to the ground.

Steve nods and smiles. "See? Told you. It ain't me. It ain't you. It's the *bender* that ain't workin'." A moment's pause, as the truth starts to sink in. "An' that ain't you, or me. It's Kim."

Relief appears on Jeni's face, followed by concern. "Oh Steve. Steve. I'm sorry. But how...?"

"She told me. Sort of. Just now. But you told me yourself why the bender stops workin'. Too fixed a view of reality, you said. Too much desirin' for what you can't have. An' what's Kim hung up on right now?"

Enlightenment dawns on Jeni's face.

Steve nods. "Yeah. Right. You got it."

"Kyle. Of course! She wants him, and she can't have him. That'd do it. About as fixed a view of reality as one can get." She turns self-critical. "I should have guessed. And I should have helped her more."

Steve grins again. "Hey, Jeni? No shoulds in this game, he said, remember? Only is or isn't, do or not do?"

Jeni at last grins in return. "Right! But Kim... Poor baby, you poor baby!" She jumps up in excitement and concern. "Come on, Steve, we've got to get back to her! Come on!"

Looking back towards Steve, she starts running towards the house. Just getting to his feet, Steve notices what's in Jeni's path: a shallow depression in the ground.

"Jeni, no!"

There's a loud crack as the ancient wooden beams of the cap give way, then Jeni disappears into the mineshaft. Steve runs to the gaping hole. "Sweet Jesus, *no!*" A brief moment at the edge. "You all right, girl? Can you hear me?"

To his surprise and relief, her voice echoes up the shaft. It's a long way down.

"I'm okay. I think. Nothing broken, anyway." A wry laugh drifts upward. "Must have slowed the self on the way down. Too busy for ownership-resistance! But I can't lift back up from here."

"Okay. I'll go get some rope. Keep yourself safe, y'hear?"

He stands up and runs down the path towards the house. Arriving at the backyard, he pulls at the rope tying the bootstrap to the trailer, coiling it as he goes. The bender's harness and helmet still rest between the seats, left there after the abortive flight-attempt at the forest track.

Remembering the last interaction with Miros, he grins at himself. "Not 'too much' rope now, huh?" He calls out, "Kim, where are you? Quick!"

Kim appears at the back door, dressed in somewhat ill-matched clothing, and noticeably less befuddled. "Hi cutie. Sorry 'bout then." She finally wakes up to Jeni's absence. "Where's Jen? She all right?"

"Fell down a shaft. Think she's okay, but we need all the rope we can get. Nearest tree's quite a ways from the hole."

Steve has most of the rope pulled from the bootstrap. But Kim is placing her still-drunken attention elsewhere.

"Oh look, we're friends again!"

"What?" Steve glances up at her, irritably.

"The bender. See, it's happy to see me."

Sure enough, the bender has started to hum, the dials showing strong sync. The 'ta-ka-te' pattern can be heard, growing stronger. The frame starts to float, weightless, bumping against the sides of the trailer. Steve throws the rope into the back of the bootstrap. "'Answer your need', all right!" he yells. "Come on, Kim, get in! Get in!"

He pushes her into the 'passenger seat', vaults over the top of the frame, clips on the bender harness, slides into the 'driver seat', and pushes the helmet down over Kim's head. He grins. "You know how to work this thing, but I'd better drive!"

She grins, then leans forward to push a couple of switches on the bender. The hum rapidly rises in pitch and volume, with the 'ta-ka-ta' pattern clearly overlaid; as soon as the flickering starts, Steve pulls upward on the right joystick, and the bootstrap leaps upward in response. "Whoah! Got it!", he calls in a mixture of exhilaration and fear.

Kim says nothing, but grips the frame with white hands, looking straight ahead, giving the bender all the attention she can scrape together.

Steve pushes gently forward on the joystick; the bootstrap moves to follow, with the 'ta-ka-te' pattern changing to a different set of syllables. As they move forward, the pattern fades away without warning; the flickering stops, the bootstrap lurches downward.

"Shit!"

On reflex, Steve, twists the joystick the other way, sending the bootstrap into a slightly different direction: the flickering resumes with a new sound-pattern. The bootstrap levels, but the sequence repeats: the sound-pattern falls off as he moves out of range, another lurch, then regaining control as he finds the sound's new direction.

Kim is near panic. "Jeez, Steve, what you *doing*?"

"Sorry! Got to follow the songline, it's the only way we can stay up."

"Bloody oath, I thought I was the one bin drinkin' here, not you!"

Steve gives a wild laugh. "'Drink, drive, bloody idiot'? Looks like we got the full house tonight, don't it?" The bootstrap continues its drunken path towards the forest.

Meanwhile, Jeni squats at the foot of the shaft, in almost the position we first saw her, as a child at school. Two side-passages are both collapsed a short way in; the damp floor is littered with small rocks, leaves and a tangle of wire and broken timber. She's covered in dust and mud, her overalls torn in a couple of places, her hair tangled, a few cuts on her face and hands. She lifts her head.

"Steve, damn you, where *are* you?"

A hum begins overhead. She looks up: there's an odd flicker in the dusk-light, at the top of the shaft, twenty or thirty metres above. Moments later, the hum fills the shaft, sending down a cascade of small pebbles. The small square of light is replaced by a harsh flickering that's hard on the eyes, revealing the underside of the bootstrap.

"Jeni? Can you hear me?"

"Yes!"

"Okay. I'm going to throw down a rope, try to pull you up. Put a knot in it to stand on. Clear?"

Jeni ducks into the shelter of one of the side-passages. "Okay!" she calls.

A moment later the rope tumbles down. It's only just long enough to reach the bottom. A large knot at the end explains Steve's ambiguous 'put a knot in it'.

"Yell when you're ready!" comes the call from above.

"Will do!"

"An' shut your eyes, an' keep 'em shut, or you'll put us all at risk!"

She climbs onto the rope, a wry grin of amusement across her face, remembering her own first instructions to Steve. With eyes shut, the reflex phrase comes out of her mouth. "Rolling!"

A moment later, she's being pulled fast up the shaft.

Far overhead, the bootstrap hovers just above ground level. Kim holds on tight in the 'passenger seat' looking straight ahead, face white as a sheet behind the faceplate. Steve looks down the shaft, one hand on the rope, feeling for Jeni's weight. The sound-pattern is clearly audible here, in a pattern like 'nu-to-wer-rong-nan-nun-ee', which seems to translate itself to describes what's going on here – 'mistake in hollow'. As Jeni's 'Rolling' call echoes up the shaft, Steve too finds himself repeating the same reflex warning.

"Rolling!"

He sits upright, puts his hand back on the joystick and lifts upward. The bootstrap leaps skyward; Jeni pops out of the shaft, jumping off the rope as soon she feels open air around her.

As she lands on the ground, rolling to slow herself down, Kim leans over the side of the bootstrap. "She's clear!" Kim calls. But she then suddenly realises where she is.

"Omigod, how did we get *this* far up? Oh *shit!*"

Instantly the bender hum cuts out, though the sound-pattern continues; the flickering stops, starts, stops again. The bootstrap is now a large metal frame with two people in it about thirty metres up, with nothing to hold it there.

With another flicker, the bootstrap disappears and reappears some five metres down and twenty metres to the side. After another flicker, the sound-pattern stops; the bootstrap stays solid, moving diagonally rather than straight down, slowing as it crashes through the branches.

It hits the ground in a shower of leaf-litter and small rocks. Steve is thrown clear, while Kim clings on as the bootstrap rolls onto its side, protected by the roll-bar. Steve jumps to his feet, runs back to the bootstrap, helps Kim climb out, then helps her lift off the bender helmet.

"Do I have to tell ya?" he says, laughing "First rule of heights: *don't look down!*"

Jeni runs up, joins in the laughter. She jumps forward to hug Steve. "You did it! You did it!"

A moment's necessary pause. Kim grins, then looks thoughtful. "So... how come we didn't fall when *you* looked down?"

"We was at ground-level then, almost. Not so hard on witness-inhibition, see? Pushin' it at thirty metres, though..."

They burst out laughing again. Jeni looks across at the helmet in Kim's hand. "See, Kim, you *can* do the lifts without me!"

"Oh." A pause. "Oh yes." Another pause, as a smile crosses her face. "Yes, I can, can't I?" A sudden firmness. "*Right!*" By the last phrase she's standing upright, looking proud.

Steve rests a hand on Kim's shoulder, with a smile to Jeni. "No ownership-resistance there, right?"

They again laugh. Steve puts his other arm round Jeni's shoulder, then stops and looks down her back. "Picked up a bit of stuff in your travels, did you?".

There's a small tangle of wire caught in a tear in Jeni's overalls. Steve pulls it out, is about to throw it towards the bootstrap when he stops and looks at it more closely.

"Uh... Jeni? You know those miners that you don't like? Looks like you've hit pay-dirt."

He holds up the tangle of wire. Caught up in the middle are three small nuggets of gold.

"A gift from the land...?" is all that Jeni can say.

There is a quiet, awe-filled pause; then Kim cuts back in. "For gawd's sake don't tell any vizzies: they'll all want to come an' have a try. Can't you just imagine it? Bootstraps bobbin' up an' down like corks, people flyin' out every which way? Wouldn't get a moment's peace..."

More laughter. Steve waves at the bootstrap. "C'mon, we'll sort this out in the mornin'. Get back 'ome. An' can we stick to the path this time?"

More laughter. They move down the forest path, arm in arm. Time to relax at last.

"Uh... Reckon there's still a bit more to do on it, Jen." says Steve. "Witness-inhibition ain't quite nailed yet..."

Kim cuts in, "An' don' even *ask* 'bout the way it moves. Talk about drunk-drivin'..."

They laugh. Jeni hugs Steve tighter, resting her head against his shoulder. "Getting close, though. It works. You've proved that. Lifting us by the bootstraps..."

They head down towards the house as the dusk-light fades.

Cargo bootstrap

At first sight, over the tarmac of a general-aviation field, it seems to be the slightly squared-off nose of a medium helicopter. Two people stand beside a standard cargo tractor/trailer, loading parcels into the body of the craft. One is a medical orderly, in blue flight-overalls with a red cross on a shoulder-patch; the other is dressed in shorts, short-sleeved shirt and fluoro jacket, with ear-protectors pushed back over his cap. The only sounds are their breathing and movement, the thump of parcels in the loading bay, and a faint background hum.

A few sleek-looking aircraft are some distance away, mostly light-cargo types. Standing beside a minibus, at the edge of the field, are a group of people who, at a guess, would be engineers or engineering management. One of them seems foreign; indeed, his brash American accent can be identified even at this distance.

The loaders finish; the one in shorts jumps onto the seat of the tractor and drives off with a wave, whilst the orderly closes and latches the door to the cargo bay. He opens the side-door and climbs in. As he does so, we can see there seem to be no rotors, no tail: the 'aircraft' is best described as a slightly streamlined brick on skids.

"All done", he says to the pilot within. "Let's go."

She nods agreement. Like the orderly, she's dressed in overalls and flight-cap, and with flight-style sunglasses and headset. This 'aircraft', it seems, is a much more sophisticated version of Steve's bootstrap. The head-rests have side-cushions to protect against the 'drunkard' flight-path; the bender unit is much the same, but its joysticks are now mounted on the seat-arms, the helmet faceplate replaced by a head-up display on the windshield. Some of the symbols are as on Jeni's display, but also a complex map of wiggly lines with aboriginal and Anglo placenames. The pilot speaks into her mike.

"Moorabbin Tower, this is Bootstrap niner-one, medicals on course for Corryong via Omeo."

"Niner-one, you are cleared for take-off."

"Niner-one. Thank you, Tower. Rolling."

The bender hum rises in pitch and volume, the 'ta-ka-te' pattern also clearly audible. The view forward flickers, indicating a smooth move upward by about thirty metres. The sound-pattern changes to a complex sequence of Songline-type syllables as the view through the screen becomes hyper-real, moving forward, fast, in an odd slightly zigzag path.

Belonging

A clear, calm gentle, sunlit morning, some days after the rescue. Steve leans against the doorway of the miner's cottage, whilst Jeni stands beside the open front passenger door of the Wirinun's ute, with the Wirinun in the driver's seat, and Kim and another man in the back, her hand on his knee. The somewhat battered frame of the bootstrap is visible beyond the car.

"Sure you won't come, love?" she asks.

Steve shakes his head. "Best I stay here. Not up to crowds. An' better finish that note to me Mum."

"Okay. We'll think of you with us. See you tonight." She turns to the Wirinun. "Still time for the train?" She gets in and closes the door. As they drive off, both she and Kim wave.

"See ya, cutie!"

Steve shakes his head in wry amusement. He walks out into the driveway to wave, then wanders over to the bootstrap. He rubs the surface of the frame, again with a wry grin.

"Not quite the magic carpet, are you? But close. Brought me to the land of Oz, anyway." He sighs. "Won't be takin' me back, though. They wouldn't know what to do with you there."

A quiet, slightly sad laugh. He walks back to the verandah, sits back in a wicker seat, stretches his legs out for a moment. On the edge of the forest a kangaroo sits, looking at him. There's a brief shift to the hyper-real, telescopic view towards the 'roo, with the 'ta-ka-te' static songline pattern coming through; then reverts to the view around him, with just birdsong and a cow lowing in the distance.

He leans over the table beside him, picks up a pen and finishes the text on a letter-pad.

'I'm staying here, mum. I belong here...'

No idea who he was

telelink::fax-class="letter"
telelink::fax-addressto: Mum
14th June
Taradale

Hi Mum

You're not going to like this, so I may as well keep it short and get it over with straight away.

I'm staying here, Mum. I belong here. That's what I've really been finding out in the past couple of months: I belong here. The crew have sponsored me for full citizenship, because that's what I've decided to go for. I'm sorry, I know you won't like it, but it's what I need to do for me, and I just hope that it's going to be okay for you too.

It's not as if I'm going to be stuck here for ever, after all, is it? Depending on what happens here, I should be over for a while in a couple of months anyway. See you soon, okay?

I'm on my own at home today: gives me some time to think, which is really what I need to do most at the moment. There's nothing to do in town anyway: everyone's gone to Melbourne. It sounds like half of Australia's there today, for the funeral of some bloke they called 'the Don'. I've no idea who he was.

Bye for now, Mum. I'll write again soon.

Steve

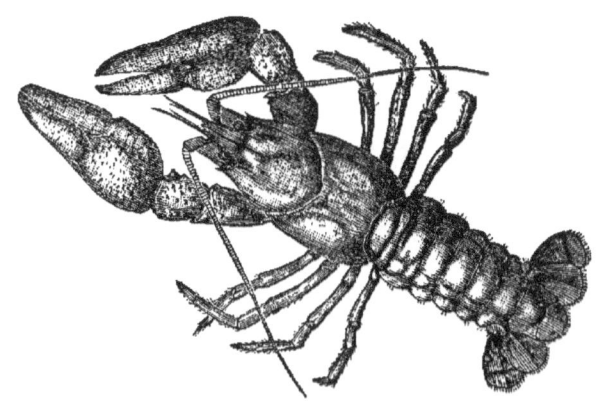

Background

It's perhaps unusual to add a commentary to a novel, yet it does seem valid here to provide some kind of background explanation.

The *Yabbies* project was born way back in late 1998 or thereabouts, and has come out in a number of different forms since then: first as an interactive website, then as a screenplay, a standalone draft novel with explanatory notes between each text-item, and finally here as a fairly conventional novel. In each case, its core structure has always been much the same, as 'story-fragments' that come together in seemingly-random form:

> Bits and pieces drift down, in any old order, all out of sequence. An' we have to make sense of them as best we can.

So although, by its nature, a book forces the fragments into a fixed order, you should be able to dip in at random, change the thread, to perhaps give a different sense or flavour to the overall story. My own view of what 'really happened' in the context of the story is in the Timeline that follows this chapter – though in reality any other timeline could be just as valid. Note, too, that at times this sequence of fragments is deliberately *not* in chronological order – just to reinforce that sense of uncertainty about the way in which time and stories interweave through each other and themselves.

Why 'Yabbies'?

In the real world, a yabby is a crayfish, a crustacean of the species *cherax destructor*, a bit like a small freshwater lobster. Common throughout much of rural Australia, they're often to be found burrowing into the walls of farm dams – hence the 'destructor' part of the species-name. They've also been an important food-source for the indigenous population since time immemorial.

I'll have to admit, though, that the link between this story and the yabby itself is fairly tenuous, because the real starting-point was the acronym YABI – 'Yet Another Book Idea'. This arose from two separate themes. One theme came in re-reading Ursula le Guin's masterful sci-fi classic *The Dispossessed*; which explores ideas and implications of a society based on true anarchist principles, and compares it with a thinly-disguised analogue of the then-current

(1970s) US society and economics. The other theme was that, whilst reading about permaculture, I had a sudden realisation that we cannot achieve sustainability without a system of law that supports it – which doesn't exist at present. Yet how could we get from here to there? What could we use as a roadmap? Le Guin's *The Dispossessed* seemed a very good place to start.

The catch, for me, was that le Guin takes a few rather important short-cuts. In particular, she places the two societies on related yet separate worlds; and the core driver for her story is that, for the first time since the societies separated, one of the people from the anarchist culture chooses to return to the homeworld, as a visiting scientist. These short-cuts do help to make her story stronger, to emphasise the contrasts, the clashes in worldview. Yet they also tend to distance the story from our own experience, in which everything and everyone must coexist somehow on the same crowded planet. So instead of le Guin's separate worlds, what if there were no boundaries? How would an anarchistic, sustainable society protect itself from predatory possessionist cultures? How could it deal with visitors – with tourists, even? That was probably where this story really started.

Why Australia?

For a number of practical reasons, I chose to place the main part of the story in Australia. I was living there at the time, and it is of course a lot easier to build a story around a place that's known. But there were other reasons too, that helped that choice to make more sense:

- Australia is a single nation on an 'island continent': it shares no land-border with any other country – which makes it easier to create and maintain a radically different social structure from other countries.
- Australia has a strong tradition of a 'fair go' – fair treatment of everyone, regardless of class, religion or (at least post-Second World War) ethnic background or race.
- Australia has a strong tendency to radical or egalitarian movements, particularly since the gold-rush period and the Eureka Stockade (1854).
- Australia is a strange amalgam of cultures, where West meets East and – in the cities especially – where almost every ethnic group is represented.

214

- Modern (i.e. European) Australia was based on the theft of an entire country – the dishonest claim that the land was 'owned by no-one' – and "began as a dumping-ground for criminals", as the historian Robert Hughes put it: "we had nowhere to go but up, and we've been going up ever since!"

However, it's a historical reality that the governments of the self-styled 'Lucky Country' have repeated almost every mistake made elsewhere, but usually ten or so years later – hence much of the 'luck' was simply that other people had had to work out how to recover from those mistakes, so that Australia could recover more quickly. We might also note Karl Marx's purported statement that the two countries he thought least likely to embrace communism were Russia and India – two countries that in fact *most* embraced his theories. So I make no real assumptions there: if the *Yabbies* scenario were ever to eventuate in real life, it could indeed happen in Australia – but it could just as well happen somewhere else.

Sustainable law

'Sustainable law' would be a system of law that actively supports a sustainable economy. The story's fictional character Dr Don Mercer, fairly early on in his 3QJ radio-interview, describes the background as follows:

> The original idea for the sustainable law project came from permaculture. [It] aims to interweave the needs of people with the needs of the environment, so that all needs are met in a sustainable way – hence permaculture, permanent agriculture. But it can't really be sustainable, at the level of the whole society, unless there's a system of law that fully supports it – which is where the idea of sustainable law comes in.

Present statute law is not sustainable. It is primarily designed to attempt to control the inherent chaos created by the possession property-model – and for the most part succeeds only in making the chaos worse for (almost) everyone. It suffers from all the problems of the money-based economic model: in particular, it fails to recognise the futility of trying to define absolute controls for inherent uncertainties. And it evades many fundamental problems – such as many international environmental issues – either by ignoring them, or abandoning them into the 'too-hard' basket. And it is far, far too complex: the formal statement that 'ignorance is no defence within the law' no longer makes any practical sense, given that in Australia, for example, tax law alone, *each year*, runs to many new volumes of impenetrable 'legalese'. Even full-time professionals can't keep up with the flood of new laws and regulations, let alone we ordinary mortals...

By contrast, the common-law mostly *is* sustainable – particularly that which deals with interpersonal issues rather than property-based ones. And there seems to be a significant difference in the wisdom available from judges and magistrates – who implement the meaning of law – rather than that from the random contortions of lawyers and the legislature – who, all too often, seem more concerned with arbitrary advantage than anything else...

The core of sustainability – as is also illustrated well in most common-law – is a clear awareness of mutual responsibilities that interweave in complex yet often unpredictable ways. Hence the key change described here is a shift in emphasis from rights to responsibilities – for example, from supposed *rights* of exclusive-possession to the *responsibilities* of stewardship.

Sustainable law places its emphasis not on individual 'rights' – as at present – but on *mutual* responsibilities. The core of the law would not be a Bill of Rights, but a Charter of Responsibilities. This does *not* mean that individuals would have no rights as such. Instead, as in current British traffic law, individual rights arise implicitly, yet directly, from defined mutual responsibilities. Any 'declaration of rights' *over* others is seen as arbitrary, and (as an *a priori* assertion) is usually indefensible in legal terms. By contrast, a reasoned case *must* be provided for any assertion of asymmetry in responsibilities – especially where a responsibility is assigned only to others – and is thus, once accepted, far easier to sustain and maintain. This also ensures that *no-one* gains arbitrary 'rights' which provides them with automatic priority over all others – an endemic problem arising from much current law.

Another key reason for this emphasis is that whilst individual rights do arise directly from mutual responsibilities, personal responsibilities are often absent from most definitions of personal rights. If mentioned at all, the responsibilities needed to achieve those rights are assigned implicitly to others, but *not* to self – hence the all-too-common notion that "*I* have rights, *you* have responsibilities". In practice, a declared 'Bill of Rights' tends to reinforce a toddler-age self-centredness – crippling the entire culture in childish fights about personal priority and privilege.

By instead shifting the emphasis from 'rights' to responsibilities, sustainable law shifts the basis of property away from arbitrary

216

'rights' of possession, and towards the explicit responsibilities of stewardship. This includes not just property-holding, but also full responsibility for property-disposal – the 'anti-property' of waste, pollution, environmental damage, exploitation and injustice for which no-one, under present law, either wants or needs to accept responsibility. This does not mean that individuals become personally responsible for carrying out all property-disposal as such, but that they *are* responsible that it is done appropriately – and also to minimise the need for property-disposal, by reducing waste and (unlike the 'consumer society!) unneeded acquisitions.

Arbitrary and wasteful exploitation of any kind becomes illegal *because* it is irresponsible: yet it is *everyone's* responsibility – not that of some arbitrarily blamed 'Other' – to reduce and minimise waste. Because the responsibilities are placed on everyone, in all circumstances and contexts, the effective rights do remain very similar to those of the present – without promoting the dangerous self-centredness implied in the current concept of 'rights'

A side-effect is that most sustainable law can be reduced to a clear set of legal principles and guidelines that can be far less complex than present statute law. This is paralleled by an awareness that so-called 'morals' are little more than a lazy-person's avoidance of ethics. Instead of hiding behind the smokeshield of 'rights', the onus is placed on everyone to show how the respective actions (and inactions) support those principles of mutual responsibility – and what to do when they don't.

Property and money

A core theme of the story here explores and contrasts the implied outcomes of two different property-models:

- *possession* – the explicit right to exploit a resource without reference to others either in the present or elsewhen, and to exclude others from access to that resource;
- *stewardship* – acceptance of the responsibility to appropriately manage a resource in the context of others in the present and elsewhen, and thus the implicit right to exploit that resource as an expression of that responsibility to self and others.

At present, the possession-based model is the norm in 'western' macro-economies: it is the key concept that underlies all 'western' property-law, including finance and 'economics'.

At present, the stewardship model is the *internal* norm in many if not most micro-economies in 'western' economies – such as with family, charity, support-group, immediate friends and colleagues, and also *within* most businesses – and on a larger scale in many if not most 'traditional' economies (though a possession-based model is often used *between* unrelated groups).

A huge practical problem we face is that the possession-model gives 'better' results in the short-term, yet is invariably disastrous in the longer-term. It usually *seems* more efficient at a local scale, but the reality is that it is usually very ineffective at a global scale – "forests precede civilisations, and deserts follow them", to quote the 18th-century French writer Chateaubriand. The key word here is *'seems'*: in essence, a possession-economy actually 'works' only by stealing from the future, and/or from others in the present or past. Its inherent logic of 'winner-steals-all' can only be run as a pyramid-game: when there's no more that can be brought in at the bottom of the pyramid, the structure is forced to cannibalise on itself, eventually to oblivion. Many of the environmental and other indicators imply that we're dangerously close to that tipping-point right now, at a truly global scale.

A return to barter is not a viable solution to the problems of the possession-economy; and the same applies to *every* would-be 'alternative currency' model that I've seen to date. The concept of barter depends on exclusion – withholding – and thus exists only under a possession-based model. Money, as a mutually-agreed standardised intermediate token for barter, likewise only exists in the special case of a possession-based property-model. It does not exist, and is not used, within a true stewardship model.

In the *Yabbies* context, the removal of money from the economy – the 'no-money' economy described in the story – is actually an inherent side-effect of the change to a stewardship property-model. For outsiders, living in a society with a possession-based property-model (i.e. the model which is 'normal' in our current society), it's all too easy to make the mistake of thinking that because there's no money, everything is 'free' – which is definitely *not* the case! For insiders, the real 'currency' is respect: the economy essentially operates on self-responsibility and mutual respect – neither of which appear to be deemed necessary (in the short-term, at least) in a possession-based economy.

A problem of power

The current politics, economics, social mores and concept of ownership in 'western' societies can best be described as based on the self-centred psychology of a toddler's possessive temper-tantrum. A key theme of the story is to explore the possibilities that would become available if we support a social psychology in which the society as a whole can grow beyond that childish state.

To make sense of those power-issues in social context, I've found it useful to build outward from a set of flat definitions, which you'll see applied in practice throughout the story:

- *Power* is the ability to do work, as an expression of personal choice – where 'work' can take any form, at any level, and needs to be understood as a synonym of both 'play' and 'learn', and also 'relate' with others and with self.

- *Responsibility* is 'response-ability', the ability to choose responses appropriate to the context. It is essential to understand that responsibility is *not* a synonym for blame, which itself is actually an act of violence and/or abuse.

- *Violence* is any attempt, in any form and at any level, to create the illusion of empowering the self by disempowering any other – in other words, any attempt to prop oneself up by putting others down is an act of violence. Trashing the environment or kicking the cat is just as much an act of violence as physical assault.

- *Abuse* is any attempt to offload responsibility onto another, or to take responsibility from any other, without their express involvement and consent.

The *only* ultimate source of power is from within the self. Each person can, however, assist others in creating that power. Power is created by individual responsibility. Violence and abuse create the *illusion* of power, but in fact reduce the overall amount of power available. The key distinction between violence and abuse is that the aim of the former is to leave the Other without apparent power; the aim of the latter is to co-opt the Other's power.

Violence and power are mutually exclusive; it is not possible to be both violent (or abusive) and powerful at the same time – and the delusion that it *is* possible is a key source (arguably *the* key source) of dysfunction in our society.

Transition

"The whole system is so fragile that, quite honestly, there is a real risk that it could collapse at any time, in a really big way. We already know that it tends to break down anyway, quite often – such as in the Depression years of the 1890s and 1920s, or the computer-driven stock-market crash of 1989 – but what we're seeing is that those problems are inherent in the system, so to speak, and that the whole thing is held together by little more than wishful thinking."

So says the character Don Mercer, in his interview with Radio 3QJ in an early part of the story's timeline. It's factually true that "there is a real risk that it could collapse at any time, in a really big way". But it's perhaps the last comment there that is the most disconcerting: "the whole thing is held together by little more than wishful thinking".

It's all the interlinks and cross-dependencies in the current overall system that make it so fragile: for example, a factory that depends on 'just-in-time' inventory-management will be unable to produce anything if there are any transport problems at all. The systematic removal of the backups and redundancies as part of so-called 'economic rationalism' has increased the fragility to the point where there are often no alternatives in case of failure. At present, the overall system can probably withstand a single failure in any single key sub-system; but with simultaneous multiple failures, catastrophic collapse becomes increasingly likely.

The 3QJ interview refers to a real incident of this type in Victoria, Australia, with disastrous impacts on the state's energy-supplies, threatening the viability of the state as a whole. The Japanese earthquake of March 2011 is another example: a huge earthquake, which then triggered an almost unprecedented tsunami, which in turn caused lethal damage to a poorly-managed and decidedly risk-prone nuclear power station. On a world scale, much the same applies: for the most part, the system is still robust enough to withstand one major failure at a time, but not multiple failures at the same time. And Murphy's Law is the only law in town...

For the purposes of the story, I chose three fairly arbitrary examples of global-scale failures, as described in the Cabinet-meeting transcript.

The first is a feedback-loop in algorithmic trading-bots, similar to the 1989 stock-market crash. Some people never learn from past mistakes – especially if it seems there's a quick profit to be made...

The second is a computer-virus that targets internet routers, conceptually similar to the Stuxnet worm that was used to target the Iranian nuclear programme. There's always some fool who fails to think about the risks of unintended consequences...

The third example, though – the impact of the 'flare' – might take a little more explanation. For this I imagined a new processor-technology called the 'Zell effect', which can pack far higher density onto each chip – obviously desirable in many ways. But the take-up of the new technology is so fast that it already dominates the market before a fatal flaw is identified: it's at risk from certain types of cosmic radiation associated with the peak of the sun's thirteen-year sunspot cycle. For commercial reasons – such as happened in the real-life case of the Ford Pinto car – the risk is first concealed, then conveniently forgotten. In the story, an unusually strong flare with a huge coronal mass ejection would destroy or damage most new technology dependent on the chip-design; the flare in turn pushes the Earth's magnetic field into an unstable state, flicking the magnetic poles rapidly between North and South, in effect acting as a bulk-eraser on any unshielded magnetic-based records. (The science is still out on whether that would actually happen – some scientists argue for a slower, more sedate reversal – but the core concept is scientifically sound.)

Even on its own, each of these impacts would be disastrous. If all three impacts were occur together, as in the story, it's clear that the results would indeed be catastrophic.

Given that events like these are real possibilities, it seems wise to at least *consider* some alternatives to the lethally fragile systems we have now... and explore how to reduce the overall risk, and how to recover from them if – or *when* – the risks eventuate.

A little bit of magic

For many people, one of the more difficult parts of the original *Yabbies* project was the inclusion of references to a variety of so-called 'intuitive technologies' – the application, *as technologies*, of various controversial phenomena such as dowsing, psychokinesis, telepathy and alchemy. It's probably true that, to quote Arthur C Clarke, "any sufficiently advanced technology is indistinguishable from magic". Yet somehow very few people seem to realise that the inverse is equally true: "any sufficiently advanced magic is indistinguishable from technology". An interesting point...

There are several reasons why I've included these 'intuitive-technologies' in the story. One is that, to me, they're part of my own everyday reality: I've been around those fields for several decades now, and have seen enough first-hand to know that there's *something* going on that may not make sense in terms of the everyday, yet still *does* seem to exist. I've taught dowsers (water-diviners) for many years now: it's long been my standard test-bed for research on how people learn the awareness and judgement aspects of *any* type of skill. I have a close friend in Australia who is a real alchemist, creating compounds with the same chemical formulae as in standard chemistry, but with radically different chemical properties. I've even seen a real example of intentional psychokinesis, by a young woman – one of my design-students, at the time – on whom I based the character Jeni Silver. (Sadly, her real-life fate was similar to that of the character Andy to whom she briefly refers in the story-fragment 'Lifter-crew'...) Sure, the whole subject-area is often drowning in a morass of wishful-thinking and self-delusion: yet unlike many self-styled 'skeptics', I do have enough experience to have some sense of what is real and what is not. (Most of the time, anyway...) And beyond all those newage inanities, there *is* something real, concrete, practical, the solid glimmerings of a tangible technology – even if, as I would freely admit, usually far from 'everyday' as yet.

Many people would no doubt prefer to dump all such things into the random grab-bag of 'the supernatural', as a source either for uncritical hype or equally-uncritical 'skepticism'. Yet in either case, it kind of misses the point. In each of the examples I'd used in *Yabbies*, current physics does actually allow for their existence: for example, the previously 'supernatural' concept of action-at-a-distance has now long been proven, at least at a quantum level, and arguably beyond. Note too that most technologies consist of taking something that is highly improbable in the natural world – a gas-explosion, for example – and providing conditions under which it becomes highly probable – such as the gas-explosions inside a car-engine. Hence these somewhat-imagined 'intuitive technologies' are perhaps not quite so bizarre as they might seem. Somewhere between science-fantasy and science-fiction, perhaps: but a lot could happen in technology in the fifty-year span of this story, as we know well within our own real world of today.

Yet what I really wanted to explore here is the way in which science itself becomes a kind of 'exclusive possession' – the notion that there is only one truth, and that no other truth is possible. I'll admit that I'm anarchist enough to want to shake people out of their comfort zone a bit, to get them into a stronger habit of challenging assumptions. And if the anarchistic philosopher of science Paul Feyerabend is right, that "the only approach which does not inhibit progress ... is 'anything goes'", then anything that purports to be 'the truth' has to be considered suspect, a vain yet ultimately arbitrary 'exclusive possession'. Or perhaps, to quote Feyerabend again, "'anything goes' is not a 'principle' I hold... but the terrified exclamation of a rationalist who takes a closer look at history". Letting go of possession of 'truth' is perhaps just as important as letting go of the delusions of possession of 'things'.

Whilst working on this edition, it became clear that I was actually dealing with at least two very different themes: the 'big-picture' focus on politics and economics, and large-scale social change over long periods of time; and the more intimate or personal side of those stories, around each person's experience of those clashes of worldview, to which that clash between the 'scientific' and magical' paradigms would add yet another useful counterpoint.

Yet each of these themes appeals to rather different audiences: as I've discovered to my cost, there aren't that many people who would comfortably straddle both worlds. So at one point I did try to split the story into two separate parts, to focus on only one of those audiences at a time. But it actually didn't work *as* a story in that form: one side become a disjointed set of fragments, and the other a simple narrative-story without any real depth. It was only when I brought the two parts together again that it started to make sense, with the political and conceptual ideas brought to life through the social context of the Troubles and of Steve's more personal journey. To me, the 'magical' themes add another layer to all of that, weaving the story as a cross-current, a counterpoint that brings up deeper questions about reality and our role within it. But if such things do annoy you beyond what you're willing to bear, it's perhaps simplest just to ignore them: they're not actually essential to the story as such. Add some other theme of your own instead, perhaps, and see where it will take you?

Yes, it's real

How much of this is real? After all, it's all fiction, isn't it? These are questions I see quite often in relation to *Yabbies*.

The short answer is, yes, the text is fiction, and the characters are fictional, too. But the issues the project addresses are not fiction at all: they're painfully real. All of the references are real as well: for example, that's the real content of the Emergency Management Act of one of the Australian states; the story-fragment on Weikart and 'Plan, Do, Review' describes what really happened; likewise the reference to the magazine 'Women & Guns'. The drink-driving poster and the 18th-century broadsheet are exactly as originally published. The references to aboriginal culture and relationship with landscape are based on formal research, whilst the terms that Steve interprets as sound-patterns are derived from an aboriginal dictionary. And all the references on 'intuitive technologies' are real, too: Kenneth Batcheldor, Julian Isaacs, Rupert Sheldrake and F David Peat are all real researchers who've published proven work in the respective contexts. Don's thesis doesn't exist, as far as I know, but otherwise just about everything that purports to be in the present or past is derived directly from real material.

Any references to the future are fictional, of course. Yet they're likewise based on a lot of careful study – the kind of assessments I do in my 'day job' as a futurist. I'll admit that, yes, they're somewhat caricatured, to emphasise the point: Tony Morrison's tendency to drop into the most appalling clichés – and somehow get away with it – is one of the more egregious examples. But there've been plenty of colleagues in Australia, for example, who regarded the depiction of the Topolski affair as too *mild* rather than too extreme.

Perhaps the most unfair portrait is that of the US under the control of 'Moral America': but the blunt reality is that it could indeed happen that way, because all the seeds for a literally 'unholy alliance' between corporatism and religious fundamentalism can be seen all too clearly in present-day US politics. The fatally-flawed logic of the Bill of Rights does point directly to an *Animal Farm*-type society in which "all humans have equal rights, but some are more equal than others". And if not the US, then some other country: the 'winner-steals-all' logic of possession in a social context leads directly to a stratified society in which some people become treated as the possessed 'human resources' of others.

(In many ways the old slave-based economies from two or three centuries ago have continued on, almost unchanged: the only difference is that much of the work of the former slaves is now done by machines – which depend on prodigious amounts of energy, from energy sources that are fast running out. When those energy-sources do indeed become scarce, expect to see the return of a true slave-economics again, though probably in disguised form at first – as in the use of literally captive prison-labour.)

The responses of the various characters to the transition, and other contexts in which they find themselves, were all straightforward enough: I built up a picture of each person, put myself in their shoes, and wrote down whatever seemed to come up for them in

224

the respective context. For those, it's not about analysis, but about *feeling*: and the feeling itself has its own logic that drives that person's decisions and experience. Very real, in its own way – even if 'only' fiction.

As for the 'Yabbies scenario' itself – the SusLaw framework – could that ever work? My short answer is, yes, I do think it would. Don Mercer's summary in his Radio 3QJ interview puts it well:

> It would be hard, for a while, but after that I honestly believe that no-one would want to go back to what we have now. The present system is so ridiculously inefficient, in every way. It would be much more effective – and, I honestly believe, much more satisfying, for everyone – to belong to a literal 'commonwealth', in which resources are owned simply in terms of use, and are used as needed. And yes, as far as law is concerned, it really is as simple as I've said: for example, we really could replace every single monetary transaction with the simple phrase "What do you need?"

Some people have said that "this goes against human nature" or some such: yet whilst myopically stupid self-centredness is indeed all too human, altruism and sharing are just as much part of 'human nature' too. And the reality is that we get the behaviour that we reward: so given that our current 'economics' actively rewards selfishness and actively punishes almost every form of responsibility, it's hardly surprising that we get what we currently get. If instead we were to provide conditions that could support responsibility, rather than punish it, does it not seem probable that we might see better results than at present?

There's far, far more that would need to be worked out, of course, and many of the true complexities and problems would only surface once it's up and running – there's no way to know beforehand. Yet as a colleague puts it, "the devil is in the details, but the angel is in the architecture" – and there *is* enough of an architecture here on which we could indeed get started.

At the very least, food for thought, I hope? Over to you…

Yabbies timeline

The following is my own view of how the story-fragments could fit together in time as a storyline, spread over a span of some fifty years or more.

Story-fragments that apply to each point in the timeline are listed in *italics* after the respective timeline-description. Some story-fragments appear more than once: if shown with an asterisk *, this indicates alignment with a concept or key previous event, rather than the action in the timeline. Any story-fragments not explicitly listed – including all of Steve's journey, and most of Jeni's story – occur almost at the end of the timeline, in the months immediately prior to the aged Don Mercer's eventual demise.

Your own view may vary, of course: make up your own storyline, perhaps?

Before the present time

About fifteen years ago

Postgraduate law-student *Don Mercer* becomes interested in Australian Aboriginal law and other indigenous legal systems – particularly the way in which their responsibility-based model of property allows for a much simpler and more stable system of law than current 'western' law – and bases his doctoral thesis on the idea of adapting their principles to present-day circumstances and technologies. After his doctorate he takes up a teaching post in the Law faculty at Derwent University, in suburban Melbourne; somewhen around this time he marries Mary Mullard, a lecturer in textiles in the University's Arts faculty.

  • *Don's thesis*

About ten years ago

Don Mercer develops the 'Sustainable Law Project' as a unit within his 'Theory of Law' course at Derwent University. The future politician Tony Morrison is one of many law-students over the years who become involved in and excited by the project.

  • *Don Mercer and Tony Morrison*

- *Don't drink and drive*

In several 'western' countries, 'emergency powers' legislation is quietly passed, under which absolute political and judicial power in a region, a state or an entire country may be assigned to a small unelected committee, or even an individual. The Australian version of this legislation is the Federal Emergency Management Act; it includes provisions for the army to be used as an armed extension of the police force, under the control and jurisdiction of individual police officers.

- *Emergency Management Act*

Meanwhile, US gun-makers – struggling to make up for reduced military sales after the fading of the Cold War – push to create a new domestic market, selling guns to women rather than men. Advertising themes such as "a woman's best friend is the pistol in her purse" bring big new sales, and big profits. Industry-funded *Women and Guns* becomes one of the top-selling magazines; Smith & Wesson even promotes its 'Ladysmith' handgun as a fashion accessory, with interchangeable colour-coordinated grips. Handgun deaths continue to rise, with gun owners or their immediate families as the most common victims.

- *Women and guns*

The public Internet, previously restricted to academic and non-profit use only, is opened for commercial use. Lawsuits fly as corporations claim ownership of individual words, as trade-marks and domain-names. Language becomes classed as 'intellectual property': in Australia, one company even manages to trademark the word 'Yes'.

About five years ago

Based on more than thirty years of practical work with thousands of people, social worker David Weikart, from Detroit in Michigan, demonstrates that the most cost-effective way of preventing crime is to provide adequate pre-school facilities in disadvantaged areas, with a focus on developing thinking skills at the earliest possible age. Other evidence shows the enormous cost of reducing crime by putting people in prison: increasing the prison population by 25 percent can reduce crime by 1 percent or less. Weikart's proven results are ignored; his funds are withdrawn in favour of an increased prison-building program, constructing two new prisons each year in Michigan state alone.

- *A quiet crusader*

Don Mercer's wife Mary is killed in a car-accident.

• *Don alone*

Pre-transition

About the present time

Partly to give himself something to focus on after Mary Mullard's sudden death, Mercer organises the first international 'SusLaw' conference at Derwent University, bringing together legal experts and traditional elders from many different cultures. Mercer is startled to discover that his 'academic exercise' is being taken seriously by many people outside the legal profession – especially as the fragility of the infrastructure on which the current society depends is illustrated during the conference, as Melbourne struggles with the aftermath of an accidental explosion at a gas-plant, cutting off most of the state's gas-supply, and only just averts a similar breakdown in the state's electricity-supply.

• *Home Matters*

• *Mercer's law*

In Australia and elsewhere, the gap between rich and poor is rising fast, causing increasing breakdown of the legal systems set up to protect it. In the USA, the prison population passes the two million mark; in many poorer black and Hispanic districts, a jail sentence becomes almost a 'rite of passage', marking the transition into adulthood. In Africa, Asia and the Pacific island-clusters, rampant corruption and 'warlordism' – often blatantly supported by multinational corporations – increasingly leads to regular rioting and near-civil-war conditions.

• *The greater villain**

House prices in 'developed' countries so far exceed viable incomes that increasing numbers of single-income couples with children become unable to earn sufficient to cover mortgage payments. In Japan, 100-year mortgages become the norm.

The conference of the World Trade Organisation, representing the world's one thousand largest multinational corporations, formally asserts that a refusal by any state to permit the farming or import of genetically-modified crops represents a breach of international trade agreements, and should be resisted by punitive tariffs – in effect, declaring that the interests and concerns of multinational corporations must have priority over national or environmental concerns. Despite strong protests by environmentalists, small-farmers' groups, and others, most governments accede to these demands.

About three years from the present

A shareholder analysis by the Australian Stock Exchange shows that more than half of all national assets are owned or controlled by overseas corporations; long-term comparisons show that this is an accelerating trend, and is likely to reach eighty percent within five years.

- *Due-diligence**

About five years from the present

The WTO annual conference demands that minimum wage agreements must be deemed illegal worldwide, since they can be considered to interfere with global competition. A non-violent if noisy protest outside the conference venue by environmentalists and workers' organisations ends in a massacre, as police open fire with machine-guns into the crowd. Subsequently, a conference spokesman applauds the police action, arguing that the protestors were illegally interfering with the rights of world trade, and had thus forfeited all legal rights of their own.

The regular 'SusLaw' conference at Derwent University is now called the 'Sustainability' conference, as it covers a much wider scope, studying synergies between technology, sociology, agriculture and law, and also concepts from traditional societies, in particular the relationship between people and place. Mercer himself initially objects to the inclusion of a session on 'intuitive technologies'; he relents, if with some qualms, when a colleague shows him the extent of the formal research supporting traditional magical beliefs.

- *Intuitive-technologies*
- *Lines in the landscape**
- *The deep-stories**
- *Belonging**
- *Lifter crew**
- *Witness-inhibition**

About eight years from the present

In the US, a new administration closes down the entire welfare system, on the reasoning that since crime rates are highest in areas with the highest rates of welfare payments, cutting off welfare should therefore reduce crime. Major rioting occurs in most large US cities; as the administration vacillates, citizen vigilante groups are formed to protect property. Legislation is hurriedly passed to permit these groups to operate a 'shoot on sight' policy, with full immunity in the courts; many of the vigilante groups join together under the shared banner of 'Moral America'.

Four hundred employees at a US agro-chemical research facility are killed by poison-gas, spread through the air-conditioning system. Terrorists or environmental extremists are blamed; in a scathing attack on what it calls the 'inadequacies' of national police forces, the WTO demands the right for its members to operate their own permanently-armed security forces, and to carry out pre-emptive operations across national borders against 'these enemies of world trade'. Even within Europe, environmental organisations are forced to go 'underground', as Britain, Germany and France quickly follow the US lead in acceding to this; in several 'Third World' countries union activists are rounded up and publicly shot whilst police stand and watch. Australia is one of the few states to refuse to condone this, and is ostracised by the WTO – even though an enquiry confirms that the original poison-gas deaths were not the result of a deliberate attack, but caused by poor maintenance at the plant and an unsupervised experiment that went badly wrong.

In Australia, climate-change brings on the worst bushfire season in living memory. The 'Black Monday' fires rage across large areas in several states: whole towns are razed to the ground, with an overall death-toll of more than a thousand people, and tens of thousands made homeless. The national Emergency Management Commission is convened to manage the recovery, with Don Mercer as chair.

• *Transition – Cabinet transcript**

Transition

Four months prior to transition

In Australia, two weeks before national elections, a telecomms technician carrying out a routine line-check accidentally records a conference call between the federal police minister, the opposition deputy leader, and senior police from Victoria, Queensland and New South Wales, all arguing about their personal shares of the 'take' from selling-on a container-load of marijuana, captured in a

230

much-publicised drugs raid and supposedly already burned. Horrified, he notifies his supervisor, handing over the tape; that evening, on his way home from work, the technician is killed in what at first appears to be a random 'road-rage' shooting – except that a freeway security camera shows that the shots come from an unmarked police-car, with an identifiable senior police officer firing the fatal shot. An hour later, anonymous copies of the camera tape and the original telecomms tape reach the news-studios – and go out to air immediately, with explosive results. An urgent national enquiry is ordered – the Bannock Commission. As the days go by, more and more evidence appears of a culture of endemic corruption at every level of police and government; the old sarcastic comment that "the only organised crime in this country is run by the police" suddenly ceases to be a joke.

- *Prelude to disaster*
- *Topolskigate*
- *Police**

With several government ministers and opposition figures clearly implicated in the scandal, the run-up to the election descends into chaos. At the end, the old party-system is all but destroyed: almost all members of parliament describe themselves as 'independent'. After an election within parliament itself, Tony Morrison takes over as Prime Minister.

- *Going independent*
- *After the election*

The moment of transition

In a matter of hours, and seemingly without warning, the world economic system spirals into total collapse. Paper values of multinational businesses and their national suppliers plummet to near-zero; in Australia, as elsewhere, the finance markets, the banks and the Stock Exchange are forced to close immediately, plunging the entire economy into chaos.

- *Transition – Prime Minister*
- *Transition – Stock trader*

In the US and in parts of Central America, rioting and looting begins almost immediately; in London, Paris and elsewhere, the respective armies hastily assemble barriers in commercial and government districts to forestall similar problems. By the end of the day, Australia is the only 'western' country not under martial law – and this only because the army refuses to place itself under the control of the now-discredited police, as required by Australian 'emergency powers' legislation.

- *Transition – Cabinet transcript*
- *Emergency Management Act**

With the agreement of the Governor-General, Tony Morrison appoints his former teacher Don Mercer to head an emergency commission, implementing the full 'SusLaw' model – in effect nationalising every asset in the entire country – as the only available alternative. The transition goes far more smoothly than expected, partly because of all the research shared at previous Sustainability conferences, but also because many politicians and senior bureaucrats are already familiar with the model – the Law Faculty at Derwent University being the classic start-point for a career in politics.

- *Transition – Last orders*
- *Shock-jock*
- *Transition – Paton's*
- *Transition – Cabinet transcript*

Post-transition

Two weeks after transition

The US death toll has already reached half a million; cholera, dysentery and typhoid are spreading fast in the ghetto areas in the cities, barricaded in by the National Guard under the control of Moral America.

- *Due-diligence**

In Europe, with fewer guns in private hands, the military maintain a fragile peace; the same applies in most of Latin America, and in most of the old 'Soviet empire' – though the Balkan region is once again a chaos of ethnic enmity.

Over in the Middle East an all-out war is raging, after a nuclear suicide attack on Tel Aviv; further eastward, India and Pakistan are in chaos, with rioting going on in every city; and China seems to be imploding, as its 'New Economy' collapses completely.

In most of the ASEAN states, and in much of Africa, military coups occur almost daily, as one self-styled 'warlord' after another tries to establish personal rule.

- *Transition – Cabinet transcript**

In Australia, by contrast, there's been no rioting at all: there's already almost a sense of 'back to normal' – though still without any money changing hands.

- *Transition – Graphic designer*
- *Transition – Musician*
- *Transition – Golfer*

Two months after transition

Australian Prime Minister Tony Morrison introduces the Citizens Charter, which expresses citizens' rights by outlining citizens' responsibilities. The key responsibilities are summarised by the old farmer's adage "live as if you'll die tomorrow, but farm as if you'll live forever". This provides the stable anchor around which the 'no-money' sustainability/stewardship model coalesces. The 'no-money' economy is operating well, and is becoming a matter of national pride amongst many Australians. It is supported somewhat shakily by a distributed work-tracking system based on the LETS model, nicknamed 'Workshare'. With previous company law effectively invalid, work-groups increasingly use the Workshare term 'alliance' to describe their collective work-relationship.

- *Negotiations with Ausam**

In another key piece of legislation, Morrison freezes asset-values at the point at which they were last valued, just before the declaration of emergency. In most cases, because of the collapse, the paper-values of most companies are frozen at close to zero.

- *Due-diligence*
- *At the airport**

The ghetto system is formalised in the US, with pressure from Moral America to enforce it in racial grounds. The surviving prison population is moved into the ghettos; exit from the ghettos is permitted only in daylight, and only under armed supervision.

- *Steve's diary**

International networks are repaired sufficient for the World Trade Organisation to reconvene and for multinational corporations to attempt to re-take control of world trade by reasserting their claims to possession of all resources. In Australia, still under the national emergency legislation, those claims are formally rejected.

Five months after transition

After a shaky start, international flights to and from Australia resume. A surprising number of tourists and foreign nationals, stranded in Australia by what is euphemistically described world-wide by the old Irish term of 'The Troubles', request to continue to stay in Australia.

A team of 'systems of systems' architects in Australia succeed in integrating the previous government and commercial systems into a single network, making the Workshare system accessible any-where in the country. Work starts on extending the system to cover availability of and needs for resources of all kinds.

- *Workshare*
- *Steve's diary**
- *What's the project?**

One year after transition

Morrison brings the official 'state of emergency' to an end, and promotes a referendum to decide on the property model to be used when the emergency legislation is withdrawn. Despite extensive campaigning by outsiders for a return to the possession-based model, in order to reclaim 'their' assets, the referendum almost unanimously defends the 'no-money' model, and finally settles the republic debate, ending the historical 'ownership' of the country by the British Crown. The stock-market does not re-open.

- *Put it to the vote*

Multinational companies clamour for war against Australia, to retrieve their 'stolen' property. The United Nations Secretary-General intervenes, supporting Morrison's argument that by the WTO's own rules, the assets have near-zero paper-value; she also notes, drily, that most of those claimed assets would be destroyed anyway in any conflict. The UN Assets Arbitration Tribunal is set up in Geneva, to negotiate compensation for all international assets 'lost' in the Troubles. The Workshare system is extended to include and take over the former banking role of international monetary transactions.

- *Due-diligence**
- *Negotiations with Ausam**
- *At the airport**

Closed-labour contracts, which are automatically renewed in case of debt, but in which it is impossible to get out of debt, become commonplace in the sweatshops springing up around the ghettos in the US.

- *Closed-debt contracts*
- *Contract-breach*

Becoming stable

Two years after transition

Angela Coulson, Tony Morrison's Education Minister, launches the new Australian primary-school curriculum. It changes the emphasis from the old content-based 'three Rs' to a focus on thinking and responsibility, linked to the precepts of the Citizens Charter: "Plan, Do, Review" replaces the old 'Reading, wRiting, aRithmetic" as the catch-phrase for early education.

- *A quiet crusader**
- *Backpacker hotel**
- *Lifter crew**

Cory Osmer's group at CCAT (Caulfield College of Advanced Technology, in the inner Melbourne suburbs) develop and test a simple biofeedback amplifier for experimental psychokinesis. Its use confirms that psychokinesis and other so-called 'psychic' abilities are in fact learnable skills, although, as Osmer comments, "making them into reliable technologies is probably many years away".

- *Intuitive-technologies**
- *Crazy scientists**
- *Lifter crew**

Labour organisations are outlawed in the US, though European nations refuse to follow suit.

Trade between Australia and other countries has settled down to routine, the only irritant being the continuing demands of some multinationals for compensation for loss of their Australian assets. Workshare manages the overall money-supply, but international purchases and sales are fully decentralised once more, under the control of individual alliances.

- *Negotiations with Ausam**
- *At the airport**

As tourism restarts, 'Visitor Zones' are defined in most Australian cities, where the money-system can still operate in ways that tourists can understand.

- *Visitor Zones*
- *Tipping*
- *In Melbourne**

Five years after transition

In the US, the ghettos are shut out of the electoral system de facto, by preventing electoral registration to take place in the ghettos 'on grounds of personal safety'. The Moral America government, now settled in what is effectively a one-party state controlled by multinational corporations, passes legislation to permit companies to buy and sell closed-labour contracts – and thus the people entrapped by those contracts. The US stratifies into a caste-based society, based in part on race, but even more on employment-contract class.

- *Mitesh**

A national election returns Morrison's government for a third term of office. With rates of pay or control of ownership no longer an issue, the party system has become increasingly irrelevant: almost all members of parliament present themselves as 'independent'.

The 'telelink' becomes available. It combines voice, video, text, handwriting, speech-to-text, email, messaging, browse and search into a single integrated system reliable and robust enough for general public use, and rapidly supplants the telephone as the standard means of landline-communication.

- *Negotiations with Ausam**
- *Letter to Dave**

Seven years after transition

Morrison dies, at the end of a visit to Geneva to finalise the 'asset compensation' negotiations. The exact cause of death is unknown, and may well be a covert assassination on behalf of a vengeful corporation, but is carefully glossed-over as a purported heart-attack. He is mourned as 'the father of free Australia'.

- *At the airport*
- *A convenient untruth*

Don Mercer retires from Derwent University, and quietly fades from public life, by choice. Although he still appears at the annual Sustainability Conference, he devotes his energies to his tapestries and weavings – "so that I can spend more time with Mary", he says, recalling the memory of his long-dead wife.

- *Love beyond reason*

Amber Inigrou, the head of research into 'intuitive technologies' at CCAT, confirms that psychokinetic abilities are more common in children in Australia than in other countries: her team's research suggests that this is linked to the personal-responsibility emphasis in Australian pre-school education. Mark Ivetic, another member of that group, adapts an existing biofeedback-based system for 'thought-control' of aircraft flight-systems into an experimental system for telempathy, enabling students with that aptitude to 'communicate' directly with networks and electronic circuits. Nicknamed 'reality-benders' – soon shortened simply to 'benders' – the telempathy systems also enhance other intuitive skills such as psychokinetic ability: combined with new selection criteria and educational tools, psychokinesis in particular starts to become a usable technology.

- *Developing the skills**
- *Lifter crew**
- *Crazy scientists*

The new generation

About twenty years after transition

After more than a dozen years of further development, Ivetic's 'bender' technology is becoming increasingly commonplace in Australia; some is even adapted experimentally for defence use. Selection techniques are refined to identify psychokinetic aptitude in school-children – most often in teenage girls. Telempathic aptitude is found to be more common in boys, particularly those with both musical ability and an affinity for technology in general. Middle-school education in Australia now includes a component on 'self-identification': mainly intended to make it easier for students to identify the type of work they most value, a side-effect is that many students learn to direct their own boundaries of self – making some forms of controlled telepathy increasingly common.

- *Scattered fragments*
- *Developing the skills*
- *Lifter crew**
- *Saber-rattling**

A new Indonesian 'warlord' – one of many still fighting for domination of that disparate nation – takes control of the country's navy and launches an attack on Darwin, in an attempt to extend his personal empire to include what he calls 'New Irian Jaya'. The night-time invasion is a spectacular disaster: electronic systems on the ships inexplicably go out of control, launching anti-ship missiles that sink most of their own fleet within sight of the Australian coast. Australian fishing boats and two naval vessels returning from East Timor pick up the few survivors; the warlord is not amongst them. Suspecting that bender technology was involved in the warlord's fiasco, US military researchers somehow obtain a unit – probably during joint military exercises in Australia's 'Top End' – but find that its key component is an electromagnet which appears to cancel its own field. They declare it useless – "a pointless fake" – but admit that they have no idea why electronic equipment sometimes becomes unpredictable in its presence.

- *Saber-rattling*
- *Lifter crew**

With international tourism increasing rapidly, the Australian visa system is simplified and the Visitor Zone scheme expanded to manage money-based transactions with 'outsiders' throughout the country – though the evident success of the 'no-money' economy is pointed to with pride by Australians.

- *Visas*
- *Visitor Zones*
- *That big blue line*

About thirty years after transition

Scientists worldwide still describe the now-extensive Australian research in alchemy and intuitive technologies as "seriously insane"; despite this, Australians have succeeded in getting them to work as reliable tools. Psychokinetic 'lifter crews' – usually young women – provide specialist industrial crane services; and although alchemical materials remain difficult to create, their special chemical and other properties are used not only in medicine, but also in some industrial processes.

- *Lifter crew*
- *Letter to Dave*
- *Cargo bootstrap*

The 'Workshare visa' – a kind of 'working tourist' visa – is an increasingly popular means for foreigners to explore Australia and its uniquely open culture.

- *Visas*
- *Steve's diary*
- *Apollo Bay*

By now, the 'New Australia' has become a very different society to anywhere else in the world.

- *Language*
- *Police*
- *Deathday*
- *Negotiations with Ausam*
- *Steve's diary*
- *Steve's arrival*
- *In Melbourne*
- *Apollo Bay*
- *Letter to Mum*
- *Letter to Dave*

The contrasts to other countries that still run on a possession-based model – particularly the extreme of the Moral America cabal – can be surprising, and often shocking.

- *Mitesh*
- *Mishie*
- *Steve's diary*

Don Mercer dies, essentially of old age, having lived into his early nineties. Despite his age and his intentional obscurity in the previous decades, his death does not go unnoticed – in his own country, at least.

- *No idea who he was*

www.ingramcontent.com/pod-product-compliance
Lightning Source LLC
Chambersburg PA
CBHW050509260626
47157CB00004B/1254